Bite-Sized Fiction

The People We Know

Farrokh Suntook

Cover by

Dean Stockton

Published by Bite-Sized Books Ltd 2021
©Farrokh Suntook 2021

Bite-Sized Books Ltd 8th Floor, 20 St. Andrews Street, London
EC4A 3AY, UK

Registered in the UK. Company Registration No: 9395379

ISBN: 9798777575029

The moral right of Farrokh Suntook to be identified as the author of this work has been asserted by him in accordance with the Copyright, Designs and Patents Act 1988

This novel is entirely a work of fiction. The characters portrayed in it are the work of the author's imagination. Any resemblance to actual persons, living or dead, is entirely coincidental.

All rights reserved. No part of this publication may be reproduced without the prior permission of the publishers

For
Maneck
and
Dinu

Contents

Mahabaleshwar   1

Bombay   39

London   107

Return   233

Mahabaleshwar

1

The end was near.

Yet, in these final moments, she felt her senses spring to life. Everything around her came into focus, every leaf etched against every other leaf, every twig jostling for her attention. Her ears twitched at the sound of unseen animals, real or imagined, furtively doing whatever they do when darkness falls. And she smelt as she had never smelt before the fragrance of moistened earth mingling with the smoky sweetness of village wood fires.

She walked past the sign pointing to *Niddle Hole*, where the sheer rock juts out over the valley and splits to form the eye of a needle. Straight ahead of her was a wide open space, saffron in daylight but now barely distinguishable from the slate grey of the distant foliage lacing the edge of the cliff.

Something made her turn round for one last time. Barely half an hour ago, under the gaze of the evening sun, she had been anxious she would be caught in the act. But when the sun melted into the contours of the mountains, the twilight that crept in offered shelter. Now, instead of the patchwork wilderness of the Krishna valley, all she could see ahead of her was a wash of blue-greys and murky browns merged in a mist of ancient desolation.

She carried on walking towards the precipice. Having reconnoitred the place the previous evening, she knew the lay of the land. She knew exactly where and how she would do what she had come here to do. And it would be easier to slip away unnoticed now that the day-trippers were beginning to disperse.

Now there was almost total darkness. And stillness. The landscape felt like a three-dimensional collage of gloom: in the foreground, jagged slabs of slate filleted with stripes of silver; further in the distance, massive mounds of charcoal shaping the horizon.

Slowly but deliberately, feeling every bump in the soil beneath her sandals, every lift of her ankles, she moved forward - towards the point at which the earth would give way to oblivion. And with every step the nausea that had been pressing on her receded.

Out of nowhere a yawning boulder loomed ahead. She let out a gasp: like some megalithic poltergeist, mouth wide open, it reared over her as if readying itself to shatter the silence.

For the first time this evening she felt her isolation, and the fear that came with it. But she walked onwards, determined not to succumb to the play of the late evening shadows.

She felt something disturb the rhythm of her movement; some creature lurking in the trees lining her pathway. Oh no, it must be the monkey that had glared at her when she arrived at Kate's Point.

Cyrus had once shielded her from an evil-looking macaque intent on snatching her banana. An inner voice cried out "Cyrus, where are you?", but the cry was met with silence. The trees had regained their stillness. There was no monkey. Only her imagination playing tricks on her.

Suddenly she lost her foothold and felt herself falling. For a heart-stopping moment of exhilaration-terror-regret she braced herself for a nosedive through space. Then she hit a clump of bushes. She realised that she had stumbled into a ditch.

She lay motionless to still the racing of her heart. Then she heaved herself up, feeling foolish she was relieved not to have twisted her ankle.

She resumed her advance. She must be approaching the brink. But now each foot was creeping forward with a desperate deliberation, as if fearful of a last-minute change of mind.

"Watch your step!"

For an instant she didn't know what to make of the voice, but she told herself to ignore it. As she edged towards the black space ahead of her, the voice, this time closer, called out, "Are you OK?"

Sheela could have decided in that split second to dash forward and jump. But the voice. It was a stranger's, yet like a voice she knew well. Her daughter Nina's. She froze, unable to move forwards or backwards.

"Can we help?" The voice was more tentative now.

So there was more than one person.

She wanted to rage against this intruder, whoever she was, snooping in the dark, frustrating her meticulously laid plans. She wanted to rage - but realised she couldn't.

Slowly, she turned round and walked up the narrow path ahead of her.

Against the glimmer cast by the lights of the shacks were silhouetted the figures of a man and a woman.

She heaved herself up the slope, her legs straining against some force dragging her back.

Why did she give up so easily?

2

"Hello, are you all right?" The woman's voice was gentle, solicitous.

As she approached the top of the path, Sheela noticed a figure that was slim, tallish, wearing trousers made of some flimsy material; suitable for the heat of Bombay but hardly for the chill of a Mahabaleshwar evening. Even closer, she saw that the woman was European, and from her accent she decided she was probably English.

And now she was going to have to talk to these strangers, when all she wanted to do was to return home as soon as possible.

Before she could say anything, the figure of a man emerged from the shadows.

"We just wondered if everything was OK. Don't know whether you realised but you were awfully close to the edge."

There was a pause. Then the words, matter-of-fact, calm, came out as if spoken by another person: "Oh thanks. Nothing to worry about really; my husband always said I had a head for heights." *God, why did I have to mention him?*

As she spoke she fixed her eyes on the craggy stones marking the end of the pathway in front of her.

But once she had reached their level she was forced to look up.

"Would you like a drink or something?"

The woman turned her head towards Baba's Bollywood Café, which claimed to sell everything from straw hats to 'strawberry with cream'. With nightfall, and the departure of most of the day-trippers, the shack had the desolate air of all shops that have to come to terms with the end of the day's business.

"No thank you, I'm fine," but the defiance she had wanted her voice to express refused to make itself heard.

"Beautiful around here, isn't it." The man was smiling awkwardly.

The couple were about her age, perhaps slightly younger - in their mid-forties. Not so long ago she would have had the energy to engage in small talk, the formulaic game played by strangers in civilised society.

After a pause, the woman said, "Are you sure you're OK?"

"Yes yes, of course I'm OK."

"In that case we must be going - it's getting quite nippy. Come on, Max."

Picking up a Bombay Store carrier bag, the woman lingered for a moment, as if reluctant to leave, before turning to join the man. The couple walked away towards the potholed road leading to the centre of Mahabaleshwar, a good six kilometres away.

"Excuse me," Sheela called out, "you've dropped something." She bent down to pick up the object. It was a paint brush with fresh remnants of green on its bristles. The woman's an amateur artist, she thought.

"Oh thank you so much. My lifeline!"

"Can I give you a lift somewhere?" And, before they could answer: "It might not be safe to return on foot when it gets dark." *Oh God, why am I offering to take them back?*

"How kind of you! Are you sure?"

What did they expect her to say? "No, I'm not"? But then hadn't Cyrus said that the English could no more avoid the little hypocrisies peppering their acceptances of offers than the Indians could resist the impulse to be hospitable by making such offers?

"Yes, yes, there's plenty of room in the car."

"Are you really sure we're not taking you out of your way?" said the Englishwoman as she looked in vain for a seat belt.

"Where do you need to go?"

The woman said, "We're staying at the Mahabaleshwar Club."

The Mahabaleshwar Club. Cyrus had been a member there, as had his parents and grandparents. Of course, Cyrus had been a member of everything, the life and soul of every party, and through him she had been accepted into the magical inner circle to which everybody who knew him wished to belong. Everybody who knew him... But what did they really know? Nothing.

Suddenly she felt the darkness around her. No light, save the car's headlights, to alleviate the gloom.

"As it happens, the Mahabaleshwar Club is on the way to my place."

"Oh, that's a relief." Sheela detected a hint of irony - or was it a flash of anger? - in the woman's nervous titter. "By the way, my name is Clarissa, and this is Max."

"And I'm Sheela Marker."

"Goodness, I never knew that Sheela was an Indian name as well!"

Here we go again - will the English never recognise that the world no longer revolves round them? "Actually, my full name is Susheela, but Sheela is what I've always been called. It's spelt s-h-e-*e*-l-a". She wondered whether the Englishwoman had detected the con-descension behind the stress on the second vowel.

Jerking his head forward, Gopal pressed his foot on the accelerator, then slammed the brakes and swerved just in time to avoid colliding with a lorry festooned with marigolds. He banged his fist on the horn and screamed at the sister-fucking lorry driver. Sheela's instinct was to admonish him, but she had the sense to keep quiet. She knew his temper was directed as much at her as at the lorry driver. When she had asked him this morning to drive her back to Kate's Point, the expression on his face had said it all: hadn't they already visited Kate's Point the previous evening, and why should he, the Marker family chauffeur, have to put up with this woman's whims, just because she happened to be the wife of his beloved Cyrus sahib?

"How long are you here for?" As she spoke she gave a quick backward glance. The couple appeared to be clutching each other's hands like young lovers; strange, given their age, and there was an unseemly desperation in the interlocking of their fingers. Perhaps they were having an adulterous affair; yes, that made sense.

"Oh, we're here for another few days," the woman replied.

Sheela didn't respond. The sight of the hands clutching each other brought back thoughts of times gone by, floating around like shards of driftwood, then converging, against her will, to a single focal point: Cyrus.

It was Cyrus who had first brought her to this place. Then it had been early evening, the sky still a bright blue. On the drive back to the bungalow, he had given her a potted history of Kate's Point. Then he had gone quiet, gazing out of the window.

"What's the matter?" she had asked.

"Nothing," he had said. "I was just thinking."

"Of what? Come on, tell me."

The story had come out haltingly. He was barely ten, staying with his parents in Lammermoor Lodge. One morning in the bazaar, he glimpsed what looked like a stretcher being carried by men with ash-daubed foreheads. There was a small bundle on the frame - a dead body trussed up in white cloth. That evening, he discovered from his parents that a girl belonging to a family by the name of Kalmani had fallen over a precipice at Kate's Point.

As she recalled the story, Cyrus's words came tumbling back to Sheela, almost word for word: "Can you imagine, Sheela, what she must have felt, realising that she was falling, falling, falling, desperately trying to get a foothold, knowing every milli-second that she was hurtling to her certain death?"

Sheela had never been able to understand how he could feel such horror even some thirty years after the event. In the early days, she would tease him for being a glutton for punishment, soaking up the pain of others. But over the years she had learnt that a squeeze of the hand, a hug - some wordless recognition of his feelings - was the comfort he needed.

Later that evening, when they had gone to bed, their four-poster cocooned by mosquito nets, she had held him tightly in her arms, wishing that moment to last forever.

And now she was without him, stuck in the car with this tiresome couple who had scuppered her carefully laid out plans - to appear a victim of an accident, as the Kalmani girl had been so many years ago.

Thr rest of the journey passed in silence until signs of street activity signalled the approach of the bazaar area.

The car turned a corner she recognised; they had almost arrived at the club.

"Well, nice to have met you."

"Are you going to be here for a while? It would be lovely if you could come over to the club for tea tomorrow. We hardly know a soul here, so you'd be doing us a favour!" The woman sounded almost grateful for Sheela's unexpected civility.

Why were they being so friendly? Here were people she had met barely half an hour ago, behaving in a singularly un-English way - showing that they meant what they said by following up civilities with concrete gestures.

"OK, what time?"

"What about sometime around 4.30 - Max will have had his siesta by then!"

On the way back to Lammermoor Lodge, she wondered why she was unable to sustain the resentment she had initially harboured against the couple. For an uneasy moment she felt they had come to rescue her, but she quickly dismissed the thought as absurd. Then a further thought she found harder to dismiss: could it be that *she had wanted* to be rescued?

She went into Nina's bedroom: in Mahabaleshwar she couldn't get herself to sleep on the bed she had shared with Cyrus. As she rested her head on the pillow, she was irked by a feeling that something hadn't been quite right when she met the couple at Kate's Point. But try as she might to give it shape, like some elusive worm it kept slithering away from the grasp of her consciousness.

She had a restless night - like all the nights she had had sleeping alone, but even more so than usual. When she raised her head to look at the time on her bedside alarm - two in the morning - the worm wriggled out: when speaking to the couple about her husband, she had used the past tense.

3

She woke up to the sound of Ramu shuffling in as usual with a tray of tea and Marie biscuits. Today she kept her eyes shut, unable to face the thought of greeting anyone, not even her faithful Ramu.

Ever since Cyrus was a child, some forty years ago, Ramu had worked as a general dogsbody, cleaning the rooms, lighting the kerosene lamps, serving meals, and tending the front garden with its profusion of roses and fuchsias. His wife Amoli had remained shyly in the background, cooking, washing the dishes and, in the days before showers were installed, carrying the pails of freshly boiled water for the early morning bath. They had never had children ("it was the will of God"), Ramu's curvature of the spine seemed to get worse by the year, and Amoli was just beginning a feeble recovery from dengue fever. On every visit to Mahabaleshwar from Bombay, Cyrus and she had made a point of buying a new *kurta* for him and a sari for her. For Sheela, Ramu and Amoli personified the nobility of Indian country folk: people taught by hardship never to take for granted what little they possessed and never to despise gifts, however small - or unwanted - they might be.

Sheela could only manage a couple of sips of Ramu's tea, and she barely glanced at the biscuits. Like a black monsoon cloud, the nausea she had felt at Kate's Point returned, assailing her with a sense of alienation bordering on disgust - with what she couldn't tell.

Morning sounds were heralding a new day: the clucking of hens in the back yard; the call of voices in the half-distance; the song of the whistling thrush. Once she delighted in them. Now the thought of another day filled her with dread.

Reluctantly, she slipped into her dressing gown and went to the verandah.

She had failed last evening to accomplish the mission for which she had made this trip to Mahabaleshwar. That damned English couple, they were to blame. And having succumbed to their blandishments to have tea with them, she was stuck for another day in this unbearable place, with its oppressive charms and stifling beauty.

She turned round on hearing a soft footfall: the sound of *chappals* on the smooth floor tiles.

"Baby, phone *hai*," Ramu said quietly. His Baba having gone, he was even more retiring than usual. She knew that he understood, that he shared her grief; after all, he had dandled Cyrus as a toddler. And of course he knew what had happened a year ago.

"*Apka bhai*," he added. He could never refer to Sheela's brother Mohan by name; it was always "your brother". Ramu, the meekest and mildest of people, had never taken to Mohan.

"Hi, Lovely darling!"

Not receiving the sign of recognition he had expected, Mohan continued, "It's Sweetie, calling from Mumbai. I came in from Honolulu earlier today and I thought you just *had* to be the first person I called, after Mumsie of course!"

"Oh hi, I didn't know you were going to be here."

"Nor did I! Only I've been invited to be the keynote speaker at this investment symposium funded by my dear friend the Maharajah of Chhota Buddhipur. And I'll be giving my usual talk - you know the one that for some reason my clients in Hawaii seem to love - *The Kama Sutra Guide for Smart Investors: Long, Short and Other Positions*. I couldn't possibly let poor old Buddy Baby down, even though that meant cancelling a number of my US speaking engagements."

"The price of being so talented, I suppose."

"Hee hee, I know you're pulling my leg - but seriously, being expected to be in so many places at the same time can be a real pain in the butt. And that better half of mine is always complaining that I'm hardly ever at home."

"Oh, how's Nandini?"

"All right, I suppose, but I wish she wouldn't constantly whine about her wonderful life back in India."

"Maybe she's lonely. Can't you involve her in some of your activities?"

"Are you crazy? How can I possibly involve her, so quiet and mousy, when she doesn't know the a-b-c of the investment world?"

Nandini was a dreary woman, that couldn't be denied. She was the peahen to her husband's peacock. But there the resemblance ended: unlike the peacock, with its aquamarine splendour, her brother had nothing to strut about; all he had was an unassailable self-belief powerful enough to convince his following of would-be billionaires that their own incomprehension only served to confirm the profundity of the great guru's thoughts.

"So how long are you going to be in Bombay?"

"About a week. And what about you, sis? Hope you're returning from Mahabaleshwar while I'm still here."

"Well, as it happens, I was planning to return to Bombay tomorrow or maybe the day after."

"Oh wonderful, Lovely, give me a ring when you arrive."

Lovely. It was her father who had first given her the pet name.

"Jeez, I really gotta rush - expecting a call from Buddy any minute now. So long, sis - see you in Mumbai!"

The peremptory click of the telephone receiver was a reminder of Mohan's ability to set the terms of any discourse between the two of them: it was he who had decided to call her when it suited his convenience, and it was he who had brought the conversation to an abrupt halt.

Putting the phone receiver down, Sheela felt the dreaded nausea coming back to haunt her like a ghost of the rage she had been trying to smother. Ever since her father's sudden death almost twenty years ago, she had learnt to inure herself against the billing and cooing of mother and son, from which she was studiously excluded. From his earliest years, Mohan had developed the unearned confidence of the favourite child; and as an adult, he enjoyed the knowledge that he was to inherit his parents' properties in Bombay as well as Poona (against the wishes of their father who had carelessly trusted his wife to apportion the family estate fairly between the two children). With Cyrus by her side, the "Mumsie-Chweetie axis" - Cyrus's quip - had ceased to matter to Sheela. But with him gone the relationship between mother and son had once again brought home to her the isolation she had tried to end at Kate's Point.

She called out, "Driver!"

Gopal bounded in with a smile. He was evidently in a good mood.

Sheela was incapable of holding grudges for long, a quality that Cyrus had found endearing, although she regarded it as the weakness of an ego too easily seduced by peace offerings. Her voice softened and the peremptory "*gari mangta hai*" that she had prepared, to demand use of the car, became "Gopal, *chai piya hai*?" When he assured her that he had indeed drunk his tea, she asked if he could take her to the bazaar in thirty minutes. She had no real need to buy anything, but she just had to get away from the bungalow.

They arrived at the end of the bazaar furthest from Imperial Stores, her destination. On either side of the main pedestrian-only street were clusters of shops, most huddled cheek by jowl, some separated by dusty tributaries normally avoided by the more affluent visitors to the hill station. Today the bazaar of old, with its hill station feel, was unable to hold its own against the tatty prosperity of fast food joints, fourth rate hotels and games arcades blaring out Bollywood music.

Sauntering towards Imperial Stores, she passed an assortment of these places, but when she arrived at Imperial Stores, she felt like the driver who has reached her destination unable to remember any of the landmarks of the road she has taken. Normally squeamish, she even forgot whether she had avoided stepping on the traces of sewage and cow dung threatening to smear the *chappals* of the unwary pedestrian.

Instead, her mind had wandered back to Kate's Point - and to visions of her husband smiling benignly with his hazel eyes.

At Imperial Stores, it was only when her gaze fell upon the battery of red, pink and orange toothbrushes that she remembered the toothpaste that had been her excuse to visit the bazaar. She was out of the store in a matter of minutes.

"Good morning, madame!" The last word was pronounced to rhyme with 'harm'.

She pretended not to have heard the call and wondered whether she could escape round some corner.

The voice came closer, "Madame, how are you?"

The nervousness turned to dread. The silvery whine of the speaker forced back memories of that day a year ago.

She turned round, clutching her handbag to her chest. "Yes, what is it?" she said, trying to stifle the tremor creeping up her voice.

"Oh, madame, what great pleezhyer to see you again!" The man, dark brown and portly, was sporting a tight-fitting Nehru jacket and flabby white trousers. His cherubic smile and round darting eyes made the hairs on her nape stand on end: the Peter Lorre of Bollywood.

"And what brings your good self back to Mahabaleshwar?" Then, with a stare that could have driven nails into the balls of her eyes, "I never expect you to return", followed quickly by the smile he had momentarily forgotten to keep fixed on his face.

"So you still live here."

"Oh madame, where poor humble village doctor like me can go? I am not one of rich citywallahs who can come and go out of Mahabaleshwar whenever they wish."

She felt a calculated menace in the pause that bore down on her.

"You see, madame, I am always grateful for the kind generosity of people like your good self." Another pause. "As you know very well, I think, madame."

"I have to –"

"Of course, you are very busy. Always so busy in city! But even city people will kindly remember those who have helped them?"

"Sheela!" a voice cut through the hubbub of the bazaar. "Sheela, I never knew you were in Mahabaleshwar!"

She turned round. "Bachoo, fancy meeting you here! How long have you been in Mahabaleshwar?"

Sheela felt her body shaking with relief. Bachoo Dhondhy was a bridge playing pal of her mother's, an archetypal Parsi battleaxe.

"For the past three weeks," Bachoo replied, suffocating Sheela with a bosomy half nelson and a smell of sweat and rose water. "And where have you been hiding all this time?"

"Oh, I've just been here for a few days." This was said softly, so that only Bachoo could hear. "Anyway, I'm *so* happy to bump into you."

Glancing sideways, Sheela found no sign of Peter Lorre. But the thudding inside her rib cage hadn't subsided.

"And I am too, sweetheart. But I'm surprised to see you here at all - I mean, with all the associations with Cy - with what happened, and all that?"

"As it happens, I planned to leave tomorrow, but now I've gone and committed myself to tea at the club with some Brits I don't know from Adam - so it will probably be the day after."

"You don't mean Clarissa and Max Alexander, do you? They're the only English couple I know at the club."

"Yes, that's them. How do *you* know them?"

"I'm staying at the club this time. Mannering Manor got flooded during the monsoon because our *mali* - lazy so-and-so - didn't keep an eye on the roof, and now I'm landed with the most massive repairs. So I've got to know the Alexanders quite well over the past few days. Such a charming couple! Mind you, the less said about their bridge the better. Oh my God, I must dash - I'm supposed to be speaking to the workmen at MM, and you know how it is - late by a minute and that's the perfect excuse for the whole jingbang lot of them to do a bunk. See you later at the club - I'll tell the Alexanders I'm going to join you for tea!"

With an anaconda embrace and a flourish of her ring-encrusted fingers in the direction of her waiting chauffeur, she was off.

Sheela was considerably cheered by the prospect of not having to cope with the English couple on her own.

With Bachoo around, nobody else would get a word in edgeways.

She retraced her steps along the bazaar, glancing sideways now and then to make sure there was no sign of Peter Lorre.

Now she felt able to take in her immediate surroundings: *mochis* selling and mending shoes and *chappals*; on the right, Elsie's Dairy and Bakery, 'estd. 1849'; and numerous stalls displaying walking sticks, fruit crushes, and jars of honey and strawberry jam.

She stopped to buy several packets of roasted chickpeas from her favourite *chanawala* and boxes of groundnut and sesame brittle from her favourite *chikkiwala*.

On the way back to Lammermoor Lodge, Sheela reflected on the humility of the poor of India: hurt that on her arrival at the bazaar Sheela had, uncharacteristically, taken no notice of them, the *chanawala* and *chikkiwala* now responded to her greeting by welcoming her like a prodigal daughter. But how could they not? After all, she had been the wife of their beloved Cyrus Baba, the kindest of *seths*, whom they had first got to know when he was barely ten, a child with a ready smile who was always at his mother's side when she went to the bazaar.

When she returned to Lammermoor Lodge, it was almost half past two. She asked Ramu to make her an *akoori* on toast. Anything heavier than the Parsi scrambled egg would leave little space for whatever the English couple had in store for her. Amoli normally did the cooking, but the Parsi scrambled egg was Ramu's speciality.

She had a couple of hours to kill before tea at the club, so she stretched the lunch by playing the part of solicitous mistress: first, compliments on the excellence of the *akoori*; then a prolonged homily on the importance of using mosquito nets to ward off malaria. All this received with the shy smiles and sideways head-shaking expected of those who ought to be thankful for the beneficence of kind masters.

Having lived in the west for much of her life, however, Sheela found it difficult to square the part she was playing here with her Guardian-reading persona. But she did want the elderly couple to know how much she cared for them. And at this moment the role fulfilled a need: the need for their company, especially now when she faced the prospect of having to meet the English couple.

As she stepped into the car to be driven to the club she found Gopal had returned to his surliest *paan*-spitting form. She wasn't looking forward to meeting the couple. True, Bachoo would be there, but the thought of Bachoo brought back her encounter with the doctor, and she spent the rest of the journey trying but failing to forget what he had said.

4

Sheela could see why the Mahabaleshwar Club, orangey-red in the blazing sun, might appeal to the English couple. The 130-year old building, with its bare gables squatting over gothic-shaped windows, was redolent of a British public school, but its russet façade and its low-lying corrugated roofing were far plainer than the turreted and crenellated exteriors of the edifices which had spewed out the rulers of an Empire. And therein lay an even deeper difference: there was something generous and welcoming about the club, with its large arches, like open *namastés*, positively beckoning the visitor to enter; whereas the institutions of privilege she had seen in England never failed to remind her of their remoteness from those who didn't belong.

As if it had been reading her thoughts, a voice cried out, "Charming, isn't it?"

In the few seconds it took for her host to approach her Sheela noticed far more about the woman than anything she had registered the previous evening. This time the person she had wanted to shove into a pigeon hole marked Stereotypical Englishwoman emerged from her compartment a flesh-and-blood individual with a distinctive gait and appearance. Her long strides did, admittedly, have something of an Anglo-Saxon no-nonsense about them, but the flowing buoyancy of her shoulder-length hair and the lissom sway of her hips, in unison with the easy swing of her arms, lent her the jaunty sex appeal often found in those blessed with the optimism and confidence that Sheela had never possessed but always envied.

As she came closer, Sheela saw a delicately fashioned face which reminded her of Botticelli, but this was Botticelli with a difference: a nose which would be regarded as classic if it weren't for the sideways tilt at the tip; aquamarine eyes with the slightest hint of a squint lending them an air of quizzical playfulness; and a mouth with an upper lip thickening quirkily on one side. It was as though Botticelli, bored with the idea of creating yet another perfect 15th century Venus, had time-travelled to the 21st century, drawing attention to his latest creation with unexpected asymmetries catering to contemporary tastes.

"Oh hello," said Sheela. Why did she have to appear so tongue-tied?

"Hi, so glad you could make it," said the Englishwoman, grasping one of Sheela's hands with both of hers. Why, thought Sheela, were the English so intent nowadays on over-compensating for their famous reserve? She remembered the outpouring of tears at the funeral of Princess Diana: "Mourning Becomes Britannia," Cyrus had quipped at the time.

She didn't yield to her initial impulse - to withdraw her hand as fast as she could. Instead she let it rest in the other woman's palms, and her face took on a will of its own, creasing itself into a smile.

"Where's your - ?"

"Oh Max, he's coming. He never took his siesta. He's become a carom addict (never known the game in England), and there's this little boy who keeps beating him, which he simply can't take. Honestly it's true - men never grow up!"

As they spoke, they drifted past the central garden towards the club building, Sheela lagging behind the Englishwoman by a few inches, partly because she didn't know exactly where they were heading but mainly because she was brought up to defer to the other party. She remembered Cyrus talking about how, beneath the commonality of language, culture and upbringing, there were crucial differences between those who were western and those who were westernised: her Indian heritage had inculcated a sense of delicacy that still made her inclined to let others walk half a step ahead of her.

"Oh, there you are!" The Englishman emerged from the main building. He looked pleased with himself. "So nice to see you again," he said to Sheela.

"So, Max, did you win?"

Everybody knew the question was unnecessary.

"I was telling Susheela what a baby you are about winning games!"

Susheela: Sheela squirmed at the obvious attempt to make amends for the earlier anglicisation of her name.

Max's tanned face flushed slightly. Looking at him properly for the first time, Sheela remembered her mother remarking on how some couples really did grow to look like each other: the slender figure of the woman was matched by a lanky angularity in the man, and in their faces too she observed a coming together. But there were differences, however slight, that seemed to match their personalities: like her he had warm greenish eyes, but they had a softer grey tint; his nose was also aquiline, but more regular; and he too had a generous mouth, but there was none of the impish quiver which threatened to break into a smile. In short, his good looks were subdued into something more gentle and retiring. Clarissa was the one to turn heads, yet it was he who wore an expression more endearing to Sheela.

But beneath the physical features there appeared to be something much deeper: a meeting of spirits, a bond that, without any conscious intent, made all others present feel like outsiders. Sheela tried to tell herself that she too had enjoyed a special relationship - but that memory only served to remind her of its loss.

"Oh, there's Bachoo," said Clarissa.

"What took you so long?"

"But I'm not late, Bachoo!" Sheela protested.

"Well, it feels as though you are. The Alexanders have been so excited about your visit that they've barely been able to eat, let alone sit down and play a decent game of bridge."

There followed a diatribe about the standard of bridge-playing at the Mahabaleshwar Club. Bachoo was well known for her impatience with partners she regarded as inept (which in practice meant most partners). But Sheela, who had spent years defending herself against her mother's jibes, found Bachoo's forthrightness, for all its ferocity, a source of comfort.

"In fact," Clarissa said with a laugh, "we've been excited about her visit ever since we met yesterday..." Her voice, playful to start with, trailed off into an awkward silence. She turned anxiously, first to Max, then to Sheela. Sheela looked away.

A huge rectangular cloud, dirty-grey like a discarded bale of cotton, lowered over the garden. All of a sudden Sheela was reminded of the desolate evenings she spent as a little girl watching the sun set over the Arabian Sea, with only Mary Ayah for company. The same sun she had recently seen set over Kate's Point.

"I'm going to be mother," Bachoo said, shakily lifting the pot of tea. "Oh God, don't say they've been using tea bags - and not even Darjeeling!"

There followed a long diatribe about how "you youngsters don't know the a-b-c of what good tea is all about". Sheela noticed Clarissa and Max exchanging glances: they had clearly never come across Parsi matriarchs who referred to anyone under seventy as a youngster.

"Sheela, did you know that our friends here plan to be in Bombay for a week before they return to good old Blighty?"

"Well, actually," said Clarissa, "we're not sure exactly how long we'll be in Mumbai -"

"In *what*? Why should we succumb to the pressure to call my beloved Bombay, the city of my birth, *Mumbye*? Anyway, returning to the matter in hand, do you know your place in Marine Drive is only a stone's throw away from where Sheela and Cyrus have their flat on the Oval Maidan. I mean -"

Bachoo was seized by a coughing fit. Sheela dropped her napkin on the ground. Bending over to pick it up, she imagined all eyes in the garden turning towards her.

"What I mean," spluttered Bachoo, "is that you could easily meet when you're all back in Bombay."

Bachoo's matchmaking prowess, much appreciated by Parsi women with daughters of a certain age, extended beyond affairs of matrimony: any opportunity to "bring people together" was seized upon with gusto.

"I'm sure that Sheela has better things to do with her time," said Clarissa.

Sheela looked up to find Clarissa smiling at her. Out of the blue she felt a surge of emotion rise in her throat. But she managed to say, "Yes, meeting in Bombay would be very nice."

"Oh good," said Bachoo, then proceeded to inform everyone about the exact location of Sunset Villas on Marine Drive and Tower View on the Oval Maidan.

"Now, when will you want to meet?" As if a pause might rupture her plans to knit the fabric of society closer together, she went on: "I tell you what - come to my place for dinner on Friday; that's four days from now. You'll all be in Bombay by then, won't you?"

The cotton cloud had long gone, but dusk was now falling, bringing with it signs that heralded the end of the day: villagers calling in the distance; crickets chirping their insistent chorus; and moths fluttering in a suicidal bid to collide against the lamps that had just been lit.

"Well I really must be going." Sheela's attempt to give Bachoo a peck on the cheek was squashed with a bear hug.

"See you in Bombay," she said, turning to Clarissa.

"Oh yes, really looking forward to that." The expression on the Englishwoman's face again stirred something that she was unable to pinpoint.

"Bye for now," Sheela said, this time to Max, who responded by cupping her hand in a *namasté*-like motion. Her instinct was to withdraw from the grasp, but when she saw his smile, tentative, verging on timidity, she held his glance and left her hand in the hollow of his palms for a fraction longer than she would have normally thought appropriate. Then, as if by silent consent, they both let go of each other.

Back at Lammermoor Lodge, the silence of the bungalow hung heavy on her. Although she had eaten very little at the club, she had no appetite for the meal Amoli had prepared. She told Ramu that her tummy didn't feel good, that she needed to go to bed and would sample Amoli's cooking the next day.

As sleep came, fitful and uneasy, she felt herself slipping into a haze of shadowy figures and hushed whisperings. The figures criss-crossed in a middle distance, dim and translucent, then floated towards her, and as they approached they merged into a single recognisable form: Cyrus, handsome and imposing as ever, wearing a Parsi *topi*, velvety maroon, like a Jewish skull cap. He was smiling; but his smile was fixed on a distant spot, and there was no love in his gaze, only a blankness.

Suddenly the figure turned away and, pulled by a cord around the neck, slowly rose towards the ceiling before receding into the night beyond. As she raised her head to look into the distant dark, she saw a pair of hands wielding the other end of the cord. Hands that looked like hers.

With the disappearance of the figure, the whisperings became louder, sounding like sibilant obscenities, all directed at her. Paralysed by fright and guilt, she kept her eyes shut. But she remembered how Cyrus - the good Cyrus, the Cyrus she thought she had known - told her that the only way to overcome fear was to invoke the forces of good; in other words, to pray. So she said the first prayer that came to mind, the Lord's Prayer, the prayer that had been taught to all the children at the Anglican school she had attended in Bombay.

With the words "deliver us from Evil," she mustered the courage to open her eyes. In the darkness she detected the ceiling lamp, the foot of the bed, the wardrobe at the far end of the room. She pressed her hands against her sides, then turned her whole body, looking around to see the familiar bedside table. It had been a delirium after all.

But she couldn't erase the image of the hands pulling at the cord.

She had to think of pleasant things. That was what her father would remind her to do when as a child she was awoken by nightmares. Now, lying in her bed, she made a conscious effort to shift her mind to something pleasurable. To her surprise, it took her to the English couple. She recalled Clarissa's smile, but however hard she tried she was unable to capture the feeling it had stirred in her.

She heard the noises of morning ablutions. She must have fallen asleep again. She wanted not to forget something, something that had come back to her in her sleep. This time, perhaps because in her drowsiness she had stopped trying so hard, it did return, with an emerging clarity that had eluded her when she was awake at night. That smile. Behind its apparent playfulness lay something akin to a profound fellow feeling, an intuitive sense of what Sheela was undergoing, above all a compassion deeper than the surface brilliance of the Botticelli exterior.

She wanted, very much, to meet this woman again, and regretted that Bachoo's dinner party in Bombay was as late as Friday.

5

Sheela swung out of bed, buoyed by the crystalline chill of the scented morning. For the first time since Cyrus's departure she relished the prospect of the day. It was barely seven. She would go for a brisk walk, then return for a shower and - the ultimate reward for her morning exercise - Ramu's gooey-crunchy *akoori*.

She decided to take the path towards Bombay Point, famed for its sunsets and its view of lights flickering like faded fireflies through the smoggy dusk of a distant Bombay.

For many years, Cyrus and she had avoided evenings, when the clamour of tourist hordes vied with the blaring of their favourite accessory - the portable radio. "Your average lower middle-class Indian", Bachoo would pronounce, "thrives on noise pollution." Sheela would make a half-hearted gesture of demurral, but she was honest enough to recognise that one reason for Bachoo's popularity lay in her willingness to do the dirty work of other people's thoughts.

She set off at 7.20, quickly turning into the narrow path that Cyrus had discovered to be a shortcut. As she trudged along the twig-strewn pathway, Sheela felt the absence of Cyrus by her side. In the past, as they walked together, she found comfort in the threads of sunlight filtering through the overhanging trees, the satisfying snap of twigs trodden on their nodes, the drone of insects whirring from leaf to leaf; now, she was aware only of the silent menace of creatures unseen.

The narrow path widened aimlessly until it merged into the main road. Coming towards her was a *dhoti*-clad man with a moustache like two belly-up crescents. As he approached he stared at her with bloodshot eyes matching the blood-red of the betel nut stains on his teeth. She avoided meeting his stare, walking purposefully ahead, realising with a fright that there was no other sign of human activity barring the distant cries of local people, so common in rural India that they had become part of its silence. As he passed her a tingle of panic spread up her spine. She wanted to run, but that risked inviting the very thing she feared. As the road bent, she noticed a cracked mirror, with reddish brown Mahabaleshwar dust in its crevices, presumably erected to warn motorists of a blind spot. She could see enough in the mirror to establish that the man was not following her. Just then she spotted another pathway veering to the right. She hurried towards it.

She walked a few yards and settled, panting, behind a massive tree sprouting horizontal branches. Thank God, no sounds of approaching footsteps. She stepped out to retrace her footprints back on to the main road, but froze when she heard a rustle in the undergrowth. Her heart whiplashed as she saw something leap from the bushes. Then what looked like a hare scampered away in a flurry of hind legs. As if warned not to return to the main road, she decided to turn round and continue along the new path, in the hope that it would somehow take her back to Lammermoor Lodge. She had no desire to continue the journey to Bombay Point.

She followed the path carefully, eyes fixed on the dusty ground, alert to every sound or sight that could serve as a warning of things to be avoided. A ghostly stillness pervaded her surroundings, yet she heard, or imagined, a hushed whispering, as if this primeval woodland were making muted complaints about the intruder disturbing its peace. Like the Forest Murmurs from Cyrus's recording of *Siegfried*. Cyrus, where are you, an inner voice cried out yet again. But what would he have done if he had been at her side? Protected her? Abandoned her? She was desperate now to return to the bungalow.

It was a smell that threatened to disrupt the rhythm of her movement. At first, she put it down to her imagination. After all, in a wilderness like this, sights, sounds, fragrances, presences, come and go. But this smell - a perfume - intruded with a memory of something that didn't belong here. And it was becoming stronger.

She stopped abruptly. There was a silent commotion somewhere ahead of her. She looked up and darted behind a tree. Sight, sound and smell converged in the form of Clarissa. There she was, beyond a sheltered glade not fifty feet away, her face clearly recognisable under a beam of sunlight which seemed to be paying court to her. Sheela then noticed another figure, mostly hidden by a thicket, but a movement revealed the back of a head she recognised. It was Max. Her first instinct was to cry out to them, in relief that she was not alone after all. Something though about the oddity of finding them in this unlikely place, at this time of morning, made her withdraw. The two main branches of the tree in front of her extended outwards to form a wishbone. She felt her pulse racing as she peered through the 'v' where the branches met. All she could see was Clarissa's head resting against a tree trunk. Her face suddenly turned in the direction of Sheela. Sheela ducked, although she realised that she was almost totally shaded by the umbrella of overhanging leaves.

She raised her head slowly, barely allowing herself to take in what she was witnessing. Clarissa's face was contorted, but the expression was not of pain. Her eyes seemed to be raised skywards, leaving in view what looked like a pair of flickering white almonds. A rhythmic rustling of the bushes surrounded the couple. Suddenly the man's head came forward, tucked in the nape of her neck. The commotion of the foliage became more agitated. The action unfolding before her could have been from a silent movie, yet Sheela was convinced that she could hear convulsive sobs. Suddenly the bushes calmed down, Max's head dropped out of view, and Clarissa slid down, head tilted upwards, until she too disappeared inside the thicket.

Sheela turned quickly, frantic to flee the forest and forget what she had just seen. She retraced her steps back to the main road.

On the way back home, an image from the silent movie stuck to her like a leech: the expression on Clarissa's face, at once euphoric and desperate, of someone drowning in ecstasy, exulting in what she possessed - yet clinging on to it as if its loss could mean the end of everything.

At the breakfast table the *akoori* was waiting for Sheela, sizzling in ghee. Ramu looked at her expectantly, waiting for her to notice the extra quantity on the plate. Sheela nibbled a tiny piece of the egg and exclaimed *"Bohut achha*, Ramu!" He signalled his appreciation of the compliment with a pendulum shake of his head, but his back appeared more bent than ever as he shuffled out of the dining room. She managed to eat half the amount he had served her, then went into Nina's bedroom before he returned to collect the dishes.

She wanted to forget the walk but couldn't stop her mind whirling round what she had witnessed. As she lay on Nina's bed, she replayed the scene with a growing sense of revulsion, but she struggled to identify precisely what disgusted her. Was it the scene itself? Was it some fixation to understand what was really going on, what the expression on the Englishwoman's face truly meant? Was it her own role as a voyeur? Or was it something else? Staring at the ceiling above her, she could scarcely believe what her thoughts were leading her to. At the club she had observed the closeness of the couple, she had noticed how others might feel like outsiders in their presence; the scene she had just witnessed had triggered the same feeling, but much more acutely. On their honeymoon, had she and Cyrus not abandoned themselves in similar circumstances - outdoors, on a hot summer's day, in a secluded copse in Umbria? But now there was no Cyrus, only this couple. An image floated before her, an image she tried to blot out: there she was, right in their midst, with her *and* with him, at the base of that tree, wrapped in their intimacy.

She swung out of bed. The commotion in her mind was not going to subside, but on one thing she was clear: she wanted to leave Mahabaleshwar as soon as possible.

She packed her bag messily, called Ramu and Amoli to tell them that she had to return to the big city to attend to some urgent business, and gave them a *baksheesh* which was even more generous than usual. They accepted the tip with modest grace, but the hint of a frown on Ramu's face showed that he was perturbed by whatever had happened to Sheela Baby.

Although clearly taken aback by Sheela's sudden decision, Gopal didn't protest as she had expected him to; perhaps he had noticed that something serious was afoot.

As she got into the car, Ramu called out and hobbled towards her like a man running a three-legged race with an invisible partner. There was a look of supplication on his face. It turned out that an envelope had been left for her earlier in the morning when she had gone for her walk. Amoli had taken it from a man. Because he was in his quarters Ramu hadn't met the man. There was something careful in the old servant's wording: he hadn't met the man, but that didn't mean he didn't know him. Sheela said there was nothing to worry about and told him to look after himself, his wife and the house.

It wasn't until the house was out of sight that Sheela turned to the envelope in her hand. On it, in neat childish handwriting, was written "Madame". With a sinking feeling, she ripped it open and found what she had feared:

Dear Madame

What a deliteful surprise to see you again in Mahabaleshwar!

It is some while since the last time we are in contact. At that time, as you know your generous contributions were most welcoming. Then I was very surprised that they stopped. If I may say, most respected Madame, I was even a little bit dissapointing. I wrote to you in Mumbai but since I got no reply I thought you were out of station. I could not believe that you did not reply purpusly!

Now I feel God has truely blessed me to meet you in Mahabaleshwar again! Now you may continue your contributions which had become interupted! Kindly put them in envelope and I will arange somebody to pick them up. No need to worry anybody find out. Also please be so kind to put your Mumbai address in envelope so I can contact you there.

I am sure I will never need to embarass you because you are lady who will never forget to do the needful!

Yours most respectfully
Dr Balram Deshpande MBBS

"Evil bastard!"

Her initial fear had turned into fury. There was nothing this slimy creep could do; not after so long. She had made sure that there would be no evidence of her past transactions with him: there were no written communications and all the payments had been in cash. Besides which, who in their right mind would believe his word against hers, especially after so long? Yes, in the worst case scenario, the Bombay chattering classes might whisper that there was no smoke without fire. But it would all become a thing of the past when something more juicy turned up. She tore up the letter, opened the window, and let the pieces of paper fly off, casting to the winds her own principles about litter vandalism.

A feeling of unease crept through her as she recalled Ramu's anxious face. I hope this bastard doesn't make things difficult for my Ramu, she said to herself. Of course, he couldn't do anything really -

Ramu was a totally innocent party; but if the swine couldn't get the better of her, he might, just out of spite, make himself an unwelcome visitor to Lammermoor Lodge. She must remember to phone Ramu to check that all was well with him and Amoli; and to make sure that under no circumstances were her Bombay contact details to be disclosed to anybody without her express permission.

She couldn't help dwelling on the English couple. Who were they really and what lay behind their behaviour - particularly this morning's display out in the open? She wished she had never met them. Perhaps she would make some excuse to avoid going to Bachoo's dinner party.

She closed her eyes, trying to ignore the raucous honking of lorries and the painful bump of potholes over which Gopal seemed to relish speeding. But she knew that any attempt to sleep was no more than a futile bid to banish unwelcome thoughts. Thoughts about the interfering English couple, thoughts about the repulsive doctor. Thoughts about Cyrus. It was possible to avoid dinner parties. But these thoughts were impossible to escape: however hard she fought to shut them out, they slithered back like worms multiplying at every attempt to crush them.

She dreaded the prospect of returning to Bombay and facing all the people she would have to face, her mission unaccomplished. She dreaded her ultimate return to London, where every moment of the day would serve as a reminder of Cyrus. Of the life she had lost.

Bombay

6

Caught in the gridlock of the evening rush hour, Sheela looked for distractions in the hubbub of the approach through the northern suburbs. After the fresh coolness of the hill station, the city's smells assaulted her more acutely than ever: savoury aromas of street food mingling with the stench of rotting garbage, open sewers and black exhaust fumes. People were everywhere, spilling over on to streets and weaving their way through bumpers barely twelve inches apart, escaping injury by an unspoken compact between pedestrians and motorists that brakes would be slammed at the very last moment. Only the profusion of trees offered relief, vines cascading along their gnarled branches like the luxuriant locks flowing down the face of the model advertising Ramtirth Brahmi oil.

Yet, however much she bemoaned the transformation of the Bombay of her childhood into the Mumbai of today, she felt her spirits lifted by the crowds, the din and the pollution assaulting her senses. It was as if everything around her were intent on reminding her that there was life beyond the echo chamber of her mind. No longer did Peter Lorre feel quite so threatening, nor was the prospect of meeting the English couple so daunting. And right now, even the circumstances that had led up to Kate's Point - the circumstances surrounding Cyrus - felt as though they had been experienced at one remove.

"My goodness, darling - back so soon?"

"Will explain in a minute, Mummy. I'm desperate!" Sheela brushed past her mother-in-law.

When she returned from the bathroom, she gave Khorshed a kiss on the cheek and a prolonged squeeze which seemed to take the older woman by surprise.

"How was it in Mahabaleshwar? Did you do everything you needed to get done?"

Khorshed had appeared taken aback when Sheela had suddenly announced her decision to leave for Mahabaleshwar, but her unerring instinct for recognising the boundary between interest and inquisitiveness ensured that she did not probe into precisely what Sheela had meant about settling matters concerning Lammermoor Lodge. So unlike her own mother who, like many belonging to the *bhel puri* and bridge set, confused nosiness with friendliness and discretion with coldness.

"Yes, yes, it was all done. And how about you? You've been taking your pills, haven't you?"

Sheela glanced at the older woman's lined face. Not for the first time she noticed how Khorshed had aged over the past year: her hair was sparser, her hands shook more, and her voice had developed a frail rasp as though shock had eroded her vocal cords. But the woman herself hadn't changed. Her grey eyes, rimmed watery with age, looked steadily at Sheela, but the gaze was comforting, not discomfiting.

"Oh the pills - yes - but you must stop worrying. I'm so glad to have you back, that's all that matters. Come, you must be hungry."

The two of them sat down at the dining table.

"Be sure to have plenty." Khorshed pushed a bowl of asparagus mousse towards Sheela. It was only then that Sheela noticed it was the Moser crystal piece that she and Cyrus had bought on the occasion of her parents-in-laws' ruby anniversary.

"Beautiful, isn't it," said Khorshed, "I've always thought it so beautiful." And then, as if fearful of relapsing into bathos, she stretched her hand out to Sheela and said, "So what are your plans now?"

Sheela told her mother-in-law about Bachoo's dinner party and the English couple who had also been invited, but before she could go on, the telephone rang. Sheela jumped up to answer it. It was past 10.30. Who could it be? *Oh God, hope nothing dreadful has happened.*

"Hi Mom!" she heard with a mixture of delight, anxiety and guilt.

"Oh darling - I was going to write you a letter. But never mind. How are you, has anything happened?"

"Oh stop being so controlling, Mom - why should anything have happened?"

"I'm not being controlling, darling - it's just unusual for you to be phoning all the way from New York, especially at this time of night."

"It's only like morning here. Sorry, I lost track of the time your end."

"Don't worry, sweetheart - it's such a lovely surprise hearing from you."

"Why is it a surprise, Mom - it isn't like this is the first time I'm phoning you! You're always, like, putting me in the wrong."

"No, I'm not - I mean I'm really pleased to hear from you."

Nina's combativeness was bad enough but her use of "mawm" and "like" in the middle of every other sentence was the last straw.

"Granny is sending you lots of love."

"Oh, I didn't think she'd be up so late." (So she *hadn't* lost track of time!) "Can I have a word with her?"

The mention of her grandmother never failed to have a calming effect on Nina.

After handing the telephone receiver over to Khorshed, Sheela left the room to go into the bedroom she and Cyrus had always used when they stayed at Tower View.

She sat on her side of the double bed. Ever since Cyrus had ceased to be part of her life, she had avoided his side, moving everything round to her end of the room - the portable telephone, the chair, the dressing table - even though the disruption had been painful.

She heard a tentative shuffling of the curtains at the entrance to her room. "Darling, Nina wants to say bye to you."

She took a deep breath before picking the phone up. "So, sweetheart, did you have a good chat with Granny?"

"Oh I love talking to Granny; she's so cool." Sheela's ears pricked up; she thought she heard a catch in Nina's voice.

"Oh Mummy, things haven't been good; in fact, things have been horrible!" At this point a series of squeaky hiccups crescendoed into an uncontrolled wail which made Sheela anxious about the reaction of the neighbours at 110th and Broadway.

"Shh, my baby, shh. What's happened, my darling?"

"Jake has... he's left me. For some bitch he met at a sorority get-together at Columbia. I saw the two of them smooching. The bitch was positively gobbling him up. I don't know how he'll survive with her."

"More to the point, how will he survive without you? He'll probably tire of her and return to you."

"Return to me? Why the hell should I take him back?"

"Look, darling, we really must meet asap. You're in the middle of your term, aren't you?"

"Well, funny you say that, Mum - as it happens we have our Spring recess in the second week of March, so maybe if I could come over to you then..."

"Wonderful - the second week in March is about a couple of weeks from now, by which time I should be back in London."

"Great, I'll return to you as soon as I get my flights organised."

Interesting how in the space of a few minutes her daughter had bounced back. Sheela wondered whether Nina had planned the week's break all along, using the Jake story as an excuse to skive off. Anything for a junket, she couldn't resist thinking.

7

At barely past 7.30 Sheela was awoken by a din which made the quiet mornings of Mahabaleshwar feel like a mirage: crows cawing their obscene chorus, *jari puranewalas* shouting their wares in a dual-note cadence like rag-and-bone men all over the world, and buses braying as they honked along the Oval Maidan.

As Sheela left her bedroom, she saw Khorshed seated in the alcove she had made into a prayer area. She had a prayer book in her hands and her body was swaying gently to the rhythm of the words she was mouthing. A portrait of Cyrus, garlanded with dry marigolds, rested on the dressing table opposite her.

Sheela bent over and gave her mother-in-law a kiss on the forehead; it smelt of old skin and eau de cologne. She felt sad - how much longer would the old lady be around? - yet comforted: the smell reminded her of Mary Ayah when she used to hold little Sheela Baby in her arms and sing a Goan-inflected version of Schubert's Ave Maria. Today, forty years later, she sought - and received - comfort from another woman much older than her, a woman she loved deeply, the mother Cyrus adored, now smiling at her with eyes that appeared more watery than usual. But as Sheela craved comfort, guilt was never far away: surely it was she, the younger woman, who should be the comforter, not the comforted?

"You know" - Khorshed's eyes had turned distant - "when Cyrus was a little boy I noticed him on one of his school holidays *pagay-parowing* much more than one is supposed to when saying one's Zoroastrian prayers. Later, when he was much older, he told me that he had felt compelled to bow down at least ten times and repeat his *kusti* prayers twice - as a sort of insurance against anything bad happening to me."

"Oh Mummy!" Sheela wrapped her arms round the old lady's neck. She took a deep breath, which remained caught in her throat as though someone else's arms were squeezing her own neck. She didn't let go of Khorshed until the older woman broke the spell.

"I don't know, sometimes I feel it was all my fault."

"What was all your fault?" The question spilt out as if in defiance of Sheela's own better judgement: it risked a return to a past she dared not remember.

"Cyrus being so nervous and all that."

"How can you say that, Mummy? Cyrus always told me you were the most doting of mothers."

"That's just it - perhaps too doting. Perhaps I should have given him more rope, given him the leeway to become more confident."

"But he was the most confident of people. He always put his best foot forward. He was a perfectionist who succeeded in - in being perfect at everything he did." Fearing that a desperate vehemence had crept into her voice, Sheela added, "Surely that speaks volumes about you!"

"Oh darling, you're very sweet. His father was of the old school, as you might have gathered - he didn't believe in being demonstrative. All too sissy for him. So perhaps I over-compensated, particularly I think in Cyrus's early years at boarding school. Something happened then - I never found out exactly what - and that more or less coincided with the time when he started becoming excessively zealous about his prayers. Whatever it was, it made him slightly withdrawn, slightly difficult to reach out to."

Sheela suddenly felt the need to escape from her mother-in-law's gaze. "Slightly difficult to reach out to." She had thought that too, hadn't she? Those times when he would relapse into a silence which all her efforts to make conversation could never penetrate. Those times when - for all his lovability, his sweetness, his kindness - she felt he was a stranger. Lovability, sweetness, kindness - such hollow words: she tried to stop her mind floating back to that day a year ago...

"Withdrawn, and at the same time - how should I put it? - sort of over-sensitive, almost secretive, about things. I remember once finding him poring over a book in his bedroom which he hastily shut when he saw me come in – of all things, something about different forms of capital punishment, as I recall - not very savoury, I suppose, but hardly anything to lose sleep over. My husband insisted that he play sports, join the Boys' Scouts, the Duke of Edinburgh's Award, that sort of thing - to 'knock that sissy morbidity out of him and make him a man', he would say - but although he did excel in those activities, I feel that this pressure just pushed him further into his shell. It was one of the few things my husband and I couldn't agree on."

"Actually, Mummy, before breakfast can I give Ramu a call – just want to check everything's OK with him."

Sheela sat on her bed, head throbbing, trying but failing to erase the associations brought on by Khorshed's recollections about Cyrus. The familiar nausea that had begun stirring inside her quickly gave way to anger: why was her mother-in-law, normally so contained and lady-like, going on about Cyrus in this way, knowing full well that, as his wife, she would have known him

better than anyone else? Or at least she should have...
Sissy morbidity, his father had said. Against her will, a
memory returned of the time Cyrus had taken her to a
pub near Hampstead Heath, where Ruth Ellis, the last
woman to be hanged for murder in the United
Kingdom, had shot her lover; for a number of days after
that, he had reverted to the subject, dwelling in
particular on the terrifying moments when the noose
was being fixed round the woman's neck.

Sheela rushed to the basin in the bathroom and
spat out a gob of yellow liquid. She gargled with
mouthwash, but remnants of an acrid taste remained in
her mouth. Back in the bedroom, she tried to focus on
something she needed to do, but her mind kept
returning to the conversation she had just had with her
mother-in-law. Seized by a sudden panic, she tried to
trace - and retrace - the thread of that conversation; no,
thankfully she hadn't blurted out anything about that
day last year.

The task in hand came back to her: she had to call
Lammermoor Lodge.

When reassured that all was well, Sheela asked
Ramu whether yesterday's visitor had made another
appearance. Ramu said yes indeed, the man had revisited the house, but not to worry, he had left the
bungalow empty of any information.

Khorshed came out of her bedroom just as Sheela
put the phone down. Sheela sat opposite her mother-in-
law under the gaze of the Nandi that she and Cyrus had
bought from one of the over-priced faux-antique shops
that targeted tourists residing in the Taj Mahal Hotel.
For years she had seen the bull as an icon of good luck,
but now the benevolence of its gaze had turned into
something closer to mournfulness.

Philomena came in from the kitchen and, without any preamble, asked in a Konkani-mutilated version of Gujarati what Sheela wanted for breakfast. She spoke Hindi fluently enough but insisted on Gujarati out of loyalty to the Markers and spite towards Sheela. Ever since Sheela's marriage to Cyrus, when she was no more than ten, she had made a great point of distinguishing the intruder who had appropriated Cyrus Baba from the rest of the family.

Sheela said she wanted tea, nothing else - and could Philomena make sure that the tea was piping hot this time; and, by the way, could she not loiter in the dining room once she had brought in the tea because she had some important matters to discuss with Khorshedbai.

As Philomena flounced out of the room, Khorshed gave Sheela an enquiring glance.

"No, Mummy, there are no important matters to discuss. I'm just sick to death of her constant hostility towards me."

Khorshed looked as though she wanted to say something but couldn't find the right words.

"Sorry, Mummy - I know this is very thoughtless."

Fearing that the conversation might return to Cyrus, Sheela told her mother-in-law that she would like to invite Shireen, her best friend from Cathedral School days, to lunch at the Cricket Club of India.

A week ago, she had not wanted to speak to anybody about her plan to go to Mahabaleshwar, but when she received a call from Shireen, she had to tell her about her trip, explaining that some problems had cropped up at Lammermoor Lodge. She had then cut short the conversation. So now it was time to make amends.

"Sheels, how lovely! Lunch at the CCI would be great - at the usual poolside place? About one? I must say I'm so glad to hear your voice. There was something not quite right when we last spoke."

"Oh, everything's fine. Let's talk when we meet."

The thought of seeing Shireen lifted Sheela's spirits. Shireen - optimistic, ebullient, funny, always by her side, always ready to lend an ear. Her father used to say that true friends could be counted on the fingers of one hand, and Shireen was certainly the best of them. Cyrus had once told her how he envied her closeness to Shireen: "You know, Sheela, your gift for friendship is so precious: there is nobody outside my immediate family I'm really close to - unlike you, no bosom pal like Shireen to confide in." This was his response to her playful observation that, in their circle of acquaintances, she was always his appendage - "Cyrus's wife", "the doctor's wife", "Mrs Marker" - but she felt no resentment because she was so confident in his love for her, so proud of him, so happy that he captivated friends and patients alike with his ready smile and winning ways. His response had struck a chord: she couldn't think of a single person she would have called a close friend of his. She had never really understood why his public popularity wasn't matched by his private relationships. Perhaps, she had thought at the time, because he was a man. Now she knew, from her later experience, that the explanation can't have been that simple - and Khorshed's recent reminiscences confirmed the point.

She had been looking forward to the lunch with Shireen, but now she wished she hadn't made the phone call.

It was a short walk along Dinshaw Vachha Road to the CCI. Just as she approached the club entrance she saw Shireen stepping out of her car.

"Sheels!" Shireen was looking as flamboyant as ever, with reddish-brown make up and scarlet lipstick, a crimson top and flamingo trousers, and four-inch sandals matched by earrings dangling in the sunlight. She looked a good decade younger than her forty-eight years.

Funny how unmarried women always age better than their married counterparts; this is what children - and husbands - do to you.

"Hi, sweetie, so nice to see you looking so glam." Sheela gave her friend a hug, and Shireen landed a cherry lip mark on her cheek.

As they walked past the few parking spaces near the main entrance, Sheela noticed a sign stating 'Reserved for differently-abled member's cars.'

"Look," she pointed to the sign, "surely somebody should have spotted the wrongly placed apostrophe?"

"God, Sheels, you're no longer competing for the English prize!"

Shireen squeezed her friend round the waist. Sheela smiled. For the first time in a while she was feeling more relaxed.

They sat at one of the tables nearest to the swimming pool. Waiters were bustling around in a state of confused misdirection, some taking orders, some appearing to avoid eye contact.

A moustachioed waiter called Selwyn ambled towards them with an air of solicitude as expansive as his paunch.

After giving their orders, Shireen stretched her arm out to hold Sheela's hand. "Sheels, I can't make out what's happened, but - oh, I don't know - are things OK? I know things can't be the same after Cyrus and all that, but I do worry about you. You seem - how can I put it - sort of wary."

Sheela assured her that there was nothing to worry about, and the conversation turned to the last time Shireen had visited Mahableshwar.

"One fresh lime soda," declared the waiter with a flourish of a napkin.

"Now, Shireen, tell me about your nice Australian friend."

"Oh, he's quite cute, but I'm not sure he's my type. Anyway, Shaun's very busy with some friends of his - an English couple who are here for a short while. Actually, I think she's Australian or something - I gather she's the one Shaun originally knew. Apparently they're all going to guess who's for dinner - Bachoo Dhondhy's! - and since finding out that I know her he's been trying to persuade me to come to the dinner as well - but obviously I can't just turn up uninvited."

The waiter brought the *puri bhaji* they had ordered.

"Mm, delicious. Sheels, why the shell-shocked look?"

"This couple you're talking about - they're not called Alexander, by any chance?"

"That's it, that's their name. Goodness, Sheels, how d'you know them?"

"I don't really know them. I just bumped into them in Mahabaleshwar."

Australian; that explains why she had sensed something slightly different about the woman - something not quite English.

"Had tea with them at the Mahabaleshwar Club, together with Bachoo. And I've been invited to Bachoo's too. Shireen, please come. I'd been thinking of some pretext to excuse myself, but if you come I'll go."

"OK Sheels, I'll come, but on condition that you tell Bachoo in advance - and you don't back out at the last minute. So what time are we supposed to be at Bachoo's?"

"Let me check - and I can tell her about you."

Sheela whipped out her mobile.

"Sheela, you haven't forgotten about Friday, have you?"

"No, in fact that's what I was calling about. What time is it?"

"Supposed to be 8pm. But knowing them, your mother and brother won't turn up until 10pm - and there's going to be some maharajah in tow. But don't worry, I plan to start serving dinner no later than 9, so, unlike the rest of your family, please come on time!"

Sheela fought hard to maintain the earlier lilt in her voice. "Oh, with the rest of my family it's going to be quite a party."

"There'll be eight of us."

"Well actually, Bachoo, I was wondering if we could make it nine - you know my friend Shireen Kapadia - she might be at a loose end -"

Shireen was shushing and shaking her head.

"Yes of course I know Shireen. Lovely girl, if a bit loud. Yes yes, nine people will be fine."

"Thanks - I'll tell Shireen. Of course she might be busy, but -"

"No problem, see you on Friday. Arrivederci!"

"Oh God, Sheels, you made me sound so pathetic!"

"No I didn't - I said you might well be busy. Anyway, it's all settled."

"As long as she doesn't think I'm gate crashing. Oh Sheels, it's been lovely seeing you - and I'm so glad you're OK." There followed a tight squeeze and two more kisses, but the *puri bhaji* and fresh lime soda ensured that there was no scarlet imprint this time.

Sheela started walking back towards Tower View. The telephone call to Bachoo had left her with the uneasy feeling of having forgotten something. Oh God, of course; she had to phone Mumsie.

"Lovely! I say, what a surprise. I never expected to receive a call from you all the way from Mahabaleshwar."

"As it happens, I'm back in Bombay."

"Really? Since when?"

"Actually, I returned last night, but..."

"But you couldn't be bothered to ring your poor old Mumsie until this afternoon. Just shows how much you care for her! When I think of your sweet little brother... he even called you when you were in Mahabaleshwar. I suppose I should be grateful to have at least one loving child."

"Yes, it was nice of him to call me. I gather you and he have been invited to Bachoo's for dinner on Friday?"

"Yes. She told me you were coming too."

"I was thinking I could come to see you before that - maybe tomorrow? I'm feeling a bit knackered today."

"Oh, you poor thing. No, I'm really very busy until Friday, so let's just meet then."

"OK, if that's what you want."

"I bet that's what you want! I really need to end this conversation now - I have important things to do."

"All right, bye Mumsie - see you on -." She heard the phone click. *Why do I have to feel so guilty? Bloody bitch.*

She decided that she would spend the rest of the day at home with Khorshed. She would try to forget about herself, about Mahabaleshwar, about the Friday dinner, about everything that bothered her. Tomorrow morning she would go to her tailors, Beverley and Hills, to fetch the sari blouse she had thought she would never need to wear again.

8

Beverley and Hills was on the other side of the Oval Maidan, in a corner street near the law courts. As she stepped onto the road after crossing the Oval, she felt a hand touch her side. For a moment she recoiled, then turned to find an elderly woman asking if she could hold her arm. Yes of course, she replied, but as she slowed her pace she worried that the bellicose taxis edging forward might not be quite so understanding.

They got to the other side of the road just as the baying of the traffic reached its usual crescendo with the changing of lights.

"I'm so sorry," the woman said, "you see, I'm really nervous I'll fall." A faded floral dress, ending above the knee, hung loosely over her skinny frame. The woman's garb, together with her pronounced nose and sallow complexion, told Sheela that she was a Parsi.

With a "thank you so much" the woman shuffled off unsteadily. Sheela sped towards her tailor, concerned that, being a devout Muslim, he might have gone for his *namaaz*.

She felt sad for the Parsi lady, not so much for her personal plight but rather for what she epitomised - a community in decline, its numbers falling so rapidly that short of drastic measures it faced extinction. She was not a Parsi herself but, having married into a Parsi family which had been far kinder to her than her own, she cared for the Parsis with a fervour that endeared her to Cyrus, even though he didn't share her concern about the community. Her mind receded to the conversations she used to have with him on the subject. Always her thoughts returned to Cyrus; like an omnipresent Pied Piper, he drew her back to everything she longed to forget. She had wanted a carefree day, but this woman, a total stranger, had ensured that this wouldn't be possible.

Sheela felt better when she saw Iqbal greeting her with a smiling *salaam*. Before leaving for Mahabaleshwar, she had had the firm intention of never coming back, yet for some reason she had decided to have a *choli* made for a sari she had bought some eighteen months earlier. Why did she do that, she wondered. Because she never really believed in the finality of her trip to the hill station? Before her musings could take hold, she dragged her mind back to the matter in hand and tried on the blouse. It fitted her perfectly.

Stepping out carefully on to the confusion of jagged stone slabs which passed for a pavement, she felt buoyed by the sense that, having seen to the *choli*, she had achieved something useful.

After getting some provisions from Sahakari Bhandar, she took a taxi back home. On arriving at Tower View, the taxi driver demanded forty rupees. Who are you kidding, she exclaimed. This was one of the few cabs that still had the old meter set at prices less than a tenth of current fares, so she demanded to see the price conversion chart kept by all the older taxis. As she had suspected, the driver should have quoted much less - twenty-six rupees, it turned out. How can you lie like that, she shouted at him, and gave him the correct fare without her customary tip. The accusation of lying was met with a shrug.

As she got into the lift, she converted into sterling the fourteen rupees by which the man had tried to overcharge her: less than twenty pence. Her annoyance at being treated as a soft touch was tempered by a feeling of shame. She knew what Cyrus would have said. Why did she always experience this in India - this sense of being manipulated into feeling guilty even when she wasn't at fault? She entered the flat dispirited and worn out.

She found her mother-in-law sitting, eyes closed, listening to music familiar to her. Khorshed gave a start when Sheela came in, then, with the music coming to a close, she heaved herself up to remove the old LP.

"Come, darling, you're just in time for lunch."

"I got you your favourite Ferrero Rocher from Sahakari Bhandar."

"Oh sweetheart, you spoil me."

Philomena came in holding a hot casserole dish. She gave Sheela a sideways glance, twisting her mouth into an awkward smile that ended up looking like a grimace. *She must be in a good mood.*

"You know Schubert's E Flat Piano Trio, don't you."

"Yes, yes."

"That lovely Andante - that's my favourite bit. You hear it again at the end."

"Yes, it was - is - my favourite bit as well."

"And Cyrus loved it of course. I remember him coming to me when he was barely twelve, asking me what the piece was."

"We used to listen to it a lot together."

Khorshed looked up sharply. Sheela bent over the casserole dish and brought it nearer her mother-in-law.

"Here, let me serve you."

"Just that little leg, please. Thanks. Now help yourself to that nice breast."

Sheela tried to disguise her sudden loss of appetite by covering the small piece of chicken she had put on her plate with tomatoes, chillies and a large helping of gravy. She was relieved that her mother-in-law, who had been watching, didn't urge her to have more.

Khorshed retired for her afternoon nap. Sheela went to the balcony, hoping for distraction. Pedestrians were hurriedly seeking shelter against an unseasonal shower. A cyclist, untroubled by the rain, was peddling forward in a meandering motion that triggered furious honking from motor cars forced to slow down. His only protection against the downpour was a white carrier bag wrapped round the top of his forehead and tucked behind his ears. He trundled off towards Churchgate Station, knees slowly rotating in a show of relaxed defiance; this man was certainly not going to be pushed around by bullying motorists, however ferociously they blew their horns. She envied his carefree nonchalance. And here she was, slumped leaden-chested over the parapet. How easy it would be to tip her torso over the edge, with just the slightest shift in her body's centre of gravity. Her mind drifted back to Kate's Point. She wasn't really serious then, was she? So how could she be serious now? She pulled herself up to return to her bedroom, switched the ceiling fan on, lay on her bed, and drifted into a half-sleep.

She woke up sweating, to find it was already 4.30.

Her mother-in-law was seated at the dining table.

"I got these done for you, darling." Khorshed pointed to the plate of hot cheese toast - squares of orange with bubbles surfacing like molten lava.

Sheela bit into the cheese toast.

"Gosh, Mummy, it's really yummy, but I know it's going to sit on my tummy. I think I'll go for a little constitutional on Marine Drive."

"OK darling, but please be careful - you never know what people can get up to nowadays."

"Oh Mummy, don't be silly - Marine Drive is full of people quite late into the night. In any case, how do I manage all on my own in London?"

"I know. I worry about that all the time."

There was a moment's silence. Both mother-in-law and daughter-in-law knew that the conversation had brought them back to the person who was their common link.

9

It was 6.45 when Sheela reached Marine Drive. Her mood lifted with the cool sea breeze and the chatter of people on the promenade curving round the Arabian Sea. This evening she preferred the company of strangers; they couldn't trigger unwanted memories. Walking towards Nariman Point, she sought distraction from the people milling around her: young couples walking together, some holding hands, some with children in tow; smiling youths sauntering hand in hand, fingers loosely interlocked; elderly stalwarts in knee-length shorts taking their evening constitutional with the rickety gusto of those desperate to ward off the onset of infirmity; and the ubiquitous street vendors - *nariyalwalas* deftly slicing the tops of coconuts, and purveyors of *makai bhutta* delicately twirling their corn over open fires.

"Hello - it's Sheela, isn't it?"

Sheela froze for a second, then walked hurriedly on, pretending that she hadn't heard anything.

But the voice had caught up with her.

"Fancy bumping into you here of all places!"

"Oh it's you -"

"Yes, Clarissa - from Mahabaleshwar. Goodness - it's almost as though we're destined to be thrown together in the most unexpected - sorry, I'm rambling; how are you?"

"Well, thank you. And how about you and -?"

"Max. Oh, we're both fine. Enjoying Mumbai - Bombay."

"I never asked you before - have you been travelling around India?"

"Well, before Bombay, we did the Delhi-Agra-Jaipur thing - and then of course came to Mahabaleshwar."

After a slight pause, Clarissa continued, "Do you often go to Mahabaleshwar?"

"Used to go there pretty often. Last time was about a year ago."

"Lovely place."

"Did you manage to do a lot of painting there? I noticed the paint brush at Kate's Point."

"Yes, how can one resist those views? Not that I would have been able to do justice to them."

"Time to turn round - we've reached the end of Nariman Point. Bachoo said you were staying somewhere in Marine Drive? Sunset Villas?"

"Yes, very appropriate name. Max and I just love waiting for the moment when the last sliver of the sun slips beneath the horizon."

"Funny, I remember doing just that as a child when we had a flat overlooking the sea."

"And did you feel the same when you saw a plane land - that exquisite moment approaching touchdown?"

"Yes yes - I know exactly what you mean. But I could never understand why."

"No, nor could I."

Through most of the conversation Sheela had been looking straight ahead of her, but the shared delight in watching sunsets and plane landings made her turn towards Clarissa with a smile. "Well, in that respect at least we must be kindred spirits!"

Clarissa returned the smile, but before she could say anything Sheela changed the subject, embarrassed that she might have come across as over-familiar. "You're coming to Bachoo's, aren't you?"

"Oh yes, we haven't forgotten about that."

"Do you know where she lives?"

"Not exactly, but I'm sure a taxi driver will know."

"Look, as it happens, you're on my way, so I could pick you up. If you wait downstairs at 7.45, that should be fine."

"Well, thanks a lot - that would be lovely."

They were now approaching the point where Sheela would need to cross Marine Drive to walk back to Tower View. They walked uncertainly as if unsure about what to say next.

Their arrival at the crossing forced Sheela's hand. "Well, I must be leaving now - it's just a seven-minute walk in that direction," Sheela said nodding her head eastwards.

"And how much longer are you going to be here? I understand you don't live here all the time."

"No, actually I'm based in London, although I come here quite often." Sheela noticed a gap in the flow of traffic speeding along Marine Drive. "I'll tell you all about it when we meet tomorrow evening."

"I look forward to that."

Sheela had dreaded anything like the cheek-to-cheek contact which had become, at least in the west, the common currency of greetings and leave-takings even among virtual strangers. The threat of a new onslaught of vehicles gave her the chance to sprint across the road and give a breezy wave without appearing to be unfriendly.

Walking back, past the CCI, she felt a sense of anticipation - although of what she had only a vague notion. Thoughts of her first encounter with the Alexanders threatened to float back, but this evening at least she managed to ward them off. She was almost looking forward to the dinner party. True, she cringed at the thought of facing her mother and brother, but ranged against them were her allies - Shireen and Bachoo and, yes, the Alexanders.

10

When she had planned this trip to India, social life was the last thing on Sheela's mind. The only evening clothes in her wardrobe were those she had left in Bombay the previous time she had returned to London. Now here she was, faced with the choice of a pair of jeans or two items Cyrus had bought her a few years before – a red floral dress and an embroidered *salwar khameez* in pale green silk studded with tiny sequins. When she placed the items of clothing on her bed, she felt quite unable to decide what to wear.

What had happened earlier in the day hadn't helped her confidence; no more did she feel the sense of anticipation, bordering on optimism, that she had experienced immediately after meeting Clarissa the previous evening. Over breakfast, the smell of burning toast had reminded her of the need to change the toaster – just one of the many things in Khorshed's flat that had suffered from neglect over the past year. Over lunch, Khorshed had entered the dining room smelling of the Yardley Lavender soap that Cyrus and she had got her the previous year. And over tea, Khorshed had lapsed into reminiscences about the holidays she, her husband and Cyrus had spent in Lammermoor Lodge, no doubt in the hope that recollections of a past so distant would cushion both women from memories of more recent times. However much Sheela tried to turn her mind away from him, Cyrus remained an ever-present absence.

There was a tentative knock on the door.

"Darling, wondering if you're OK."

"Oh Mummy, please come in," Sheela said, leading the old lady to the chair. "So glad you're here.

Please help me decide what I should wear at Bachoo's. Jeans are too informal, but I just can't see myself wearing those other clothes."

The two women looked into each other's eyes. Khorshed held out her arms, and Sheela fell into them. Kneeling beside her mother-in-law, she laid her head on her lap. Then, against all her instincts, she found herself letting go, not caring that her tears were wetting the older woman's dressing gown.

"It's all right, my darling. It's all right." Sheela felt the thin arms, skin loosely hanging from their bones, tightly folded round her shoulders.

She stayed there for what might have been five minutes, until she felt herself getting a crick in her neck. As if anticipating this would happen, Khorshed placed her hands on her cheeks and moved them gently upwards.

"Come," smiled the old woman, "you are going to wear something nice."

"But I can't. Cyrus gave them to me."

"Perhaps that's all the more reason why you should wear one of them. I think the *salwar khameez* will look lovely on you. Wearing something nice is not a betrayal or anything, you know."

Sheela rose, delicately placing the hands holding her cheeks on to her mother-in-law's lap. She picked up the jeans and the floral dress and hung them back in the wardrobe.

She turned round to find that Khorshed had already managed to get on to her feet unaided.

"In the next hour or so I'm expecting to see you looking beautiful and happy, all set for the party." Before Sheela could give her mother-in-law a helping hand, she was out of the room.

Sheela arrived at the Alexanders' place on the dot of 7.45. She saw them from a distance, tall figures silhouetted against the sun setting over the Arabian Sea. They looked as if they had been waiting for a while.

"Hello, really good of you to pick us up!" said Clarissa. "Thank you," she added, flashing an uncertain smile at Gopal, who had jumped out to open the door for her. He acknowledged the thanks with a vigorous sideways oscillation of the head.

Forcing a smile, Sheela said, "Hi, nice to see you both."

"Very good to see you," said Max, "and, yes, so nice of you to give us a lift - just as you did -"

"I told you, Max, didn't I, that Sheela and I bumped into each other yesterday on Marine Drive."

"Yes I know, what a coincidence!"

"Not as much as you think - I live pretty close to you."

Why does the conversation feel so stilted today? Not like when we were alone together on Marine Drive.

Sheela turned her head. "So, how've you both been?"

"I'm afraid Max went down with food poisoning."

"Oh no, what did you eat?"

"I don't really know - when it comes to food, I'm the first person to go down with something horrible. Being Indian, you don't have that problem, I suppose."

"Actually, that isn't true. My husband was just like you."

Oh God, I've done it again - why the hell can't I just bite my tongue for a change? It was as though lurking somewhere at the back of her mouth was a self-willed gremlin bent on breaking all her taboos.

An acrid gust of wind blew in, bringing with it the memories she wanted to shun: of evenings spent strolling hand in hand with Cyrus, all the way from Nariman Point to the far end of Chowpatty Beach; of street food wolfed down by her, always turned down by him; of the stale-sweet saltiness that settled on even the more salubrious parts of the city's seafronts.

"Oh did you see the sunset today?" cried Clarissa. "You don't get sunsets like that in England."

"No", said Sheela, "but I prefer the sky there."

"You're joking! It's so tame in comparison."

"That's just it. I find the tameness safe and comforting."

There followed a discussion about how the landscape in India was different from that in England. Still so stilted, thought Sheela, as though we are all beating around the bush.

"Clarissa tells me that you live in London?" Max asked tentatively, as though the question might appear intrusive.

"Yes, in Islington."

"Goodness, coincidences never cease. So do we! Now don't say you live near Upper Street?"

"Actually I do – close to Highbury Fields. Why, do you?"

"Yes, Clarissa and I live not too far from Theberton Street - you know, previously run down Georgian terrace renovated by developers and converted into flats ridiculously expensive for their size. Oh how I envy you all that green space!"

"Yes, we - I used to go for a constitutional around the fields, but for the past year or so I'm afraid I've been rather lazy."

Sheela was relieved to be interrupted by Gopal asking when the car would be needed for the return to Tower View. They were minutes away from Bachoo's bungalow off Nepean Sea Road. The journey had been remarkably quick. Sheela slipped a one hundred rupee note into Gopal's left hand, asking him to return within a couple of hours. She was sure his meal would cost far less than a hundred rupees. "Every evening out," she once said to Cyrus, "is a nice little earner for Gopal", to which Cyrus had responded, "Should we begrudge him the little extras he can earn? After all, what's a hundred rupees to us?"

"Well, we're almost there. It's that bungalow further up on the left."

11

In the dusk it wasn't possible to see the peeling paintwork on the porch. Like much of Bombay, Bachoo's bungalow was shown to best effect when darkness hid the decay and dirt infiltrating even the poshest parts of the city. It stood silhouetted against a dense blue sky partially silvered by a half moon, its delicate profile made all the more poignant by its forlorn position as one of the few remaining bastions of old Bombay, standing its ground against the depredations of the tower blocks closing in on it.

"Oh there you are!" Resplendent in a shiny maroon sari, Bachoo swept to the car just as Sheela got out.

"So glad you could make it," she added, turning to the Alexanders.

"So nice of you to have us over."

"Yes really," said Max. Sheela looked up at him. *There's something diffident, almost wimpish, about him. You expect handsome men to be vain and cocky, but clearly he isn't. But nor, for that matter, was Cyrus.*

"Come in, welcome to my humble abode."

Bachoo beckoned the Alexanders into a vast drawing room which combined splendour and decay in equal measure. Everything that could fray had been allowed to slip into genteel decline: red velvet curtains, brocade upholstery, a pink Persian carpet - all motheaten and worn at the edges; and all around the room, walls with damp patches and flaking plasterwork. But everything that could survive the passage of time continued to flaunt the wealth of better days: an opulent crystal chandelier like a sparkling wedding cake; a proliferation of Meissen figurines, heads tilted, arms raised in silent appeal; a Steinway grand gleaming ebony in the far corner of the room; two mahogany settees and four matching chairs, their backs filigreed with carvings of flowers and leaves scrambling upwards in a frantic bid to distract attention from the sadness of the upholstery they framed.

"What a beautiful piano! Do you play?" Clarissa glanced at the music scores on the piano stool.

"I used to be not too bad in my younger days, but now I just tinker with the odd bit of Chopin - you know, the Raindrop Prelude, the Waltz in C Sharp Minor (that's his loveliest waltz, of course) - but the quick bits nowadays are a bugger for me, excuse my language. So you like classical music, do you?"

"Oh yes - Max is in fact the first violinist in one of the London-based quartets - the Caracalla."

"You don't mean the one I saw at Wigmore Hall?" There was a note of grudging respect in Bachoo's question.

"Yes, they do play at Wigmore. Max, Bachoo might be interested to know more from you."

Sheela wanted to leave the room. The Waltz in C Sharp Minor, one of Cyrus's favourite Chopin pieces, and now the Wigmore, one of his favourite haunts.

The doorbell rang.

"I wonder which of my disgracefully early guests have just arrived."

The cloud of voices outside soon cleared up to reveal the identity of the next arrival. Shireen, never a shrinking violet, sounded positively demure as she tried to make herself heard between the stentorian explosions of welcome that greeted her. Sheela got up immediately to meet her friend.

"I'm so glad you've come." Sheela's hug was so extended that it seemed to catch Shireen by surprise.

She took a step back. Her friend was wearing a shimmering green outfit and a necklace and bangles that looked like jade.

"Glamour, thy name is Shireen! And where's lover boy?"

"Shh, he had to return to Australia. I'm so relieved - too much of a windsurfer type for my liking."

"Sheela, I don't know what the two of you are *ghoos-ghoosing* about, but let me introduce your friend to Max and Clarissa."

Introductions had barely been made when the doorbell rang again.

"That must be your mother. Miraculous, she's only half an hour late," said Bachoo, glancing at her watch. "Perhaps she should take a few turns round the block to make sure she's *respectably* late."

Sheela wondered what the Alexanders were making of the trio who had just entered the room.

First to walk in was her mother, in a deep gold sari with a red border. A streak of white swept up from her forehead across a mass of black hair rolled up into an enormous bun ("the genuine article, not like Indira Gandhi's"). Under the light of the chandelier her face had the crinkly shine of make-up applied to conceal the ravages of age. And her mouth reminded Sheela of a joke she and her brother had shared as teenagers: Mumsie, Mohan had jibed, "had a touch of the Joan

Crawford" about her, a reference to the extravagant smearing, well beyond the lip line, of their mother's favourite *Rose Blush Delight*.

Immediately following her mother were Mohan and the Maharajah of Chhota Buddhipur.

Her brother had developed a prosperous paunch in an otherwise scrawny body, and sported a shock of frizzy shoulder-length hair which reminded Sheela of a faux Satya Sai Baba. His pockmarked skin was fashionably spiked with a two-day stubble, and blood-red signet rings adorned fingers tipped with nails bitten to the quick.

Next to him stood a portly man wearing a shiny black Nehru jacket that was too tight for his frame. He had a baby face, grey and nondescript except for a bulbous nose and gimlet eyes which made him appear permanently on the make. The sort of guy, Sheela decided, who must have sweaty palms.

"My, Saroj, you're early - as usual!"

"Darling, you don't know what the traffic was like today." Saroj shot Sheela a glance before turning to the Alexanders: "So you must be the friends from England."

"Yes, we're here on holiday." To Sheela's surprise, it was Max who had spoken. She glared at her mother, who appeared bent on leaving it to the last to acknowledge her daughter.

But Mohan made up for Saroj. "Oh Lovely, how lovely to see you!" He ran towards Sheela and lifted her off her feet before she could push him away. "Buddy, meet my big sister Sheela."

"Plizzed to mit you," said the maharajah with a perfunctory *namasté*, but his eyes had already wandered towards Clarissa. "You must introduce me to those Britishers," he murmured to Mohan.

"Sheela!" shouted Saroj, who was now seated with Max on one of the settees. "Aren't you going to give your Mumsie a pecky-wecky?"

"Hi Mumsie." She walked over and bent down to kiss a coquettishly upturned cheek.

"What is this, avoiding your poor Mumshie; first, not bothering to contact her when you return to Bombay, and now no hello." Then, with a sideways glance at Max: "If it weren't for my gorgeous friend here, I'd have been plunged into depression." A flush crept up Max's face.

"Come, sit next to us." Saroj patted the space to her left, shoving her bulk so that her ample right thigh was comfortably nudging Max's left. Sheela sat on the edge of the settee.

She suddenly felt her face twisted sideways.

"Mumsie, what are you doing," she mouthed ferociously, hoping that Max wasn't noticing.

"I was just looking at you under the light, darling, and I see that you are *really* looking pulled down. I don't know *what* Mahabaleshwar has done to you." She extracted a compact from her handbag and proceeded to apply its contents to the bridge of Sheela's nose.

"For God's sake!" Sheela withdrew her head sharply.

"Come come, *beti*. Your poor Mumsie is doing this for *your* sake, not hers. See, already so much better - my my, your nose is quite transformed, almost a retroussé! Now you can really call yourself Lovely!"

"I need a drink," Sheela muttered. Getting up from the settee, she noticed that Max had suddenly developed an interest in the chandelier. She felt herself shaking as she walked towards Shireen, who had emerged from the group clustered round the piano, a gin and tonic in one hand and a bright smile on her face.

"Hi Sheels, what's the matter?"

"Oh, nothing. Just my mother being a pain as usual. So what have you been talking about?" Turning her head towards the piano, Sheela saw her brother, the maharajah and Bachoo all appearing to be talking to Clarissa at the same time.

"Oh it's so revolting, that third-rate princeling has been rolling his eyes up and down the Australian woman's bust ever since he set eyes on her. But *she's* lovely, and I don't mean just physically. There is a sort of - how can I put it? - fragility about her that is really attractive."

Sheela felt a pulse of recognition; her friend had this uncanny ability to pinpoint the essence of a person. But when she traced where her own discernment of Clarissa's vulnerability sprang from, the line of memory returned her to the bushes of a secluded copse in Mahabaleshwar.

"Now what's happened, Sheels? You've gone all morose again."

For Sheela, dinner turned out to be an excruciating affair: her mother expressing outrage at the unequal treatment of the poor in India, then launching into a tirade about how every one of her four servants failed to turn up for work the day before; Bachoo casting significant glances at Sheela as she asked Saroj, "the patron saint of egalitarianism", if she intended to divide her wealth equally between her two children; Mohan, pretending not to have heard Bachoo's remark, proclaiming that his Mumsie's compassion made her the guardian angel of the downtrodden - and in the next breath singing the praises of the maharajah, his dear Buddy Baby, without whose opulent palace it would have been impossible to accommodate the 500 guests so eager to attend his sold-out symposium *The Kama Sutra Guide for the Smart Investor*; the maharajah, encouraged by Mohan's accolade, inviting Clarissa to his "peliss" where he could show her "the best picocks in India", adding, as an afterthought, that she could always bring her husband along "if he wishes to avail of my facilities"; Max icily informing the maharajah that he and Clarissa did everything together – and there was absolutely no time to visit his palace; and Clarissa, wide-eyed, lips parted, looking as if she was silently begging Max to change the subject. The frantic, upturned face of Clarissa in the Mahabaleshwar woods once again flashed through Sheela's mind, and with that image stirred inside her a feeling she couldn't quite pinpoint.

"So who will have coffee?"

Sheela was relieved that the dinner was coming to an end. The *sali ma chicken* and mutton *dhansak* were delicious, but no compensation for the conversation that had accompanied the food.

"We won't, thanks - we try to avoid coffee in the evening," said Max almost immediately. Sheela looked up at him: he certainly seemed to be the dominant partner now.

"Nor will I," said Sheela.

"I won't either," said Shireen.

"That settles it – lovely having you all over."

"Oh, we wouldn't want to break up the party," said Clarissa.

"You're doing nothing of the sort," said Bachoo.

"Well, *we* could have done with some coffee, but we know when we have outstayed our welcome. Thanks for the evening." Saroj gave a half-hearted air kiss, which was withdrawn the moment Bachoo stuck her neck out to receive it.

"The food was wonderful," said Sheela. As Saroj waddled out of the dining room, Sheela couldn't help feeling every wobble of her mother's departing hindquarters bristling at her.

When her mother, brother and the maharajah had driven away, Sheela turned to Shireen: "Come with us, we can all squeeze into the car."

"No thanks, Sheels. I've brought the old Maruti with me."

Watching Shireen drive away, Sheela said, "I worry about her."

"Yes I know, but you need to look after yourself as well." Bachoo put her arms round Sheela, and the two women held each other tight. The painful lump rising in Sheela's throat was stopped in its tracks only by the sight of the Alexanders peering at the *gulmohar* trees lining the driveway.

"Better be going," Sheela said to the couple, "are you ready?"

"Oh yes," said Clarissa; then, turning to Bachoo: "Thank you again so much for the splendid meal."

How vulnerable this beautiful woman looks, Sheela thought as Clarissa glanced at her with the hint of a smile before dipping her head into the interior of the car. It was only then that Sheela recognised the feeling that had earlier eluded her: she wished to protect Clarissa - and it was this protectiveness that had made her want to whisk the couple away from the dinner party as quickly as possible.

12

"I've eaten far too much," Clarissa said as they left they left the driveway.

"Indian hospitality demands that one overeat."

"It puts us to shame," said Max.

"What do you mean?" Sheela asked, but she knew the answer: how many times had she and Cyrus entertained neighbours like the Johnsons with elaborate teas - a tarte tatin from Euphorium, *bhajias* from Drummond Street, a homemade red pepper quiche, and Orange Pekoe Darjeeling tea to wash everything down? All very successful and very pleasant, ending with effusive thankyous and insistent repetitions of how 'you really must come over to our place'. And the final outcome? Awkwardly enthusiastic good mornings and how-are-yous when the neighbours couldn't avoid bumping into them in Highbury Fields, typically followed by 'a nice day, isn't it', and ending with 'we really must be going, so nice talking to you'.

"Well, look how inhospitable the Brits are in comparison."

"So, Max, we must make amends for that, mustn't we? That means, Sheela, you must come over when we are all back in London."

"Oh, there's absolutely no need for that."

Sheela heard the reprimand of her daughter's voice: "Mum, you resent the neighbours not returning invitations but then when people do make overtures you shy away from them, as if they've got some axe to grind."

"We don't need to but we do want to - don't we, Max?"

Before Max could respond, Sheela said, "That's really kind - I'd love to come over."

"And you live so close to us," said Max.

"Yes - Calabria Road."

"Oh I know," said Clarissa, "that's where Esther, one of my painting partners, lives." "Painting is obviously a serious hobby for you."

"More than a hobby. Clarissa is a professional artist. Her current exhibition has been getting rave reviews."

"Max, the way you're going on Sheela will be horribly disappointed."

"I have a feeling I won't - but I'll need details about timings and location."

"Yes of course," said Max. They agreed to exchange mobile numbers.

As they approached Sunset Villas, Clarissa said, "You must be frightfully busy, so I don't suppose we'll see you before our return to London?"

"Probably not," said Sheela, sinking into her seat. She had been looking forward to something, which she just realised was the prospect of meeting the Alexanders again, but now Clarissa had closed the door to that possibility.

Then, as if another Sheela had taken over, she heard herself say, "Actually, I do have a little time to show you the shops if you'd like me to do so." The Sheela of old hadn't broken away entirely: they needed to know that she was the giver, not the taker; that she didn't really need their company.

"Oh thank you - that would be great!" said Clarissa.

"Well," said Max, "if it's shopping you want to do I'll leave the two of you to it."

The two women agreed to meet at 11am the next day. Clarissa leant forward and kissed the side of Sheela's half-turned face. Max clasped the hand Sheela had extended with both of his; this time it didn't even occur to her to withdraw it from his grip.

As the car moved away, Sheela turned round to give the couple a wave. She stopped short when she saw the silhouette of Max holding Clarissa by the waist, his head bent as he kissed her forehead. A deep tenderness seemed to be holding them together. A memory came back to her of Cyrus and herself walking hand in hand in Hampstead Heath, his face turned towards her with a smile so protective that it was impossible for her to imagine that anything could ever disrupt her idyllic existence.

13

The next morning Sheela was stirred from her sleep by the sound of tapping. She felt a familiar lurch in her stomach. Over the past year, it had become an anxious receptacle of bad news, real or imagined, and anything unexpected was liable to trigger a bout of panic.

More alert now, she realised that the tapping was nothing more than the sound of rain - fat drops, unusual for this time of year, smacking the window pane like Diwali fire crackers.

She entered the dining room to find Khorshed reading the Times of India. A plate of dry toast lay on the table.

"Good morning, Mummy. Oh you shouldn't have waited for me - your toast must be quite cold."

"Much more fun eating cold toast with you than hot toast without you."

As Sheela bent over to kiss her mother-in-law on the forehead she saw that, for all her wisdom, Khorshed couldn't resist minor vanities, one of which was the discreet application of black crayon marks on exposed areas of the scalp.

"I wish everybody were as sweet as you," Sheela said as she took her place at the table.

Sheela put a piece of toast next to the *akoori* Khorshed had asked Philomena to make for her.

"Why, darling? What has 'everybody' done to you?"

"Oh, I don't know. Last night was pretty ghastly. I told you about the English couple - or Australian, I never quite know what they are - who were invited to Bachoo's, didn't I? Anyway, some maharajah friend of my brother's kept on making passes at the woman, annoying everybody else in the process. Well, everybody else except my brother... and my mother."

"Oh, how is she?"

"Fine, I suppose. By the way, I'm taking Clarissa - the Englishwoman - shopping later this morning."

"How nice. But, not meaning to interfere, have you visited your mother since you arrived this time?"

"Well, we've spoken over the phone - and I did meet her at Bachoo's."

Khorshed broke off a piece of her toast and proceeded to chew it slowly.

"Look, Mummy, you know how I've never felt particularly welcomed by my mother - and how she's blatantly favoured my brother over me."

"And how is he?"

Sheela respected her mother-in-law's discretion, but there were times when it froze out the possibility of visceral love, the type of love that would have had her say - or at least think - "Yes, I know what a bitch your mother has been to you!" Instead her response felt like a silent reproof.

"Oh, very full of his success in getting his maharajah friend to sponsor some event at which he is going to be the star turn." Pausing for a moment, she added, "Now, Mummy, you've made me feel all guilty! I'd better make an appointment to see my mother. As usual, you're right."

"*Hell*o." The familiar voice rang out, stressing the first syllable to make it sound like "hell". Believing in the power of the gracious telephone voice, Saroj had told her children, "You never know, there could be somebody important at the other end of the phone, so always remember to say '*hell*o' just like this if you want to give a good impression."

"Hello, Mumsie."

"Oh, it's you." The gracious tone was quickly dropped. "Well, what do you want?"

"I was just phoning to say I must see you before returning to London."

"Oh how very kind of you. Sparing your Mumsie a few minutes before you rush back to London. Well, if you must know, your poor Mumshie is *very, very hurt* with her Lovely's neglect." There was a fraction of a pause before she continued, "OK, it's extremely inconvenient for me, but come over for pot luck tonight. My Sweetie might be around before he goes off on his jaunt."

"Great! Will 7.30pm be OK?"

There was no response. Saroj had already put the phone down.

Sheela left her room to find Khorshed reading her *Khordeh Avesta*. A devout Zoroastrian, she wore her religion lightly. She immediately put the book aside and turned enquiringly to Sheela.

"I'm going to my mother's for pot luck."

"Oh good. I'll tell Gopal that his services will be required this evening."

"Thanks, Mummy. I dread his reaction when he knows it's going to be two late nights in a row."

"Look, sweetheart, you know I hardly ever go out, so his life is pretty cushy. It's only when you and Cyrus are around - I mean when - oh dear, I've now gone and dropped the book. Sorry, darling."

"No problem, Mummy." Sheela picked up the *Khordeh Avesta*.

"Shouldn't you be getting ready to take your English friend around?" Khorshed seized Sheela's hand as the *Khordeh Avesta* was returned to her lap. "Listen, I'll make sure Gopal is ready for you."

14

As the car approached Sunset Villas, Sheela felt a curious mixture of elation and guilt. Surely she shouldn't be feeling so light-hearted?

Clarissa was already waiting downstairs.

This time Sheela was sitting at the back, and it seemed natural for the two women to hug as Clarissa slipped next to her.

Because Clarissa was mainly interested in getting cushion covers, Sheela suggested trying Fabindia.

When the car stopped outside the store Gopal turned round to say he was running a temperature.

Sheela was about to question him when she noticed that sweat was trickling down a face that had turned mustard-grey.

She turned to Clarissa to explain that Gopal wasn't feeling well and that they would need to take a taxi after they had finished with Fabindia.

As the two women got out, they were confronted by the sight of three cab drivers lounging along the front seats of their stationary taxis, grimy-soled feet sticking out of the driver's windows. A strong whiff of body odour assaulted the two women as they walked past them.

"Oh I love the hubbub of this place!"

Sheela smiled: Clarissa was a woman too tactful to reveal that anything met with her disapproval - or, perhaps more likely, she simply wasn't the disapproving kind.

Shopping became a strained affair. Clarissa couldn't make up her mind what to buy and Sheela spent much of her time assuring her that there was no need to apologise for wasting her precious morning. Finally they left the shop, Clarissa with a carrier bag containing four cushion covers.

"Shall we have a bite now? We could go to the India Tea Centre - it serves snacks, both Indian and Continental - and of course tea."

"Sounds great."

Sheela hoped her smile didn't look too forced. How on earth was the next hour going to pass?

"Taxi!" she shouted at one of the sleeping cab drivers. He rubbed his eyes and heaved himself into a seated position with a yawn which she decided was a deliberate show of insolence.

At the first set of traffic lights, a beggar tapped at the window groaning for money in a practised monotone. Sheela looked straight ahead.

As the taxi jolted forward, Clarissa said, "Must be very difficult to know when to give money to beggars."

"Did you want to give her something?"

"I'm not sure. If I'd been on my own, I might well have, but in the circumstances I didn't feel it was appropriate."

In the circumstances, stuck in a taxi with this heartless Indian woman. Why should an accident of birth require her to feel more responsible for the poor of India than someone who happened to be born elsewhere?

"Perhaps it's easier for those who don't confront this sort of poverty every day to feel confident about the right thing to do."

"Well, truthfully I wouldn't have known whether following my instinct was really the right way to respond."

"Precisely - one never knows; if you give, are you encouraging further begging? If you don't, are you depriving the genuinely needy of the few rupees that can make a real difference to them?"

Having come to a truce of sorts, both women felt a slight release of the tension that had been building up.

But the truce didn't last long. When they arrived at the Tea Centre on Veer Nariman Road, Clarissa insisted on paying the taxi fare and gave the driver a five rupee tip.

"They don't expect a tip, you know."

"But it's nothing - barely seven pence in English money."

"As you wish." But Sheela knew who Cyrus would have agreed with.

Sheela had always regarded the Tea Centre a closely guarded secret of the Bombay cognoscenti, hidden as it was in a sandstone-coloured building that managed to look nondescript notwithstanding its art deco style. The unpromising entrance gave way to a room which felt like a cosy relic of a bygone era. Placed on each linen-covered table was a little brass bell, a survivor from earlier times when it would have been regarded too crude or too effortful to beckon a waiter with a shout or a hand gesture. The waiters here were dressed in suitably decorous uniforms - tunics and trousers held in place by red cummerbunds. Only the background Muzak, with its medley of incongruously juxtaposed tunes, shattered the illusion of a throwback to the early 20th century.

Today Sheela felt there was something tiresome about the anachronistic charm of the place - and why did the waiters, sweetly attentive though they were, always look so aimless in their well-meaning scurrying?

A waiter beckoned the two women to the only table available. The place was packed with office workers, although there were a few Lonely Planet-type tourists.

Sheela asked the waiter to return in two minutes, then turned to Clarissa: "So what will you have to eat and drink?"

"What will *you* have?" Was this question a request for a recommendation, or part of the social jousting match played to establish the power of the host?

On Sheela's suggestion, Clarissa opted for apple tea, but left the food order to Sheela.

"OK, now where's the waiter gone?"

Instead of the waiter, a corpulent figure came waddling towards Sheela.

"Don't you remember me?" Sheela couldn't place the woman but recognised the squeaky voice and the round face with beady eyes glinting behind horn-rimmed spectacles.

"He*llo*!" Sheela exclaimed.

"No, you don't remember me, do you," the woman smiled triumphantly.

"Well, your face -"

"Perin Anklesaria. I used to be a seamstress at the Ratan Tata Industrial Home when your mother-in-law came to have her saris done."

"Oh yes, of course!"

"When I saw you enter the room I thought I must come over to pay my condolences. *So* sorry to learn about your husband. Must have been a *terrible* blow for Mrs Marker." Without waiting for a response she lowered her voice: "How come so sudden?" The woman had an eager smile on her face.

"Oh, here's the waiter, at long last."

The woman looked put out by Clarissa's interruption.

"Well, sorry for disturbing you. Please give my regards to Mrs Marker." The woman turned towards the exit. Sheela could have sworn there was disappointment and spite in the heave of her backside.

She turned to Clarissa: "Thank you."

"Silly, nosy woman," said Clarissa with a laugh, lightly touching Sheela's hand.

"You see, my husband died suddenly about a year ago."

"I'm so sorry - but listen, you don't need to explain anything."

Somehow she understands, Sheela thought. She only withdrew her hand when she became aware of the shuffling of the waiter.

After giving the order, Sheela turned to Clarissa. "I feel I sort of owe you an explanation."

"Why on earth should you owe me anything?" Clarissa said with a smile. Her eyes were penetrating yet gentle.

Sheela felt the urge to abandon her natural caution and confide in this virtual stranger - maybe because she was a stranger. Like an acrophobe, she felt herself teetering on the edge, terrified yet tempted to jump off a cliff, never mind the consequences.

"I don't know why."

"That day in Mahabaleshwar -"

"Goodness, that was quick! Our order has arrived. Help yourself before it becomes cold."

"Mm, wonderful," said Clarissa, sipping her apple tea.

Sheela bit into a square of chilli cheese toast. "You were saying something about Mahabaleshwar." As the words spilled out, she could hardly believe that it was she who was returning to the subject.

"Yes, I was saying that Max and I felt that something very - very dramatic - was about to happen that evening at Kate's Point."

"Gosh, it all sounds very exciting."

"I'm being quite serious." Clarissa's face looked grave, but the gentleness hadn't left her voice or her smile.

"Listen, I'm sure it's all OK now," she continued, resting her hand on Sheela's arm.

Sheela was finding it painful to swallow the food in her mouth.

"You're very kind," she managed to blurt out.

Then, in front of the waiters and the other diners, Clarissa got up from her chair, bent over and kissed her on the cheek, discreetly wiping away the tears that Sheela had been trying to fight back.

"Sorry making such a fool of myself." Then, gently steering Clarissa to an upright position, Sheela added, "You'll do your back an injury."

"Oh don't worry about my back. It's rock solid, with all the Pilates I do."

"Oh, I do Pilates too - we should go to the same class!"

"That would be lovely - I'm not too keen on the guy who takes our class."

"I can give you the details when we meet in London."

When, not if.

"It'll be so nice to have somebody I already know in the class. It can be a bit intimidating otherwise."

"Are you really the type to be intimidated in a new social setting?"

"So what type do you think I am?" Sheela felt that, behind the playfulness of the question, Clarissa was genuinely curious, even anxious, to know how she regarded her.

"I see you as someone with no reason to feel intimidated - your looks, charm and intelligence dazzled everybody at Bachoo's party."

"You're teasing me, I can see" - but Sheela was happy to note a flush of pleasure in Clarissa's face.

Then Clarissa hurried on to say, "But I *can* honestly say that you - don't laugh because I know it sounds absurd - you are like a long-lost soulmate; it feels almost like the real reason for my coming to India was to have found you."

"Now *you* are teasing *me*." Sheela looked up as she sipped her tea. "But if you're not, it's the nicest thing anybody has said to me, at least since my husband."

"Your husband, he was a very special person, wasn't he?"

Sheela nodded. She looked round, managed to make eye contact with the waiter and scribbled in the air.

"Yes, that would be one way to describe him." She paused, aware that her response may have sounded bitter, but right now she was past caring.

"It was all very sudden," she added.

"I'm really, really sorry. And that was the reason - for Mahabaleshwar?"

"Yes. But I suppose I have something to fight for. I have a daughter - Nina."

"Pretty name. Of course, one must fight on, although that sounds glib." Then, hesitantly, came the next question: "But why then?"

"It was the anniversary of Cyrus's - the day my husband left."

"I see." The words didn't sound like the usual response to an explanation; rather, they felt like a confirmation of something already suspected.

"Come, enough about myself. You haven't really told me about all the things you've been doing in Bombay."

"Well, where can I begin? Oh yes - the other day Max and I had lunch in this wonderful place called Britannia – the guide book referred to it as the go-to Irani restaurant in Bombay. You know it, I'm sure?"

Sheela scanned the room for the waiter, then, avoiding Clarissa's gaze, she added, "Yes, I've been there dozens of times."

Clarissa looked up sharply. "Oh dear, I fear I've put my foot in it."

"No, don't worry. My husband loved their chicken berry *pulao*."

"I'm sorry."

"Nothing to feel sorry about. Hardly your fault that somehow everything brings me back to my husband."

Clarissa sipped what remained of her apple tea. It must have been cold.

"It's just that remembering him sometimes feels a bit much for me. But not remembering him, actually trying to forget him, is impossible."

"I understand."

"Do you really?"

The waiter came round with the bill. Glancing down at it, Sheela continued, "You see, it's not just sadness I feel – it's also anger."

"Well, that feeling is entirely understandable, isn't it?"

"Oh, you're always saying the right things! You can't understand. Nobody can, unless it's happened to them. Because with the anger comes guilt. When somebody leaves the way he did, the feelings are - complicated."

Clarissa looked lost for words.

She doesn't know what to say, yet it feels as though deep down she does understand something - something intuitively if not factually.

Sheela left a tip for the waiter and said, "Well, I hope you enjoyed the meal."

Clarissa's response surprised her. "I really enjoyed the food - thank you. But I can't say I enjoyed the meal.

I feel upset because you're upset - and also somehow responsible."

"Responsible? What are you talking about?" But the words felt false, because responsible was precisely what she wanted Clarissa to feel. She had been eager to vent her anger on anybody who could be made to feel bad; in other words, anybody kind and sensitive enough to care.

She looked up at Clarissa. "I'm so sorry. I'm taking things out on you. On you of all people, who've been so good to me."

They were both up now, proceeding to the door. "Absolutely no need to be sorry." Clarissa put her arm round Sheela and gave her a squeeze.

"We are quite close to Sunset Villas, so I'll walk you there."

"No, please don't bother. I know my way, and you've already done so much for me today."

"The truth is you've done even more for me."

They hugged each other. Clarissa moved away, then turned round: "Don't forget to get in touch when you're back in London. I really do want us to meet."

"Will do. Happy landings!"

As she strolled back home, what stayed with Sheela was the sight of Clarissa walking away, her hair glinting red and copper in the afternoon light, her dress shimmering green in the heat, her gait giving off a cool fragrance undefiled by the sweat and pollution of the city. The afternoon had turned out so well after the earlier tension. Yes, she would definitely get in touch with her when she returned to London.

Yet, as she approached Tower View, she had a vague awareness of something troubling her. They were becoming habitual, these thoughts that needed to be nudged out of the recesses of her mind. Had she given away too much about herself? Had she said too much about Cyrus? Not really. Clarissa still had no idea how it had all happened. But the troublesome niggle refused to be dislodged.

Her thoughts turned to the invitation she hoped to receive from the Alexanders; after all, they did genuinely seem to want her over. She would have to give them a gift - something meaningful they would really appreciate. Perhaps some table mats and napkins from Contemporary Arts or the Prince of Wales Museum shop.

As she entered the lift in Tower View, the niggle that had been troubling her wormed itself out: it wasn't that she had revealed too much of herself; it was the fact that the Alexanders, for all their warmth and friendliness, had revealed virtually nothing about themselves. *She didn't really know them at all.* How can you have a soulmate you don't know? But then, come to think of it, she really knew nobody: not her mother-in-law, so shrewdly observant behind that benign exterior of hers; not her own daughter Nina, whose affection yo-yoed with the needs of the moment; most of all, not Cyrus, the love of her life, the person she had trusted more than any other.

As the lift rose to the third floor, she felt herself sinking to the bottom of the shaft.

15

"So you had a good afternoon?" As if something was telling Khorshed it was best not to wait for an answer, she continued: "You know you'll need to get ready now to see your family."

"What family? You - and Nina of course - are my only family."

"Don't say that, darling. Of course you're very precious to me, but blood is thicker than water - I still think there's something in that."

"Oh yes, thick with spite, favouritism and hypocrisy. And now I have to decide what I'm going to wear."

"You know what? I'm so happy that you find it difficult to decide what to wear - that means you still have something to live for."

Khorshed's eyes were burning bright with a keen humour, as if egging her daughter-in-law not to succumb to the weight of the past.

"You're sweet, Mummy. I suppose I'd better get myself ready." Sheela planted a kiss on Khorshed's forehead.

Saroj's flat was in a six-storey art deco building called Beethoven, constructed by a Parsi builder who reportedly worshipped the composer.

The doorbell sang the first few bars of *Für Elise*. A dhoti-clad man, with knobbly knees and shaky hands, opened the door. He looked not much younger than 80, but Sheela knew he was in his early seventies.

"*Kaisé hain*, Raju?" Sheela greeted him.

"*Theek*, Baby." The man wheezed so forcefully with the effort of speaking that it was impossible to believe he was well.

The sitting room into which she stepped was decorated in what Cyrus had once described as the Anglo-Hindu style: a carpet with large green vine-festooned peacocks against a background of pink and maroon flowers, surrounded by heavy mahogany settees and armchairs whose voluptuous flourishes were intended by Saroj to match the line drawings along the main wall of naked couples copulating: here the prurient could feast their eyes on balloon-shaped bosoms with upturned nipples, grotesquely outsized genitals, pouting cupid bow lips, and bottoms and limbs so fleshily entwined that only the closest scrutiny enabled their owners to be identified. Saroj had bought these from a street vendor near Khajuraho. On the opposite wall hung a large print of Goya's La Maja Desnuda ("So bold of him - that reclining nude with those gorgeous protruding breasts and that teeny-weeny hint of hair down there - all done in the time of the Inquisition, can you imagine!"). Against another wall stood a glass cabinet, some six foot high, with curved mahogany panelling and thick round legs the points of which, on closer inspection, turned out to be linghams. The cabinet was crammed with artifacts and curios: a plastic bust of Nefertiti, crystal bowls, silver-plated vases, porcelain cups, an age-blackened Victorian cruet set, a Wedgewood plate, figurines picked up from gift shops in Europe and a plethora of souvenir dolls.

Sheela sat on an armchair and picked up a copy of Mumbai Mirror which was open on the *Ask the Sexpert* page. Q: "*I am 26 years old and my wife is 23. While having oral sex, a liquid comes out of my penis. My wife does not like its taste. Can we apply chocolate to it just to add flavour? Will it harm the penis?"* A: *"You can apply ice-cream and use a napkin to wipe it."* Against the answer was scribbled in her mother's large, loopy handwriting: *Surely he could have suggested something classier - like zabaglione!*

Sheela glanced at her watch. Typical, she thought, deliberately making me wait; always playing games.

At last she heard a shuffling coming down the corridor.

"Oh my, what have I done to myself!" Clad in a red velvet dressing gown, Saroj flung herself on to a settee and brushed the back of her hand against her forehead.

"Oh dear, what's happened?"

"What a question to ask? But then I shouldn't be surprised - the number of times you bother to see your poor ailing Mumsie."

"Well, what -"

"The whole of Bombay knows about this excruciating arthritis in my hands - except, of course, my own daughter!"

Sheela decided not to respond. She watched her mother fiddle with her bead necklace with fingers which were remarkably plump and nodule-free. She thought of Khorshed.

"Well, if you must know, if it weren't for you coming, I would've drowned my sorrows in bed with a Miss Marple DVD."

"Look, Mumsie, I can always come another time -"

"Oh, the alacrity with which she says that!" Then, after a slight pause: "And you haven't even greeted your Mumshie with a little kissy-wissy!" Sheela duly gave her mother a peck on the cheek.

"Come and sit near me, *beti*." Saroj patted the sofa with her right hand. "You mustn't quarrel with your poor Mumsie all the time - she's getting old, you know." It was true that, without the make-up and the hair coiffed to Indira Gandhi perfection, her mother was showing her age. The wrinkles were more pronounced, the features were more bulbous, and the skin gave off a whiff of old leather. Sheela placed herself next to Saroj. Saroj clasped Sheela's left hand. No, definitely no sign of arthritis in that grip. For a few seconds the two of them sat together in awkward harmony.

"I've got the cook to make some prawn curry and rice - and your favourite cheese soufflé."

"Oh thank you, Mumsie!"

"I thought of telling you before you came, but then I said to myself: 'No, if she knows beforehand, how can I be sure that she really wants to see *me* and not her favourite soufflé?' Now I know you did come to see me after all. Oh, Lovely" - a sharp intake of breath - "I can't tell you how much I'm suffering! Still, some of us are fated to grin and bear things." Then, with a further squeeze of the hand: "I know you've had a lot to grin and bear. All this year I've being feeling so much for you, *beti*. But I wish you'd open up a bit - I'm your mother, you know."

"Thank you, Mumsie. It's just that some things are difficult to talk about."

"Like what happened to Cyrus?" Saroj turned to face her daughter: "Look at you getting all rigid. Why is it so unmentionable? It was very tragic - such a lovely handsome man disappearing from our lives. But keeping stoically silent about it isn't good for your health. And think what I'd feel if something happened to my Lovely?" Sheela feared that the catch in her mother's voice was about to break into a flood.

"Mumsie," Sheela tried to sound matter-of-fact, "I promise that when the time is right I'll stop being so stoically silent. But at the moment it doesn't feel right. Please understand."

"But I feel hurt that you won't open up to your own Mumsie. I bet you've told everybody else - most certainly Saint Goody-Goody whom you choose to live with! Anyway, I hope you're happy to know that Sweetie is going to join us. He had to go to dinner with some VIP friends of his, but when I told him you were coming he said 'How could I possibly miss dinner with my Prodigal Sister?'. See how much we all love you - but you just seem to push us away."

The doorbell rang. Saroj sprang from the settee like an excited schoolgirl, the arthritis quite forgotten. "That must be my Sweetie!" she cried.

Sheela braced herself for the next phase of the evening.

"Mumsie darling!" she heard Mohan cry out as if he hadn't seen her for years. Then came a series of *mwah-mwahs*. A whisper loud enough to hear - "Has she arrived?" - was followed by a silence that Sheela imagined was a turn of her mother's head in the direction of the sitting room.

"Lovely *dar*ling!" Mohan strode forward, followed by Saroj. "Mumsie, isn't our Lovely looking quite lovely?"

Sheela had long ago decided that nobody was fooled by the emptiness of his rapture more than Mohan himself - which was why it was difficult to feel angry in his presence. The resentment would surface only afterwards when she reminded herself that, at some intuitive level, her brother knew how his behaviour had always allowed him to get what he wanted, even if necessary at her expense.

"Hi Mohan," she said, submitting to the bear hug of Old Spice and *garam masala* which was about to smother her.

Mohan sat down next to her, his arm around her shoulder. For all his American façade, he's so Indian, she thought, never giving space, always assuming that physical proximity signalled warmth of feeling.

Saroj sat on one of the armchairs.

"What's up, mawm," said Mohan, "you've suddenly gone all quiet. As though you're upset or something."

"Nuth-*thing*," said Saroj, looking away from her children. Sheela decided that the spectacle of her children so close to each other was making her mother feel left out.

"Mumsie, the look on your face is making us feel guilty!"

"Well, Sheela, if you feel guilty, you must have something to hide."

"Mumsie, you're a scream!" Mohan jumped up and extracted a CD from a cabinet below the Khajuraho-inspired drawings.

"What are you doing?" Saroj's yell was almost inaudible as Bill Hayley's ear-splitting voice called on all the residents of Beethoven and beyond to rock around the clock.

"Come, Mumsie," cried Mohan, grabbing Saroj from her armchair and forcing her to gyrate to the rhythm of his swaying hips and shaking head. "Stop it, stop it at once," shouted Saroj, but she was soon whirling with a gusto which belied her years. Sheela saw behind the puffing breath and the wobbling buttocks the girlish spark that must have attracted her father when he had first met her.

The music ended. "No - no more," Saroj panted. "With all that exercise, we'd better have some food."

"RA-JU" she screamed. Raju emerged, hobbling anxiously. "*Khana taiyar nahi kiya hai*?" Looking nonplussed, Raju mumbled that he hadn't been asked to get dinner ready but, not to worry, the food would be served in a minute. He scuttled away as quickly as he could.

The dining table had already been laid. White plates with flowery gold and red motifs were flanked by Kishco Cutlery's most ornate efforts. The drinking glasses were a deep maroon, with gold petals plastered all around them; Saroj claimed to have found them in Murano, but Sheela suspected they were imitation pieces picked up from Chor Bazaar.

Seating herself at the table, Sheela felt the absence of something. She looked round the room, searching for clues, but found none.

Raju came in, pushing a trolley with a bowl of wobbly soufflé, a large dish of rice and a pot of masala-red prawn curry.

"Oh Mumsie, that looks delicious!"

"Well, I thought that I'd prepare something that might occasionally remind you of your poor Mumshie-Wumshie."

Sheela's eyes fell on the empty silver fruit bowl on the table. For a moment, she was distracted by the tangle of fork-tongued serpents carved over its surface.

Then, like a dormant jack-in-the-box jolted into action, the missing item jumped to the fore of her mind.

"Mumsie, where are the peacocks? You know the ones Daddy gave me."

"What peacocks Daddy gave you?"

"The cruet set. The silver peacocks with ruby eyes and enamelled plumage - the ones I never got round to taking back to England. You always kept them on the dining table."

"Oh those!"

"Come to think of it, I'll take them back this time, if that's OK with you."

"Come," Saroj said with a sellotaped smile, "let me help you to some curry-rice."

"Thanks, Mumsie. Not too much. But where are they?"

"Oh, they must be around somewhere. Sweetie, please pass the *nimbu*."

"Sure, Mumsie. The peacocks Lovely's talking about - are they the ones you gave me - ?" Mohan darted a quick glance at his sister before shifting his gaze back to his mother.

"What's this about giving Mohan my peacocks?"

"*My* peacocks?"

"Yes yes - MY peacocks. You know full well that Daddy wanted me to have them."

"Oh don't try this daddy's girl sob story on me - your father was so vague and dithery, he would say one thing one minute and the opposite the next."

Saroj's lips quivered, her nostrils twitched and her eyes glistened at the brim.

"Oh Lovely, see you're making Mumsie cry!"

"Wow, have you got a bucket ready?"

"Oh Mumsie darling, please don't cry. Take no notice of her, that's just the way she is." Then, turning to Sheela, Mohan snarled, "You know, if you're so keen on those darned peacocks I'll get them fucking Fedexed to you."

"See how noble he is," cried Saroj between sobs. "Why must you be so greedy?"

"*I* greedy? You've given virtually everything to him, and the one precious thing Daddy gave me - even *that* you pass on to him!"

"Daddy! As though your Daddy knew anything he was doing, such an impotent jellyfish!"

Sheela pushed her chair back, strode towards her mother and shook her so violently that the Indira Gandhi lock came tumbling down her forehead.

"How dare you talk like that about my father, you evil bitch!"

"Arré Chweetie, she's going to kill me!"

"Get your bloody hands off my mother!" Mohan tugged Sheela's hair so hard that a clump came off into his hand. His eyes narrowed and his lips were pursed as if readying themselves to spit venom.

Sheela swung round and Mohan smacked her on the cheek. Sheela grabbed the fruit bowl and whacked it onto the side of Mohan's head. His eyes widened like those of a demonic Ravana in a Kathakali dance. Before he could slap her again, Sheela smashed the serpents even harder into his face. She saw with a satisfaction tinged with alarm that his nose was bleeding profusely.

"Oh Mumsie, Mumsie - see what she's done. You're right - she's trying to kill us!"

Mother and son were now sobbing wildly in each other's arms.

Sheela walked to the door, banged it shut and stumbled down the staircase.

Gopal was waiting for her, with the knowing look of a witness to the drama in the flat, but he behaved in his usual nonchalant way, as if to say that all this domestic violence was just another manifestation of the everyday brutality of the city.

On the journey back, Sheela re-imagined every step of the drama, but as she re-played it the whole episode drew further and further away until there was nothing left for her to savour - none of the pleasures of victimhood, no moral triumph, no sense of vindication. The reality had been far less satisfying. If only Mohan had slapped her, if only she had bashed his face with the bowl, if only she had called her mother an evil bitch. Instead she had merely protested that her father was certainly not a jellyfish; Saroj had sighed and exchanged "there she goes again" glances with her son; Mohan had reiterated with a resigned smile his offer to Fedex the peacocks she "coveted so much"; and Sheela had found herself mumbling a thank-you.

Back in her room, she changed and lay on her bed, but the knot of fury gripping her belly made sleep impossible until the early hours of the next morning.

She woke up with vague memories of a dream with characters drifting in and out too slyly for the eye to rest on them: her mother and brother giggling like secret lovers; a distant figure lost in a vast landscape of snow dunes; Khorshed fighting a losing battle to scrape off the rust of decline; Clarissa and Max somewhere remote, eyes only for each other; Cyrus cloistered in his study, unreachable, then fading into something phantom-like and preternatural, leaving behind only a sense of his being. As she got out of bed, trying to navigate her mind through this world of smoke and mirrors, she was overwhelmed by a feeling of isolation. She felt no connection with anything or anybody. Perhaps she was the lonely figure in the snowy landscape.

She wished she had succeeded in Mahabaleshwar.

London

16

As she stepped into the silence of the black cab waiting at the airport taxi rank, Sheela yearned for the sounds, sights and smells of Bombay, so distant now, yet so immediate in her memory. Not that there was anything unusual about this feeling: after the chaos of Bombay, entering London had always been like stepping into a hushed cathedral. The traffic gliding by was like some ghostly funeral cortege wending its way along the naves and aisles of the city that had become her home. The humid silence was a balm to the ear but a dampener to the spirits.

When the cab came to a halt in Calabria Road, Sheela remembered she had to phone Nina. How times had changed. She no longer needed to think twice about making international calls to mobiles: Cyrus, ever resourceful, had discovered a provider charging unbeatable rates. A year ago, she had thought it would be impossible to cope without him. But a self-induced coma had somehow helped her to go through the motions of each passing day. It was only about a month before the anniversary, when she had come across an old photograph of Cyrus, that she had been shaken from her torpor. The photograph, taken by one of his patients, had "For the best doctor in the world" scribbled across the bottom. Those words could have been written by any one of his patients: "Dr Marker is always there for you," they would say, "always gentle and kind, never stinting on time." The whole house must have been convulsed by the grief she felt as she read the tribute; later her neighbour Rhoda had knocked at the door to enquire if she was all right.

As she reached to pick up the telephone, she noticed the blinking of the messages light.

The first message was from a man exhorting her to press nine if she had been mis-sold insurance.

The second started with a clearing of the throat, followed by a female voice. "Sheela," it said, "you must be home by now. Hope you had a good trip back. Do call us when you can. Bye!" Sheela's immediate reaction was to wish the call had never been made. In the chilly reality of a damp Spring evening in London, it was difficult to recapture the warmth she had felt for the Alexanders in Bombay. She would return the call - that was the decent thing to do; Cyrus would have done it. More important, they had surprised her: the English, she used to say to Cyrus, were all talk and no action. But she wasn't in the mood to call them today. Tomorrow would do.

The third message started, "Hi Mom! Hope you're OK." Nina had beaten her to it. The familiar guilt returned. "I've got great news for you - Jake's back! Realised what a bitch that girl was. Even better news! The Spring recess is earlier than I thought. It starts in fact this Saturday, so I've booked a flight arriving first thing Sunday morning. And you know what? Jake's coming with me! Mom, can't wait to see you. Bye for now, and lots of love!"

The guilt was erased by annoyance. Sunday was two days from now. And what was all this talk about the boy coming with her? He would have to sleep in the guest room; sharing a bedroom was out of the question. She would have to talk to Nina about this straightaway.

"Mm, did you get my message? Isn't it great? We'll be able to spend even *more* time with you in London! Can't tell you how happy I am Jake saw sense and told that slut to like fuck off!"

"Nina, must you use swear words?"

"There you go again - lecture, lecture, lecture."

"Oh honestly! Anyway, when are you going to turn up? I'll have to rustle something up for you."

"Oh stop fretting, Mom - we can just go to the local pub or something. You remember the cool place in Barnsbury we'd go to with Dad - the Albion?"

Sheela wanted to put the phone down. She hadn't unpacked, she hadn't even gone to the bathroom. And here she was arguing with a daughter who insisted on reviving unwanted memories.

"Mum? Are you there?"

The hint of alarm in Nina's voice gratified Sheela. After a pause she hoped was sufficiently unnerving, she responded. "Do what you like. You said first thing Sunday morning, so I'll expect you some time mid-morning. Don't forget to get some warm clothes - the weather's always unpredictable in this bloody country."

"You're not angry with me, are you, Mummy?" The voice at the other end had turned little girlish. Where did Nina learn to be so manipulative? She wasn't going to respond.

"Mummy? I didn't mean to upset you - I mean by talking about the Albion. Reminding you of Daddy and all that."

"Oh darling, no, no - that's all right."

"Mummy, I know what you've been going through this year. But" - Sheela caught a fractional break in the girl's voice - "you know you're not the only one missing him."

"Yes, my baby, I know," she said almost in a whisper. She stopped. Over the past year, the pain in her throat, the pain of silence, had become quite familiar, almost a friend: at least it concealed from her daughter the depth of her grief.

Or so she thought. "Mummy, I know you're crying. Oh Mummy, Mummy, I wish I could be with you right now." The familiar wail threatened to turn into a gale force howl.

"Shh, my baby, it's all right. I'm all right." Funny how the expression of sorrow by another person, especially your child, helped you to regain your calm.

Just then Sheela knew no better way to show how much she felt for Nina than to let silence fall between them; or rather to let that silence bind them in the love that none of their habitual jostling could tear apart. She was convinced too that in that moment both felt the presence of Cyrus, the husband and the father who had been the catalyst for love, healing and reconciliation in a frequently fractious mother-daughter relationship. 'Blessed are the peacemakers, for they shall be called the children of God' was his favourite Beatitude, Cyrus would say. Indeed it must have been, for the Cyrus she had known was the most peaceable person she had ever met: peacemaker at home, without appearing to take sides; peacemaker at work, smoothing the ruffled feathers of wounded colleagues, grumpy receptionists and disgruntled patients. Sheela would call him a child of God, only half-teasingly, but he would insist that his peace making only reflected the cowardice of the person who shirks confrontation.

Time to break the silence: "I'm really looking forward to seeing you. Can't I pick you up from the airport?"

"No way, but if we take the Heathrow Express to Paddington, maybe you fetch us from there?"

"OK, must end this call now."

Sheela put the phone down. What was she feeling guilty about now? She had ended the call too abruptly. She wanted to call Nina back, to say that she should really take care of herself - no, that she would take care of her. But her bladder was bursting now. She rushed up the stairs, avoiding the gaze of Cyrus's parents and grandparents in the black and white photographs lining the wall. She had tried to put away all the photos of Cyrus himself, but she didn't have the heart, or the energy, to clear his family out as well.

After she finished with the bathroom, she returned to the phone and dialled.

"Mum, what's happened?"

"No, no, nothing to worry about. I - I just wanted to say I was really looking forward to seeing you."

She waited for a nonplussed "But you already said that!" but instead she heard her daughter say, "Mummy, really, really can't wait to see you too."

"I've just got to unpack now - but look after yourself and lots and lots of love to you, my sweetheart."

"And to you too, Mummy."

Sheela heard a kissing sound before the phone clicked.

17

The next morning she made herself a cup of tea and tackled the pile of mail stacked on the dining table. The sun was streaming through slits in the old wooden shutters. The grandfather clock - a Marker family legacy - chimed nine.

Fortified by the tea, she braced herself for the next task at hand.

"Er, is that Max?"

"Yes - it's Sheela, isn't it? How are you? When did you return?"

"I'm fine, thanks. Returned yesterday" - adding "evening" would have sounded too eager - "and got Clarissa's message."

"Yes yes. Wait, let me get Clarissa for you."

"Hello, Sheela!"

"Oh hi," she said in a tone of voice that she hoped was open to different interpretations.

"How nice to hear from you. Actually, I'm so glad you rang back today. You see, Max is performing at Wigmore Hall tonight - he is a sort of last minute replacement for the first violin of this other quartet - and we have complimentary tickets, so we wondered whether you could join us?"

"Oh how kind of you! Let me think. Can I come back to you - I just need to check something."

Sheela put the phone down quietly, as if she didn't want anyone to hear. She felt her heart beating. The last time she had been at Wigmore Hall was well over a year ago, with Cyrus. *Glad I didn't accept straightaway. That would have looked needy. Besides, why did they prioritise me over all their other friends? There was something false about the whole thing. I really don't think I should accept.*

As if he had overheard her thoughts, Cyrus came back to her, gentle and reasonable as ever: "Sheela my darling, we need to give people the benefit of the doubt - even if that means taking emotional risks - if we are not to remain perpetually distrustful and timid about our relationships." Max's eagerness to pass the phone on to Clarissa - no, it wasn't a sudden cooling off; it was the awkwardness of modesty: getting Clarissa to inform her about the concert saved him the embarrassment of telling her himself.

Further delay would give room for further doubt. She picked the phone and dialled the Alexanders' number.

Now what was the next task? Oh yes, she had to make the bed for Nina; and, damn, she'd also have to tidy up one of the spare rooms for that philandering boyfriend of hers.

But suppose they wanted to sleep in the same bedroom? No, she couldn't possibly countenance that. Some beefy gum-chewing American taking advantage of her child. No no - she would not succumb to the pressures of a liberal upbringing; she would clear up the spare room, however backbreaking that might be, and make sure that Nina's room was out of bounds.

The spare room smelt of dust and dead moths. The mauve carpet was covered by a coat of white fur. Packages and cardboard boxes, accumulated over months of neglect, had dug into its pile.

As she bent down to scoop a pile of papers stacked in the corner of the room, a small cardboard box hidden in the middle of the pile slipped from her grasp, spilling its contents. She grasped a number of stiff A4 pages. *Milton Letherbury School*, she read at the top of one of them. It was a school report, smudge-marked, yellow and crinkled with age. A faded crest showed a heavily burdened Atlas carrying the motto *Semper Persevera*. Just below the crest she read 'Cyrus Marker' written with the slanting flourish deployed by institutions inclined to venerate their own history. At the bottom right-hand corner of the page was a blurred signature - Rathbone - dashed off in the fluid strokes of a fountain pen.

Sitting on the bed she had just made, Sheela managed to decipher the words behind the smudge marks:

Marker continues to prove himself to be an exemplary student. His exam results were again excellent, but his talents extend far beyond the classroom: he was a superb captain of the cricket team, and it is no surprise that he won the Trevelyan trophy in the singles tennis tournament; and he led the team to a convincing victory in the inter-school debating competition. Given his current performance, he will have no difficulty getting a place at Oxbridge or one of the top London colleges.

The body of the school report showed teachers' comments for individual subjects. A remarkable talent, said the art teacher; excellent was the verdict for physics, chemistry and biology; in his maths exam he had got full marks; in English he showed considerable insight and powers of expression; and so it went on.

Only French was disappointing: he had achieved a paltry B plus. And some comments from a Mr Runcorn (designated 'Moral Tutor') struck a slightly jarring note: while endorsing all the accolades of the other staff members, he added, "Perhaps he drives himself too hard. He aspires, indeed seems to have a desperate need, to excel in everything he does - an admirable quality, no doubt - but might he also be putting himself under undue pressure? It is also noticeable that, popular and admired though he is, he seems to find it difficult to let his hair down. It is almost as though, having become a model of achievement and good behaviour, he has been placed on a distant pedestal that the other boys daren't approach and that he cannot risk stepping off because of the constant pressure he finds himself under to 'set an example'. At our most recent quarterly meeting, I felt that he was holding something back, that he needed somehow to unburden himself - not uncommon in my experience of high achievers who carry the burden of being exemplary at all times. Something perhaps for his parents to note?"

Holding something back. Sheela tried but failed to fight off a fleeting recollection of a conversation from some years ago: "You know something?" Cyrus had said. "What?" she had responded, attempting to sound light-hearted. Something in his tone of voice had made her dread what he was going to say. Cyrus wasn't the type of person to confide; he was much more likely to be the confidant, the person who cherished his independence and privacy; the person who would sometimes shut himself off in his study for no apparent reason and avoid eye contact with her as if to spare her the disquiet that, without warning, would on occasion shadow his face. She would put this behaviour down to a bad day at the surgery. But this time he had sounded as though he had wanted to talk about something that had been haunting him for a while. "I'm sort of expected to be in command of everything," he had said, "when in fact I long for somebody else to be in control for a change. It's absurd, but I feel everybody - even you, my darling Sheela - expects me, with all my faults, to be some sort of paragon." Sheela remembered that his self-deprecating smile had failed to soften the bitterness in his voice. "So what are these mythical faults of yours?" she had responded with a light laugh. He had looked at her for an unnervingly long time, but in his gaze there had been something uncharacteristically vulnerable. Then, with a "Never mind", he had turned his face away. Relieved, she had quickly changed the subject. If only she hadn't. If only she had responded to the plea for help lurking behind those eyes. He had wanted to get something off his chest, and by not encouraging him, she had failed him. Now she was almost certain about what he had wanted to say – but it was all too late.

Feeling the familiar nausea stir in the pit of her stomach she opened a packet wrapped in torn cellophane sheets held together by a rubber band: old black and white school photographs - of Cyrus being handed a tennis trophy; of Cyrus accepting a book (presumably an academic prize) from a genial middle-aged man (Mr Rathbone?); of Cyrus in cricket whites together with other boys similarly attired; and several of Cyrus in blazer and dark trousers sitting in the front row of a group of students, usually near the same middle-aged man and flanked by other male teachers sitting cross-armed with the awkward look of those constrained by the camera to appear more important than they felt. In some photographs Cyrus looked slightly older than in others, but in all there was the same optimistic smile, bright eyes and open expression that she had grown to love in the man who had become her husband.

"This is my husband," she heard a voice in her head. "This is the love of my life, my beloved darling perfect husband."

"That was my husband," she corrected herself. The photographs told her that he hadn't changed: the boyish amiability of the model student was immediately recognisable in the man she had known for some twenty-five years. With a shock she realised that the boy in the photographs was younger than Nina was today. *This boy became Nina's father, this boy became my husband.* She wanted to wrap her arms round the person in the pictures, hold him close to her, protect him from harm - protect him from the harm awaiting him so many years later; but she no longer knew who it was she wished to embrace: the boy who, if he were alive today, could be her child, or the man who was her husband. Her eyes were now stinging, with the dust released by the reports and the photographs, and with a choking sense of bereavement.

Bereavement - and anger. *Perfect husband. How hollow that sounds now. What a load of humbug.* Yes, she should have responded to his plea for help - but how could she have imagined what was to come, something so completely beyond her ken? Yet, when her eyes fell once again upon the open-hearted face of the young Cyrus, she couldn't stem the surge of love that coursed through her.

She noticed a cobweb-smeared carrier bag tucked behind the dresser. She wiped the bag with a duster and shoved the school reports and photographs into it. Later, when she had time to collect herself, she would decide where exactly she would keep them. She walked down the stairs to the first floor and placed the carrier bag in a corner of her wardrobe.

18

"Darling, I was getting a bit worried - thank God you've phoned."

After making her apologies for the late call, Sheela told her mother-in-law about Nina's imminent arrival and the chamber music concert she was attending that evening.

"Well, so glad to know you're keeping so busy, darling. I was thinking that after the hustle and bustle of Bombay it might be difficult, you know, to sort of get used to -"

"The empty house?"

"Well, I wasn't thinking of anything in partic -"

"Look, Mummy, there's absolutely no need to worry about me. Now tell me - how are *you*? I felt you sounded a bit -"

"Oh, *I'm* perfectly all right."

"So who isn't?"

"Nobody really. It's just that Ramu rang from Mahabaleshwar. He was rambling on a bit. I couldn't really understand what it was all about. He asked if he could talk to you."

"What exactly did he say?" She hardly dared ask the question.

"Just couldn't tell. All I could get out of him was that it was something to do with a year ago."

The ticking of the grandfather clock was beginning to get on her nerves.

"But look, darling, I'm sure there's nothing to all this - you know how domestics can create a melodrama out of nothing."

"But you're definitely all right?"

"Of course I am, darling! Listen, this call must be getting expensive. Thank you so much for ringing, and have a lovely concert."

"Thanks, Mummy, will be in touch. And promise you'll always phone me, you know, if there's anything..."

"Yes, of course I will." The response was automatic; Sheela knew that her mother-in-law wouldn't dream of phoning unless she felt she were on her last legs.

As she put the phone down, Sheela wondered how close she really was to the older woman, always so disciplined, so astutely observant.

She slumped into one of the dining chairs. Her mother-in-law knew more about Ramu's call than she was letting on. She may not have known exactly what happened, but something, call it a mother's intuition, was pushing her towards the truth. And one day she might know the whole truth and live to tell the story. But she was old and frail; she probably wouldn't last the course. To her shame, Sheela found comfort in that thought.

But Ramu had told Khorshed something about a year ago. Oh no, was he going to spill the beans? Could it be that the ghastly doctor had returned and said something to upset him? The old servant's ramblings might have been incoherent, if Khorshed was to be believed, but what was to stop him from blurting everything out the next time he phoned Tower View? She had always believed that the man's loyalty would guarantee discretion, but now no longer. Yet ... he too was getting very old ...

She was startled by the cracking of crockery slipping in the sink. Was this what she was reduced to? Wishing people dead, people she thought she loved?

She dragged herself into the sitting room area. Cyrus having gone, she had avoided this part of the house. All their treasured possessions had become objects of repulsion: the Victorian chaise longue; the antique mahogany settee (a Marker family heirloom); the two Daniell aquatints of Indian temple scenes; the oatmeal raw silk curtains and the pale-green batik wall hangings. Everything, so impeccably tasteful, now felt like one big pretence: the outward decoration of a marriage she had believed to be perfectly whole, only to be splintered into two halves, of which just one remained, jagged and tormented, to endure the anguish of being left behind.

She slumped into the settee. A bird was singing in the garden. It had to be a blackbird - only blackbirds trilled so beautifully. She lay her head against one of the Rajasthani cushions she had picked up from a stall at the *Kala Ghoda* festival. She wanted to be lulled by the birdsong, lulled into a stupor in which all memory could be magicked away. She let her eyes focus on the crest of the agave which formed the centrepiece of the garden; everything else became a comfortable blur.

Then her gaze fell on the glass of the garden door. It blinked images at her - images of swaying leaves, of shifting shadows, of frantic life forms flitting around like giant butterflies. They merged into a form distantly familiar as it approached, then dissolved into shapelessness as it withdrew. And so this visual trick continued, now approaching, now withdrawing... until the form lunged into focus.

"It's you," she said with a sharp intake of breath.

"Hello," he replied. His voice was recognisable, yet not quite the same, as if refracted by the absence of a year.

"I didn't think you'd come back. Are you happy to see me?"

"I've always been happy to see you."

"Then why did you leave me?"

"If I left you, it doesn't mean that I wasn't happy with you."

She looked at him. The wetness in her eyes blurred her vision, but she noticed that he seemed young, almost as young as in the photographs.

"Don't cry." He spoke gently, as he always did, but he appeared to be withdrawing, melding with the double glazing of the garden door.

"Why don't you come in and comfort me, as you used to?" She wanted to feel his arms round her waist, his body pressed against hers, the warmth of his breath. She wanted to recapture the Cyrus she had known and obliterate the memory of the Cyrus who had become a stranger.

"I would like to."

"Then come in." She reached her arms out, ready to embrace him.

"Do you really want me to?"

"You know the answer."

"But do you?"

"Oh come in, please COME IN!" As she called out, she saw that he was no longer in the room. Outside the garden door a shadowy figure rose slowly, dangling in the air, before dissolving into the arc of the overhanging trees.

She found herself on the floor. Her head was throbbing. She must have hit it against the piano stool. She looked up at the garden door. Nothing. Just the blackbird singing. Then in some inner chamber of her mind she heard a piercing cry: *Oh God, why did I let him go, again?* There was no comfort. The blackbird's song was hateful, every twisted warble like a spike of barbed wire clawing at her heart.

Against her will, her mind stayed with Cyrus. She sought comfort in the thought that he had almost returned to her. Theirs had indeed been about as perfect a marriage as it was possible to have, or so she had wanted to believe. She could hardly recall the last time they had a row. Oh yes, it had been about something that at the time seemed so silly - she had inadvertently opened an Amazon delivery parcel with what looked like diving gear in it. Cyrus had become unusually testy, telling her she had no business opening post that was addressed to him. Quite typically, he had apologised almost immediately, explaining that he had had a difficult day at work, and that his annoyance was more with Amazon than with her for having sent the wrong item - he had ordered a pair of swimming trunks in preparation for their trip to Nice. As she remembered all this, she tried to return to the love she had felt when she saw the photographs of the young Cyrus. But now it was anger, not love, that seized her; anger brought on by the memory of what happened a year ago.

A chime of the grandfather clock jolted her into her immediate surroundings. Astonishingly, it was already five - time to get ready for the concert. She imagined the Alexanders and their friends exchanging knowing glances as she approached the entrance of Wigmore Hall - all of them able to read her mind and discover the secret she wished to hide from everyone, including herself.

Heaving herself off the floor, she felt a lump on her forehead. She told herself she was in no condition to go out, but without conviction: once you have made a commitment, she heard her father intone, never back out of it.

19

As it slid behind the terraces of Highbury Fields, the sun cast an apricot sheen on the couples lolling on the grass. The trees, filigree-fresh, were so unlike the voluptuous foliage of India; their young leaves, tickled by a rising breeze, flittered and flashed in the evening light. A flock of seagulls swooped down the length of the fields, screeching like new-born banshees.

Sheela felt her spirits lift. People might not after all notice the bump on her forehead, which she had spent five minutes in front of the bathroom mirror trying to disguise with foundation. When she was trying to pat it away, she was aware of nothing else; but now, as she walked to the tube station, what struck her was the handsomeness of the face: the tight bone structure; the aquiline nose with its broad bridge narrowing along its length to a tip bent slightly downwards; and the wide forehead framed by hair, thick and black, swept back like her mother's (although with no Indira Gandhi streak of white - at least not yet).

When she got out of Bond Street tube station, a tightly-scarved woman approached her with a low beseeching moan reminiscent of the beggars of Bombay. Funny how beggars, like rag-and-bone-men, formed a fraternity of habits, behaviours and sounds that crossed national boundaries. But time and place had altered the identities of the underdog: in contemporary Britain it was the people of Romania and Bulgaria (from which this woman no doubt hailed) on whom the garbage of the country's problems could be dumped; some forty years earlier it had been the Ugandan Asians. And now yesterday's warned-against were posting their own warnings with the same blind conviction: just the other day, she had seen a *babu*-accented Asian complaining on television about East Europeans "flooding our country". Sheela wondered how many white families listening to him had thought: "Why doesn't that Paki git set an example and go back to his fucking village?"

She avoided eye contact with the East European woman and strode ahead until the woman gave up in search of more malleable prey.

With Wigmore Hall a few yards away, her nervousness at the thought of meeting the Alexanders had become inseparable from her anxiety about appearing musically ignorant. As she walked into the iron and glass canopied entrance, she overheard a couple of bow-tied men throwing snippets of murmured conversation about the Rach 2 and the Brahms 3 just loud enough to remind her of her cultural inferiority.

She caught sight of Clarissa standing by the ticket desk, half hidden by a cluster of young people, probably music students, guffawing with the eager confidence of those belonging to an exclusive club. Her face was bent towards a programme in her hands, but every now and then she looked up, her head darting anxiously between the figures in the student group. She looked smaller than she had done in Bombay, and, perhaps because of the play of light in the foyer, the sockets below her eyes appeared sunken and dark against the whiteness of her cheeks.

"Clarissa!" cried Sheela as though she had just spotted her.

"Oh Sheela!" Clarissa nudged her way through the group, and the two women wrapped their arms round each other.

"You've lost weight!"

"Have I?" Clarissa laughed, but her eyes fluttered evasively.

"But you look more beautiful than ever," Sheela added quickly.

"You flatterer. Anyway, lovely to see you looking so well. Not well, positively stunning. Where on earth did you get that outfit from?"

"Now who's the flatterer? From a roadside stall on Colaba Causeway. I'll have to take you there when we're next in Bombay."

"Well, I'll definitely take you up on that offer! But for now we're here, about to enjoy what should be a lovely concert."

The two women went to their seats, M3 and M4.

Sheela tried to follow the notes in the programme Clarissa had just handed to her - Piazzolla, Haydn's Sunrise Quartet, Schubert's C Major Quintet - but she struggled to concentrate. Seats 3 and 4, the aisle seats favoured by Cyrus because they were on the piano side; the Haydn quartet: she could hear Cyrus insisting that Mendelssohn must have been influenced by the opening bars of the Sunrise when he started composing his octet; and the Schubert quintet, a favourite of Cyrus's and, under his tutelage, soon to become a favourite of hers.

"Are you all right?" There was concern in Clarissa's gaze.

"No - yes, yes."

Clarissa smiled and squeezed her hand.

The four players, led by Max, strode on to the stage. As Max sat down and led his colleagues through the usual tuning process, she felt a surge of something akin to pride. This was quickly followed by embarrassment; how absurd it was to countenance feelings that could only belong to his wife. She looked sideways and caught Clarissa's eye; her companion's smiling face showed no sign of having noticed anything untoward.

The Piazzolla was jauntily tangoesque, as she had expected it to be. Not her cup of tea. But she couldn't help noticing Max the performer: so focussed, so energetic - almost athletic in the way he negotiated the strings on his bow and tapped his foot to the rhythm of the music. That surge of feeling came over her again, and she felt compelled to move her eyes back to the programme notes.

The audience was clapping politely; the Piazzolla was clearly the regulation *amuse-bouche* for the meatier fare to follow.

She felt she ought to say something appropriately anodyne about the piece, but stopped short as she caught Clarissa looking across the hall: her eyes were wide open with what could have been shock, or even fear, but the expression vanished so quickly that Sheela wondered whether it was a figment of her own heightened state. She cast a quick glance to the right, but found nothing more than a few latecomers scurrying to their seats.

As the performers resettled themselves on to the stage, Sheela found herself dreading the launch of the first movement of the Haydn quartet. Curled up on the sofa next to Cyrus, she would tell him that a sunrise was indeed what the rising notes of the first bars evoked. But now as the strings started their ascent a worm in her throat threatened to explode into a coughing fit. Something was shoved into the palm of her left hand and she immediately popped it into her mouth. The lozenge eased the irritation, but not the constriction she felt around her neck.

When the movement ended, Clarissa turned towards her, but not before Sheela noticed that she had again been looking across the middle section of the auditorium. There was something strained about her smile; it was as if some ghost from the past had made an appearance. Sheela gripped Clarissa's hand - whether to comfort or to be comforted she wasn't sure.

The adagio felt agonisingly slow and even the last two allegro movements went by like a tiresome distraction. It was as if the music was disturbing her train of thought, preventing her from grasping something that she should but couldn't understand.

Clarissa didn't immediately join in the applause which erupted at the close of the piece, but her face couldn't conceal her pride. All the four players bent over in almost perfect unison, as if the bowing was part of the performance. As he straightened himself Max glanced in their direction, with the hint of an extra smile for Clarissa.

"Shall we go backstage? Artists rarely, if at all, see family and friends during the interval, but they are having celebratory drinks for the cellist, who's leaving the quartet, and apparently he has to rush home immediately after the performance. Max insisted that we pop by, if only for a few minutes."

Clarissa held Sheela's arm in a surprisingly tight grip and steered her towards the stage. "This is the way," she said, looking straight ahead. When they reached the front of the auditorium, her gaze seemed fixed on the stage. "We just need to take this door," she said, still not turning right to look at Sheela. *She wants to hide something from me. No, that isn't right: she wants to hide from something - or someone - in the auditorium.*

Max greeted them at the door of the Gerald Moore Room. The room had an upright piano, an old fireplace, and walls covered with photographs of famous performers. The place could have been the drawing room of a small late-19th century stately home.

Max introduced the second violinist to Sheela. "Oh, you must hail - let me guess - from the sub-continent? Yes, quite wonderful - concertgoers from your part of the world aren't exactly two a penny. Is this your first time at Wigmore?"

"Sheela's a Londoner and she's probably been here many more times than the rest of us. Come, Sheela, let's have a look at the photos." Clutching Sheela's arm, Clarissa whispered. "Why on earth does Max have to perform with Neanderthals like him?"

"Don't worry, I've come across his type before, although not for a while."

"A drink?" The second violinist had returned, offering Sheela a glass of red wine. "I'm sorry, I think I said something stupid."

"Oh, not to worry. So, how long have you been playing the violin?"

The man launched into a narrative about his pushy mother, but Sheela's attention had drifted away.

Suddenly aware that there was no hand holding on to her arm, she looked round the room. Standing next to the piano, Clarissa and Max appeared to be in animated conversation. Moving away to place her glass on a table, she managed to snatch a few phrases spoken by Clarissa - "...definitely here", "...how we'll manage"; Max's responses were inaudible, but he gave the impression of trying to look composed. Something had happened this evening - something to do with the way Clarissa had been glancing across the auditorium.

The conversation between Clarissa and Max came to an abrupt halt. Clarissa walked over to Sheela, hands outstretched, eyes bright, and mouth stretched into a smile so tight that Sheela imagined her own jaw muscles hurting. Max had meanwhile gone to join the other members of the quartet.

She took the outstretched hands. "Are you all right?"

"Oh, you shouldn't worry about me." Not "Of course I am". Sheela wrapped her arms around Clarissa's waist; her chest was pressed so hard against Clarissa's that she felt she knew every contour of her friend's fragile frame.

"Come, we really must get back to our seats." Sheela held Clarissa's left hand and made sure that when they passed along the front of the hall she was on the side facing the auditorium.

She had been dreading the Schubert quintet. But today it wasn't difficult to let her mind wander away from Cyrus: for a change, she was putting someone else's problems before her own. There was somebody Clarissa wanted to avoid. Who was this person, why was she upset, what exactly had she and Max been talking about?

She couldn't help glancing sideways, but Clarissa was giving away nothing. Her gaze was fixed, not at the performers on the stage, but straight ahead. The skin covering her cheek bones, limpid and white, looked stretched to the point of splitting. She must protect this woman, come what may, but protect her from what? The compulsion to find out was tempered by a fear of discovering the truth.

The applause caught her by surprise.

Clarissa turned towards her. "Did you enjoy that?"

"Not sure one can call it enjoyable. The usual word is 'sublime'."

"Unbearably sublime."

The performers returned to the stage to give more bows and feigned surprise when presented with the customary gifts.

"We'd better leave now. Max said he would be waiting for us in the car."

"Oh, but I can take the tube."

"Certainly not, you live a stone's throw away from us, besides which we'll have the chance to talk."

They walked down the aisle, Sheela holding Clarissa's arm. Clarissa lowered her head as though intent on minding her step.

In the foyer, they had to weave their way through the people filing out like attendants at a funeral service. Finally they were on the pavement outside the main entrance.

"This way - Max has parked the car on Welbeck Street." Clarissa spoke so softly Sheela could barely hear her.

They were reaching the corner of Wigmore Street and Welbeck Street when a man some distance behind them gave a shout. Clarissa appeared to quicken her step.

They were turning the corner when Sheela heard the man's voice again, somewhat louder now. She caught a word that sounded like 'air' but the shout was drowned by the diesel roar of a taxi. Clarissa was now a number of paces ahead of her. As she was about to turn into Welbeck Street, Sheela looked back briefly: a young couple were walking arm in arm towards them, and, further back, a stocky man in a suit looked as though he had been hurrying in their direction and then decided to slow down.

Max opened the front passenger door for Clarissa, and then the back door for Sheela.

"It's getting quite nippy," he said, with a slight smile.

Sheela noticed that Max locked the doors the moment he was in the driver's seat. They were on Wigmore Street in a matter of seconds, but their way was blocked by a taxi waiting to let in a couple of concertgoers.

Finally, they managed to edge forward past the Wigmore entrance towards Cavendish Square. Sheela looked to her left. The crowd had largely dispersed. But the stocky man was still there. He looked up as their car passed. She had a fleeting impression of a bald head shining under the street light and spectacles glinting into the distance, like a central European character from *The Third Man*. Sheela couldn't be sure whether he had seen them. What she did notice was that Clarissa's head was no longer visible. She had evidently bent over. As if reading Sheela's thoughts, she said, with an airy laugh, "I've dropped the programme, and I just can't find it!"

The search for the programme continued until they passed Cavendish Square. It was only when they had reached Mortimer Street that Sheela felt she could break the silence.

"Well, I must thank you both again for the lovely concert."

"Did you really like it?" Max sounded as though he wasn't just trying to appear modest.

"Well, with your wonderful playing of course I did – although I wish I understood more."

They had reached a set of traffic lights on Goodge Street.

Max turned round, looking straight at Sheela. "We often understand without knowing it."

"How do you know how much I understand?" Sheela laughed lightly. She couldn't decide if she should feel flattered or disturbed by Max's direct gaze. When he had looked at her his eyes were no longer soft and retiring. He looked as though he was a man in charge - a man who might even wish to take charge of *her*.

The light went green. There followed a silence which remained suspended until they reached Gower Street. It was as if ending it might take the conversation into dangerous alleys.

"Further back there," Sheela pointed her finger to the left as they turned right into Gower Street, "was where I studied."

"Oh UCL! You know, Max and I were saying how little we really know about you. And your husband?"

"He went to UCL as well."

They had just passed Russell Square. Russell Square, where she would spend summer afternoons with Cyrus, trying to do her revision but mostly unable to concentrate because of the distraction of the handsome young man sitting cross-legged in front of her.

"You know, Sheela," Clarissa turned round, "I was thinking of that silly second violinist assuming you were visiting Wigmore for the first time - being Australian, I think I understand exactly what you must feel. We're somehow in the same boat - outsiders."

Sheela felt a vague sense of disquiet. She did feel like an outsider, acutely, in whichever circles she hobnobbed: because she "hailed from the subcontinent"; because she couldn't claim membership of any exclusive group; but most of all because of what happened a year ago - an experience so rare that it was well beyond the comprehension of all but a tiny minority. And now this couple claimed to be outsiders as well. How were *they* outsiders? How could the mere fact of being Australian – white, hardly distinguishable from your average Brit – justify Clarissa's claim to be an outsider? Yet her claim rang true, in some way that Sheela couldn't quite fathom. Somehow, like her, this couple didn't belong. Somehow, as Clarissa put it, they were all in the same boat. A feeling of exhilaration swept through her: she was not alone. Her mind drifted back to the bald man outside Wigmore Hall. Yes, they, like her, had a secret to hide - and this man was a part of their secret, perhaps central to it. As Cyrus was to hers.

"To get to Calabria Road you need to go round and turn left on Corsica Street." They had just reached Highbury Corner.

"Corsica - you remember our holiday there, Max." Clarissa turned round to Sheela: "Have you been to Corsica?"

"No, never." The fellow feeling - the feeling that they were all outsiders - was slipping away: Sheela was reminded that she was about to enter an empty bed in a lonely house. They would return to their shared bed and make passionate love to each other. As they had done in a copse in Mahabaleshwar.

"Thank you so much for the lift. I feel I've really been a nuisance."

"No, no nuisance at all," Max said, pushing his seat back to get out of the car.

"No, I insist, please don't come out - I'll be quite all right."

"Bye then," Clarissa said, extending her arm.

Sheela pretended not to notice it. "Thank you again for inviting me."

The couple waited in the car as she walked to the front door, but Sheela resisted the temptation to turn round.

It was too late to eat, so she changed and lay on her bed. The springs squeaked in the silence. In Bombay she found solace in the noise of traffic persisting late into the night. Here there was no such refuge. She looked at the empty pillow next to her, but quickly turned over the other way. Cyrus couldn't return, so imagining him there, next to her, eyelashes curling upwards over closed lids, breathing softly (he never snored) - all such daydreaming was futile and depressing.

Pleasurable daydreaming meant letting your mind wander towards things that might be attainable in some however unlikely future. So her reverie turned to the couple she had just left: to her right was Clarissa, in a negligee so gossamer-thin that the delicately pert contours of her body were discernible under its diaphanous folds; there she slumbered, lips slightly apart, artlessly alluring, like some latter-day Ariadne as depicted by a 21st century Waterhouse.

And to Sheela's left was Max, head bent over her, fingers caressing her side. She stared at the ceiling, willing the cornice to banish the image of the bodies on either side of her.

20

A chime of the grandfather clock, distant and reproachful, jolted her out of bed. It was 8.30. She had to get dressed because Nina would be calling very soon. *Hopefully, God willing.* Over the past year she had become increasingly anxious about everything - global heating, wars, refugees, terrorism, plane crashes. Anxious, above all, about Nina.

When she reached the bottom of the stairs the phone rang.

It was Nina informing her that they were about to take the Heathrow Express.

"Oh thank God, sweetheart - I'm just so relieved you got here safely."

"What's wrong, Mum, you never used to worry like this. Anyway, really can't wait to see you!"

When the phone clicked, Sheela felt the deflation she often experienced when a moment of anxiety had passed. She could never quite understand it. What had she been expecting? A bomb in the aircraft? *Stop it - I'm tempting fate. God forbid that anything bad should ever, ever happen to my Nina.*

At exactly 9.45, she saw the slight figure of her daughter, in animated conversation with a young man who looked pale and blond in the morning light.

She got out of the car and waved her arm as enthusiastically as she could. Nina pounded along the pavement, rucksack bouncing on her back, to greet her mother with a hug smelling of aircraft seating and sweat that hadn't quite turned from fresh to stale.

"Darling, you look ravishing!" And then she heard herself say, "More and more like your father."

Nina's face was shining, and the hollows below her enormous eyes made them look larger than ever. Her complexion seemed lighter than before. In fact, she did look more like her father. Cyrus, so handsome, and Sheela, so plain in comparison, had produced a daughter who, for most of her girlhood, was said to take after her mother, to the chagrin of everybody except Cyrus and Khorshed. "She looks just like you," Saroj had said when Nina was at primary school, "but still, you never know, ugly ducklings can turn into swans." Now the ugly duckling had indeed turned into a swan.

"You're looking pretty good yourself, Mummy." The girl moved away as she spoke.

Sheela was almost relieved when the young man caught up with them.

He swayed with the simian gait of a fervent bodybuilder, his vein-swollen muscles bulging through the armholes of a singlet. Sheela was vaguely disappointed to find no sign of tattoos.

"Mum, this is Jake." In Nina's voice and smile, there was the strain of a girl unsure of the welcome to be accorded to a new boyfriend. Sheela felt out of her depth. What made Nina choose this philandering oaf, endowed no doubt with nothing but a vacuum between his ears?

"Hi," said Jake, revealing a tuft of golden armpit hair and an upturned palm which, to Sheela's surprise, showed an excellent hand: a clear round life line, a flawless fate line joining a perfectly shaped head line, and a deep Sun line travelling from the bottom of the life line to the base of the fourth finger. Although she had always pooh-poohed palmistry as mumbo jumbo, Sheela found herself reluctantly concluding that this young man was destined to go places. But she was pleased to note that his mount of Venus was thick and fleshy *(a sure sign of a lecherous type - quite unsuitable for my Nina)*.

"Oh hello," Sheela said, looking down as she fumbled for her car keys.

Nina and her boyfriend clambered into the back seat. *How mannerless, treating me like a glorified chauffeur!* Never mind, with time and perseverance she would see to it that her daughter was hitched to a nice Parsi boy, or, failing that (because presentable Parsi boys weren't exactly two a penny nowadays), a nice Sikh boy or even an English boy if he came from the right sort of family.

Initially she and Nina did most of the talking, the boyfriend offering the occasional grunt. But it wasn't long before the focus of her daughter's attention drifted towards the young man. The conversation was now reduced to whisperings interspersed with occasional fits of girlish giggles. At the Penton Street traffic lights, Sheela glanced at the couple through the rear-view mirror: Nina's head was nestled in the boy's left armpit - *chhee, to think of her hair smelling of his BO!* - and his right arm seemed to be making a circular motion. *Shameless - rubbing her thigh like that (God knows what else he's up to)!* She tried not to think about the cavorting they must have indulged in during the flight.

Less than ten minutes later, they alighted from the car.

"Mum, it feels like just yesterday that I was here - everything's like the same as ever."

"Well, nothing much has changed, has it?"

Nina looked up sharply.

"Well, Nina, you know where your bedroom is. While you settle in, I'll show your friend his."

Nina stared at her mother and flounced up the stairs.

The boy followed Sheela. The creaking of the floor boards reinforced the awkwardness of their silence.

"Well, Hank, I hope you find the room comfortable," she said as she pushed the bedroom door open.

"Jake, actually. Oh, I'm sure I will. Thanks for the trouble. But as a matter of fact, I won't be here long. I'm visiting my parents."

"Your parents?" Sheela hoped her relief didn't show in her voice.

"Yes, they live in Berkshire."

It was from the pronunciation of the last word that Sheela realised this boy wasn't American at all. Earlier he had spoken with a transatlantic accent which had left her wondering whether he was an American trying to impress her with an English accent. But then she noticed his speech was peppered with glottal stops - clearly a 21st century attempt to conceal a privileged English background.

"So that's where you did your schooling and everything?"

"Actually, my parents sent me to a boarding school close by."

"Not Wellington?"

"How did you guess?" A blush crept up his face. Scrape off the carapace of transatlantic-Estuary, and what do you find? A kernel of upper middle class conventionality. Sheela had to admit that she was beginning to feel more comfortable with the boyfriend. And the lines in his palm didn't seem so incongruous after all.

Why was she being so mean to him, she asked herself as she walked down the staircase. The boy was shy, even timid; and she had been a bully. But he did have a fling with another girl.

In the dining room she found Nina gazing out of the window.

"Why are you being so horrible to Jake?" The words came spitting out in a whispered staccato.

"Listen, we had a perfectly civil conversation on the way up to his bedroom. You're just feeling tired after a long journey."

"Stop patronising me, mum!"

"Well, I suppose you'd prefer to be told you're behaving like an ungrateful brat!"

"You're so nasty! I don't know why I bothered to come. I took pity on you, and this is what I get."

"PITY ON ME? I didn't ask you to come - you invited yourself. Of course, I was happy to have you come - but what cheek to turn the tables on me like this!"

"Look, Mum, you're not the easiest of people. It's so difficult to read your mind - you're so uptight. After all, look what happened to - I really, really don't know what actually happened with Dad, and I have no idea precisely what you've been doing since - then. I wish you'd at least acknowledge things instead of pretending not to understand."

"What is it that I'm not acknowledging?" As the words sprang out, Sheela wished she could retract them.

"For one thing, you won't acknowledge that you can't stand Jake. No, don't interrupt me - for another, you've always been so bloody secretive about Dad, for example that time when that crazy patient of his accused him of - of God knows what, but I'm sure he'd have been ready to talk if you hadn't been so paranoid about hushing things up, so in the end I was kept in the dark. And now you go on as though nothing happened a year ago - Daddy may as well have not existed."

Sheela sank into the dining chair by her side and let her head drop. Without looking up she said, "You don't know what you're talking about."

"Speak out, Mum - I can't hear you." Then, before Sheela could respond, Nina said, "I'm sorry if I've upset you."

Sheela didn't know what to say. She couldn't succumb to the darkness threatening to take over, not in front of her daughter; she couldn't make light of the situation because that would be false; she couldn't change the subject because that would prove the truth of Nina's accusation. In the end she chose silence, partly to punish the silly girl but mainly because she was at a loss for words.

"Mummy, please talk."

Sheela looked up and saw a little girl with fright in her eyes. She didn't want to, but some external force willed her to get up and envelope her child in her arms. She felt Nina's shoulders heaving with sobs and she had to bury her own face in the arm she had placed round her daughter's neck so the girl wouldn't notice the wetness on her cheeks.

"Mummy, I'm sorry." Sheela held Nina closer, but the girl wriggled free. "Oh hi, Jake! How're you feeling?" she said brightly, sweeping a wrist over her cheeks.

"Oh, I'm great! You have a really cool shower, Mrs Marker."

If the boy had noticed that something was amiss (which surely he must have?), he wasn't letting on. The beefy bodybuilder was more sensitive and intelligent than he appeared. And his interruption had rescued Sheela from her daughter's probing.

She smiled at Nina, who smiled back at her; the tears shed a minute ago seemed to have lent an added lustre to the girl's eyes. Perhaps she too was relieved. Sheela had managed for a whole year to keep the full truth about Cyrus from Nina. It was almost as though her daughter were an accomplice in this subterfuge, prepared to press only so far in case the truth should turn out too awful to bear.

"Goodness, it's late. Must get the lunch out. Hope you don't mind - it's just some cold cuts and salad."

"Mum?"

"Yes, dear?"

"Jake is going to see his parents tomorrow, and they've asked me to come too."

"Oh how nice. When do you plan to join Jake?"

"As it happens, they've asked Jake and I to come together tomorrow."

"Jake and me," Sheela blurted before she could stop herself; but she was glad that the correction slipped out. "But you've hardly been here!"

"Well, if you're going to be upset about it, I won't go."

"Don't be a silly billy, little one, of course I'm not upset about it. Just slightly surprised."

"Why surprised? You remember how you - and Dad - always told me it was more gracious to accept than to refuse an invitation, unless there was a good reason to turn it down?"

"So what time do you propose to leave?"

"Er, the train leaves sometime around 9am," said Jake, sounding as though he was keen to opt out of the conversation.

Oh God, I hope the silly girl hasn't imposed herself on them. "Are you sure that your parents are happy about this?"

"Oh Mum, why shouldn't they be?" Again turning to Jake, the girl added, "My mum really knows how to make me feel wanted, doesn't she!"

"Yeah, Mrs Marker," said Jake, as though he hadn't heard Nina's remark, "my parents are always happy to meet my friends."

"What's that supposed to mean, Jake? Don't your parents know that I'm - like - your *girlfriend*?" The girl's voice had dropped to a furious hiss. Sheela didn't hear the boy's reply. He had moved towards the sitting room, and Nina followed him.

"I need to go to the loo." Sheela started walking up the stairs.

There was no response, just a quiet rustling. Nina's probably sulking, and the boy, being a peaceable sort, has no doubt wrapped her in his arms to snog away the hurt.

145

21

"I've got to get some groceries from Waitrose." The truth was she wanted to escape the pressure of coping with her daughter, of being civil to the boy and of feeling unlikeable.

She was at Waitrose for perhaps fifteen minutes, buying non-essential items which could have waited.

Not wishing to return home so soon, she decided to take a walk around Highbury Fields. She felt the tickle of a light drizzle on her nose. A smudge of cloud threatened to turn the drizzle into a downpour. She decided to take shelter under a large plane tree. She was grateful that she never thought of taking her umbrella: the rain would provide the excuse for her late return to the house.

She leant against the tree and watched the joggers puffing past her, the pain of effort lining their faces. A young couple lazed in the grass, unfazed by the shower. Perhaps she was imagining, but they appeared to be casting furtive glances at her. She felt that others too were starting to eye her warily. Reluctantly, she decided to wend her way back to Calabria Road, having succumbed to the pressure of a thousand gimlet eyes she imagined peering through the windows of the Georgian terraces surrounding the fields.

She decided to walk on the grass, past the benches bordering the fields. A muscular personal trainer was shouting to a couple of girls "one two - c'mon, don't flag - one two, one two", until one of them slumped on the grass, her heaving breasts the only part of her anatomy still willing to obey the man's barking orders. On the next bench a woman was sitting still, hands on thighs, eyes shut. The next bench was empty, and on the one after that was seated a man holding the Daily Mail spread out in front of him so that all she could see was his podgy fingers and a headline about benefits scroungers.

A minute later she approached the walkway cutting across the fields. As she turned the corner the scene she had just witnessed suddenly struck her as curious. Why the Daily Mail? Surely this was the armchair-socialist epicentre of Guardian-reading luvviedom. She turned round as if drawn by a magnet. The man had his newspaper laid on his lap. He moved his head quickly in the opposite direction, but not quickly enough for her not to notice that he had been watching her. She turned away and advanced along the walkway. She felt goose pimples creeping up her spine. The creeping turned into a shudder when she realised that she had seen this man before; he was the man Clarissa had tried to avoid at Wigmore Hall. What was he doing here, in Highbury Fields of all places? The answer was obvious: he was following her. Why? And how did he know she lived in this area? She quickened her pace, and turned round when she reached a corner. For a moment, her knees shook with the relief of finding that he was nowhere to be seen. Relief turned to panic when she noticed a portly figure emerge from behind a tree and walk down the pathway she had taken only a few minutes earlier. She turned back, stumbling on a paving stone. The man would find out where she lived unless she disappeared from his sight. As she turned right into Calabria Road, she dared to turn round once more. *I can't see him, so please, please God, let him not discover where I've gone.*

"Hello there!"

Sheela let out a squeal and broke into a run.

"Sorry, did I startle you?"

She recognised the voice; it was that wretched Johnson man. She pretended not to have heard him.

She fumbled to get the front door key out of her purse, dropped it, picked it up and had to lay the shopping bag near her feet so that she could hold her right hand with her left to stop it from shaking as she slid the key in and opened the door. She closed the door softly and hurried to the dining room to draw the shutters. Because they were Victorian, they had a few cracks which in the past she had found useful as peepholes.

Through the cracks she saw the Johnson man walking by on the other side of the street, gazing at her front door. She imagined that he looked put out, and for a moment the satisfaction of this thought blotted out the Daily Mail man.

"Mrs Marker..."

"Oh my God!" She turned round, arms raised to defend herself.

"Mrs Marker, are you all right?"

She looked up to see an anxious Jake torn between a fear of invading her space and a desire to move forward to comfort her.

"Oh, yes – yes. Thanks."

She was grateful that he wasn't asking questions.

"Where's Nina?"

"She was getting a bit worried about you, so she's gone to look for you - at Waitrose or Tesco or something."

Oh my God. Suppose that man accosts her.

She turned and peered through the shutters.

"Oh no!" Her daughter was at the far end of the road talking to the Daily Mail man. The panic she felt recalled the time the three-year old Nina had got lost at Euston Station.

She rushed towards the front door.

"Mrs Marker, what's ..." The boy followed her like a disembodied robot being pulled in different directions. Even in her state of alarm, Sheela saw a child wanting to be a man but at a loss to know how he could make the transition.

She opened the front door and ran onto the road, only to find her daughter approaching her with an airy wave. The man was walking away, disappearing round the corner where Calabria Road takes a right angle towards Highbury Fields.

She flung her arms round Nina and dragged the girl back to the house.

"Mummy, why are you in such a state?" Nina was pressing Sheela to her chest, as if she had anticipated the sobs convulsing her mother's shoulders.

Sheela locked the door.

"What was that man saying to you?"

"Oh Mum, what are you getting, like, so *hysterical* about? He was asking how he could get back to the tube station."

"Was that all?"

"Oh, and whether there was any Indian-looking woman living around here."

"So what did you tell him?"

"Obviously I said I didn't know. But Mum, what's the matter?"

There was a pause, as if everybody in the room was waiting for somebody else to speak.

"So is it OK to go to Jake's parents' place tomorrow?"

"Oh yes, of course it's OK."

"I mean I'd like to go, but not if you're in this state."

"I'm quite all right. It's just that I don't like you talking to strangers. You can never be too careful." Sheela turned to Jake, conscious that he should not feel left out of the conversation.

She wasn't at all sure what she wanted. She didn't want to be left alone in the house, but neither did she want Nina or her boyfriend for company. The only person she wanted could never be with her. She thought of her old friends in London. But they were never really her friends. They were his; proxy friends who had melted away into their Georgian terraces and weekend homes when there was no more to be said about the happy times they had shared as couples. The only room for newly single people like her was one filled with an embarrassed kindliness which, as the weeks passed into months, had begun to suffocate all its occupants.

But there was one couple who had made a point of befriending her. Precisely why, she couldn't understand. When away from them, doubts crept in and she suspected their motives; but when she was with them, the doubts vanished in the face of their frank gaze. For reasons quite mysterious, they had genuinely sought her friendship, genuinely taken to her. And they were connected to this Daily Mail man. She must phone them.

The next morning she found Nina and Jake waiting for her in the dining room. It was already ten past eight.

"My darling, have a lovely time with Jake's parents." Sheela gave Nina a hug. Nina buried her head in her mother's shoulder. Sheela noticed an uncertain smile on Jake's face. Then the boy walked away to the sitting room. *He really is sensitive, this boy, knowing when to let people have their private moments.*

Nina held her mother tight, not looking up, not wanting to let go. The way she clung on to her reminded her of a time when Nina was five or six. She and Cyrus were going to a dinner party, leaving Nina with Ute, their German au pair. Just as they were about to leave the house, Nina rushed to them, begging them to remain with her. They had stayed on for a while, comforting her, and when she had calmed down, she had said, "I don't want to get married." "Why, darling," Sheela had said, "it's nice to get married; you can have a lovely house and lots of lovely children." "No," the little girl had started to whimper, "I don't want to get married." "Darling," she had said, "if Mummy and Daddy hadn't got married, they wouldn't have had you." "No, no, no," she was screaming now, "I don't want to get married!" Cyrus then took over. Picking her up, he said, "OK, sweetheart, you don't need to get married if you don't want to. You can stay with Mummy and Daddy forever and ever." Nina quietened down immediately, quite happy now to let her parents go to their dinner party.

That was always the way it was: always Cyrus who knew the right thing to say, always Cyrus who knew the right thing to do; however hard she tried, she couldn't match her husband as a parent - or, for that matter, in any other way.

With the years she had learnt that it was often best not to say anything. So now they stood together, stuck in each other's arms like two intertwined Lladro figures.

"Shall I come to the station with you?" A slight movement from Nina had signalled that it was time to break the silence.

"Don't be silly, Mum - besides, Jake is here to look after me!" The boy had just returned to the dining room. He put his arm round Nina's waist and said, "Don't worry, Mrs Marker, that's what I'm here for." If she had read his words on a page, she would have concluded he was being facetious, but he looked at her so earnestly that she found herself saying, "You're sweet. Thank you." She gave him a hug, which, after a fractional pause, he readily returned.

Turning to Nina, she said, "Please don't forget to let me know when you plan to come back here."

"You will be OK, won't you, Mummy?"

"Yes of course, darling. Now run along and have a lovely time." Sheela gave her daughter a kiss on each cheek, a smacking lip-squeeze of the kind dispensed liberally when Nina was a child, not the perfunctory peck brought on by teenage years of rebellion and anger.

She waited at the door, waving every time the two youngsters swung round to give her a wave, until they reached the end of the road and turned the corner.

She struggled to push her mind back to something she had to do. What was it? Oh yes, she was going to ring the Alexanders to thank them for the concert.

"It was such a pleasure having you with us, Sheela. Actually, Max and I were wondering if you could make it to our place for dinner tomorrow. We realise it's all very last minute, but we've asked a few friends over - so it would be lovely if you could come."

"Thank you - as it happens I'm not doing anything tomorrow." Or any other day, she could have added.

Sheela took down the details of the Alexanders' address off Gibson Square. She was relieved that she wouldn't need to make a point of contacting them about her experience with the Daily Mail man. But how was she going to broach the subject with other guests around?

22

Tomorrow came very soon. Over the past year, Sheela had perfected the art of filling time. Buoyed by the prospect of meeting the Alexanders, she found more energy than usual to fill the hours of the day that had just passed.

"Thank you so much for coming." Clarissa greeted Sheela with a prolonged hug.

She looked so English, with her porcelain beauty. So English, yet so Indian in her demonstrativeness - at least as conventional stereotypes would have it. Sheela drew back to look at her, then held her in a protective embrace: the porcelain seemed even more delicate now than at Wigmore Hall, as if liable to crack under the slightest pressure. When she turned to Max, the kiss she received on each cheek was warmer than the usual arms-length greeting perfected by the English.

She was introduced to an elderly woman called Gladys who, it turned out, had done her early schooling in India.

"How interesting, you probably know more about India than I do."

Sheela had expected the old lady to brush off the compliment, since for the English middle class the appearance of modesty was a compulsion bordering on fetishism. Instead, Gladys's immediate response was "Oh, quite possibly." Then she added with a mischievous smile, "But you probably know more about England than I do. I can see you've been here for a while."

Gladys had the name of an Agatha Christie chambermaid but the face of a Miss Marple, a Joan

Hickson lookalike, all delicate features, wispy white hair and watery eyes brimming with cornflower-blue perspicuity.

"Sorry," Max interrupted, "but should I give Jolyon a ring? He's normally pretty punctual."

"Maybe give another fifteen minutes?" Turning to Sheela, Clarissa added, "Jolyon is Max's best friend from school days. And with your interest in music, you'll be fascinated to hear that Gladys is one of this country's leading post-modern composers - in demand all over the place."

"Oh go on, Clarissa - you flatter me!"

"So Gladys, why don't you play the first bit of *Anticipation* for Sheela?"

"Oh well, if you insist." Gladys wiggled her bottom to the edge of the armchair and heaved herself up.

"Oh no, Clarissa, Jolyon's having a problem. He's just texted me to say there was a burst water main that buggered up the traffic, and now he can't find a parking place. Sorry to interrupt the party, but I think I'd better go and help him. Shouldn't be more than twenty minutes."

Gladys was already seated on the piano stool. *Oh no, she looks like one of those who won't stop once she's got going.*

For the first time, Sheela noticed her surroundings. Although spacious, the room was functional: apart from the piano, the stool and an accompanying music stand, there were two armchairs, a cane settee, a small dining table surrounded by dining chairs, a nest of Kashmiri side tables, a shelf stacked with CDs and a stereo player. The only concession to opulence was the piano - a Bechstein grand. But if the room looked spartan, the walls were certainly not: there must have been fifteen works of art, striking for their variety - some figurative, some expressionistic, some abstract, and one unclassifiable piece that interwove a wire mesh recalling the fishing nets of Kerala into thick layers of paint swirling across the canvas. The place looked more like a makeshift art gallery than a home that had been lived in for any length of time. Sheela's eyes fell on two pieces hanging on the wall nearest to her, one abstract and the other a charcoal drawing of an Indian girl with a bundle of hay stacked on her head. In the bottom right-hand corner of each canvas was the same signature - *Clarissa A* - written in a fluid slant but so faint that it was barely noticeable.

"Have some nuts." As Clarissa bent over, a bowl of nuts in her hand, her hair and her side face glinted gold under the light of the ceiling lamp. Once again Sheela felt herself caught by the singular beauty of this woman, but it was a beauty shot through with countervailing currents of strength and fragility, self-possession and self-doubt.

Gladys's piece was pleasant enough, and she was clearly an accomplished pianist, but it was with relief that Sheela heard the doorbell ring just as the piece came to an end.

"Gosh, that was quick," said Clarissa.

"Don't get up," Sheela said. "I'm near the door."

She felt a flutter of anticipation. *Maybe that's what Gladys's piece is really about. No, stop it, you're going crazy.*

She opened the door, but instead of the smiling figure of Max, there was nobody. "Funny," she turned to Clarissa, "somebody must have rung this flat by mistake."

She moved to close the door, but before it could click shut it was pushed wide open. Sheela let out a gasp. The portly figure that had stepped out of the shadows of the landing was now facing her with the hint of a smile on its round face. It was the Daily Mail man.

Before Sheela could take in what was happening, the man had got into the flat.

"Hello, Claire. Well, well, long time no see, as they say." The man tipped something vaguely Tyrolean to reveal a shiny pate. His accent was almost trans-Atlantic, except that the vowels sounded as though they had been modulated by some other part of the world, quite possibly Australia.

"What do you want?" Clarissa's voice was cold, her body taut. Sheela wanted to shield her, but didn't dare to move.

"What do I want? Well, now that's a strange question to ask. Surely it can't be hard to guess?"

"Go away. Please. You have no business barging into my flat like this."

"I know, very naughty of me. But then this wouldn't have been necessary if you hadn't tried so hard to avoid me at Wigmore Hall."

"What are you doing here?"

"What are *you* doing here? You ran away, so I had to find you, didn't I?" The man's gaze turned towards Gladys, then to Sheela, who returned it with a glare, hoping that he wasn't able to see the beating of her pulse.

"Get out. Get out at once, otherwise we shall call the police." Gladys had got up from the piano stool and picked up her stick, almost losing her balance as she tried to wave it at the intruder.

"I don't think you would want the police to be called, would you, Claire? All that unpleasant publicity."

The fear in Clarissa's eyes jolted Sheela into action. Glancing sideways, her eyes fell on the fireplace nearby. She turned round and rapidly bent over to pick up the tongs lying by its side.

She gripped the tongs hard to stop the shaking of her hand.

"Leave now," she said, barely audibly.

The man raised his eyebrows in mock surprise, but from the darting of his eyes behind his thick browline glasses she could see that he was taken aback. This gave her the courage to look at him properly for the first time. He was maybe in his 60's, stocky, no taller than she was, dressed in a double breasted beige suit with the triangular tip of a red handkerchief peeking over a pocket. His hands were chubby and the nails of his fingers short and wide but the tips were manicured to snow-white perfection. He was wearing a red bow tie and a pink shirt. His face and neck shone with the hint of hidden sweat. He smelt of Eau de Cologne. Altogether he gave off an air of dapper seediness.

Sheela's eyes followed the man's left hand as it slid towards a bulging trouser pocket. Bulging with what, she wondered. Not keys or coins – something far larger. *Oh my God, could it be a weapon of some sort?*

"Johannes, please leave!" Clarissa cried out.

The man's upper lip was now beaded with perspiration.

"Oh thank you, Claire, how kind of you to acknowledge me in front of your friends." He let out a sigh.

"But," he continued, his voice thickening, "this is so distasteful. You know I'm not some boorish gate-crasher. I am an artist. I paint. I listen to Bach, Mozart, Bruckner. I don't barge - as you so graciously put it - into people's homes. But it's your fault, isn't it, that I have been reduced to this. Isn't it? ISN'T IT?" His left hand was now stroking the bulging pocket in nervous circles. Sheela tightened her grip on the tongs.

"So, my dear Claire, what do you intend to do? Be sensible and return to where you belong? Or stay with that bastard who stole you from me?" His face was now red - suffused with grief or rage; more likely rage, thought Sheela. Her nerves felt as though they were hovering a hair's breadth away from a live electric current, and, as if fearful that the slightest movement could precipitate a massive shock, she remained rooted to the spot where she was standing.

"So what is it to be, Claire? No response. By that," he paused, "I take it you would rather cling to that - to that Lothario of yours than do the decent thing. But I forbid you - I will make it impossible for you to - " His voice trailed away into a barely audible choke.

Sheela saw his thumb fidgeting with the lining of his pocket. As if her arm had a will of its own, she felt her whole body follow its trajectory. The tongs hit the man on his left leg, just below the pocket. He stumbled, then, recovering quickly, he staggered upright and, to her surprise, made for the door. He turned round briefly to look at Clarissa. The rage had gone. His shoulders had slumped. His glasses looked wet, and she thought that, behind the fog of the lenses, his eyes too had misted. His lips were parted, as if trying but failing to say one last thing to the woman he called Claire. He turned his back to them as he reached the door, then, once more, looked round.

Sheela braced herself for another confrontation, but she needn't have feared. No longer did she feel the terror of a minute ago: as the portly figure staggered into the shadows of the landing outside, all that was left was pity - and shame.

23

Sheela slept uneasily that night. Fragments of the previous evening flitted through her half-wakefulness like pieces of a film still to be edited, a dislocated montage which didn't always follow the logical chain of events. Securing the chain on the door; standing still to stem the shaking in her body; turning to find Gladys with her arm round Clarissa's bent shoulders: all that she remembered clearly. What did she do next? Did she go to comfort Clarissa? No, probably not; something had held her back. Who was this man? Who was this woman he had called Claire? How could she like, let alone love, a woman she didn't know? What the evening had proved was that this woman, this Claire, this Clarissa, could not be trusted - and nor could her husband (or partner or whatever he was). Hiding things. That's what they were doing. But hadn't she been hiding things as well?

At some point she had got up to get water, more for comfort than from thirst. Or perhaps she had dreamt of this.

Then she recalled Max and Jolyon entering the flat. How relieved she had been to have them there, Jolyon in particular - a man who sounded like his name: jolly and bluff, exuding the imperturbable bonhomie of upper crust Englishmen who had been taught from their suckling days that life, for all its ups and downs, should be treated as a hoot. Max and Jolyon, the best of friends, yet as different as chalk and cheese.

Some time that night she saw Max and Clarissa kissing each other passionately in full view of their guests. This clearly hadn't happened, but what was certain was that, having entered the room with Jolyon,

Max had gone straight to Clarissa and held her in his arms. The next thing she knew they had *her* wrapped in their arms, thanking her - for what, she couldn't tell. As she remembered this, the sense of belonging returned, replacing the earlier feeling of estrangement: whatever had happened with the intruder, she felt her life inextricably linked with the lives of her two hosts.

Of the meal itself all that remained was an impression of going through the motions: dishes served, compliments murmured, wine bottles opened.

As morning light streamed into her room, Sheela felt she had to get up. Dragging herself out of bed, she heard the phone ring, shrill and insistent. She rushed to the hallway, wondering whether the caller was Nina.

"Sheela?" It was Max. She thought she heard suppressed breathing, as if he had been running away from something but didn't want anybody to know.

"Yes, Max?"

"Listen, I need to talk to you about - about last evening, for one thing. Can we meet somewhere?"

The conversation was brief. When she put the phone down, her chest was heaving, as if she had caught Max's agitation down the phone line. He had suggested meeting in an hour. Why the urgency? Why did she agree so readily? And why just him?

When she stepped out of the house, she was seized momentarily by the panic of being followed by the Daily Mail reader. Then she remembered that the man, so sinister in his anonymity, had become so pathetic in the flesh. But, although the fear had gone, the memory of the man had cast a shadow over her immediate surroundings. Her mood wasn't helped by the weather - grey, rainy and chilly in a way that only London weather could be.

Max had suggested meeting at the Highbury Fields branch of Barclays Bank, but there was no sign of him when she arrived there even though an hour had already passed. People were waiting their turn at the Barclays ATM. At the head of the queue was a thin man whose face she couldn't see but, from his stoop and his loose-fitting raincoat, she assumed him to be on the wrong side of middle age.

Sheela decided that she would leave if Max didn't turn up in five minutes: he had no business being late - after all, it was he who had asked to meet. She turned towards Highbury Fields to see if he was taking shelter under a tree, and as she did so, she noticed the man at the ATM edge away. When he raised his head, it took a few seconds for her to realise it was Max, looking as though he had aged ten years.

"Sheela!" In an instant he was hugging her as though he hadn't seen her for ages. Yes, it was the same Max with the smiling eyes and the finely-chiselled features. But no longer youthful. Something had happened.

They agreed to go to a café a few minutes away. He offered his elbow as if it were the most natural thing to do, and without thinking Sheela slid her hand through the crook of his arm. Then, conscious of Clarissa's absence, she made a move to withdraw it, but almost as though he had anticipated her second thoughts he pressed his elbow gently but firmly to his side so that any further attempt to extricate her hand would prove awkward. As they walked past Highbury

Fields on their left, she was aware of a tension, although it wasn't clear how much of it came from him and how much from the conflict she was experiencing - between the pleasure of his proximity and her loyalty to Clarissa.

The café was tiny. On one table lay a coffee-stained cup and a copy of the Guardian, but right now they were the sole occupants of the room. Sheela sat with her back to the wall; at least that way she could let her eyes roam around if she wanted to avert his gaze.

"Two coffees - one ristretto and one black with milk on the side - and one orange cake."

"Here," said Max, cutting the piece of cake not quite in half and giving her the bigger portion. She curbed her instinct to protest.

There followed a chat about the excellence of the coffee and the cake, how it compared with the fare offered by the patisserie places in the vicinity, how one was spoilt for choice living in Islington.

"Listen, Sheela, enough of this beating around the bush." Max's voice sounded unnaturally thick. A scattering of red spots had begun to pockmark his face. His right hand was clenched, as if trying to control a tremor.

"Yes?" she said in a matter-of-fact voice, turning her gaze to the Guardian headline about hostage decapitation.

"I - we, Clarissa and I - wanted to thank you again for yesterday. We owe you an explanation for the turn of events."

"Look, you owe me nothing. But if you feel you need to explain things, please fire ahead."

"Well, it all started when Clarissa left Australia."

Sheela looked down to pour more milk into her coffee. She didn't want her face to betray anything - neither her curiosity to get behind the secrets of this couple nor her fear of where that curiosity might lead the conversation.

"The man who came to the flat was Clarissa's husband." Apparently encouraged by the nonchalant expression Sheela wore on her face, he added, "Technically, he is still her husband."

Sheela was trying to hide her disappointment. So all this came down to nothing more than the usual sordid tale of wife leaving husband for another man.

He bit into a piece of the cake. "She left him before," he paused on the last word, "we came together." He looked up at her, his face flushed. "It's not easy telling you all this, with you" - his mouth broke into a twisted smile - "so sphinx-like."

"What do you expect me to say?" She gave a little laugh to cover up the vehemence of her reaction. "In any case, all this is none of my business."

"It *is* your business - because of what happened last night. Clarissa gave me all the details after you left. About how brave you were, how if it weren't for you - "

"Oh, I just reacted instinctively - I'm simply not a heroic type!"

Suddenly a lump rushed up her throat. She pushed her mouth against her napkin and coughed into it.

"Excuse me. I need to go to the loo."

The toilet was in a basement area. Sheela locked the door. She bent over the basin, her belly taut as if clamped on all sides. Without warning, the lump surged up in a bubbly discharge of coffee and spit. Her nose was dripping and her eyes were blurred. But the lump had subsided.

When she came out of the toilet, Cyrus floated before her eyes, gazing at her with an inscrutable smile. But as she climbed up the stairs she made a determined effort to wipe him away.

Max looked up anxiously as she approached the table.

She glanced at her reflection in the mirror on the opposite wall. Not as revealing as she had feared.

"So," she said with a composed smile, "Clarissa left Australia and came here. And when did she meet you? Sorry, again none of my business."

"No no - why should you not know? But that's a bit of a long story, so perhaps we can leave that for another time?"

She felt the conversation come to an abrupt halt. With a creeping sense of foreboding, she was convinced that the real reason for his wanting to see her hadn't yet been disclosed. Everything said so far had been like a dress rehearsal. She didn't dare to let her gaze linger on his face for fear of what it might reveal.

"It's my turn to go to the loo. It was downstairs, wasn't it?" He was trying to smile.

Before waiting for an answer, he got up and made for the side door.

"Would you like anything else?" The waitress spoke with a pleasant tone of finality that told Sheela it was closing time.

"No thank you." She was grateful to have the excuse to leave this place; cosiness had turned to claustrophobia. She got up to put her coat on.

Max returned so quickly that she wondered if he had really used the lavatory. She was relieved to see something of the old Max - smiling, this time without effort, and less hunched.

"Sorry to keep you waiting. I see we're ready to go."

A blast of cold Spring air smacked their faces as they walked out of the café. She was relieved. If he had wanted to tell her something awful, he wouldn't do so now.

When she turned down his offer to take her to her place, he didn't insist. Instead, he gave her a hug - of the arms-length kind.

As she walked the short distance back to her house, she felt the relief of the past few minutes tainted by something missing, something vaguely disturbing.

At her front door, as if she had been half-aware of it all along, came the realisation of what had been bothering her: why hadn't Clarissa come with Max? When he had phoned to request a meeting she had found it curious that he had used the first person singular. But then followed a more disturbing line of thought: why had Clarissa's absence not been acknowledged? and why had she avoided asking him the obvious question?

She was no longer able to separate the mystery of what lay behind this couple - so warm and yet so alien - from the mystery of her own behaviour, the behaviour of a woman quite estranged from the Sheela she thought she knew.

24

She heard the phone ringing as she inserted the key into the front door.

It was Nina calling to say that Jake's parents had invited her and Jake to stay on a bit longer. Normally Sheela would have been relieved to receive this news. But today she felt like a piece of charred toast picked up and dropped on a whim by a daughter unable to understand that need was a two-way thing.

"Fine, by all means stay with them as long as you like. Give me a call when you think I'll be - useful."

"But, Mummy, I -"

"Actually, Nina, I was about to make an urgent call when you phoned, so I must ring off. Hope you have a good time."

She put the phone down.

Oh no, I was too harsh. Oh God, I hope nothing bad happens to her. I must phone her back.

But before she could reach out to pick the handset, the phone rang again.

"Mummy."

"Oh darling, I'm so sorry, I must have sounded - distracted."

"You sounded like really put out. Sorry, Mummy, if I've upset you in any way."

"No no, my sweetheart. I've just been a little - tired - that's all."

"Are you sure it's just that?" Sheela heard the hope rising in the girl's voice.

"Yes yes, of course. Just let me know beforehand when you plan to return. Promise to look after yourself - and have a lovely time."

She had a task at hand. She needed to call the Alexanders - to be precise, Clarissa, if only to expunge the shame of having consented to meet Max on his own.

"Oh Sheela!" To her chagrin, it was Max who had come to the phone. "You've heard?"

"Heard what?"

"It's been in the news. Johannes - you know, Clarissa's ex - well, he tried to kill himself."

"What?"

"Yes, bullet in the neck, but amazingly he just grazed it, missing all the vital parts. He's in hospital - UCH - to be treated for shock more than anything else, I think."

"Thank God." Sheela couldn't understand the intensity of her relief; after all, it wasn't her problem - the man was a stranger to her.

"We were going to ring you. Can you come over some time - we were thinking tomorrow - for a mid-morning coffee?"

The question sounded more like a plea than an invitation. She recalled Clarissa that evening at Wigmore Hall; she had looked haunted - haunted and hunted - like a beautiful gazelle desperate to escape from the clutches of a stalker.

"Yes of course. I'll be there elevenish."

25

Max answered the door bell.

"Thank you for coming." He gave her a peck on the cheek which seemed almost studied, as though he had rehearsed his greeting in advance.

He looked gaunt and hollow-eyed, the lines on his face accentuated by the white morning light; and the hair looked tired, not tousled in the boyish way she had found so attractive. His shirt cuffs, rolled half-way up his arm, were frayed at the edges.

Clarissa was seated rigid on the cane settee, staring at the window, apparently unaware of Sheela's arrival. But as Sheela approached her, she got up and, without a word, fell into her arms. The only sound she made was barely audible, something like a whimper. She had been crying. Finally, she looked straight into Sheela's eyes. In her gaze, Sheela caught a glimpse of a face fast-forwarded twenty years - as beautiful as ever, but somehow ravaged by remembrances of times gone by; or fears of times to come.

"Clarissa, what's happened?" As she pressed her cheek into Clarissa's nape, Sheela thought she felt a vein pulsating against her face.

They held on to each other, both reluctant to stir, as if, by prolonging this moment, eyes shut, each of them could ward off the reality of the world with its awkward questions, dreaded answers and uncertain turns of fortune.

The tinkling of coffee cups broke the spell. Simultaneously both women relaxed their grip and looked at each other, tentative smiles hovering around their lips.

"Come and sit near me." Clarissa led Sheela by the hand, and the two women sat close to each other on the settee. Sheela noticed that some of the coffee Max had just poured had spilt on to her saucer even though the cup hadn't been filled to the brim.

Max sat on the edge of an armchair. He looked as though he was readying himself to make a speech.

"Max feels we should tell the police what happened the night you came for dinner."

Clarissa took a gulp of her coffee. Then she looked up intently at Sheela. For all her delicacy she exuded an aura of power, the sort of power driven by the desperation to carry through whatever the pressure of circumstances demands.

Sheela knew that Clarissa wasn't waiting for a response.

"But I don't think so. Besides which, how would it help?"

"It mightn't help. But somehow it feels right to tell them. What do you think, Sheela?"

Sheela didn't know whether to feel flattered or bothered that the couple seemed so dependent on her opinions.

"You said his condition wasn't life threatening?"

"Yes, apparently," Max said quickly, almost eagerly.

"Then the police will no doubt interrogate him. If he wishes to tell them about you, he will, but if he doesn't, would you have the right to deny him his privacy?" She had reverted to her fallback position - to consider the practical consequences of the choices to be made - a consideration which, she had to admit, came across as taking precedence over what was right and proper.

She noticed the tension drain away from the faces turned towards her. She couldn't help feeling pleased that she had managed to turn the moral argument on its head - even though she recognised that her point was no more than a rationalisation for the real reason why she had made it: her desire to protect this couple.

"Brilliant! Didn't I tell you, Max, that Sheela would somehow get to the core of the matter?" Turning to Sheela, Clarissa said, "You don't know how - how grateful I feel. No, somehow that's inadequate."

Clarissa moved closer to Sheela and tucked an arm round the back of Sheela's waist. Sheela placed a hand on Clarissa's knee, just as she had done to comfort Nina when she had had a bad day at school. But Clarissa wasn't her child: for Nina the feeling had been clear, uncomplicated, maternal; for this woman, the feeling was indefinable, quite beyond her conscious experience - and it made her uneasy.

She felt a shadow creep behind her, and then a hand, masculine but finely wrought, placed lightly on her shoulder. Out of the blue an image came to her of Paul Newman, impossibly handsome, all broad shoulders and bulging biceps. But Max's attractiveness had none of that brute physicality. Then her imagination returned to the track it had wanted to pursue: it was a picture of Newman's wife, Joanne Woodward, her face split three-ways, on a Hollywood poster advertising *The Three Faces of Eve*. It seemed to her now that she was herself split into different identities - if not three, two individuals so separate that they were strangers to each other: one, the Sheela of old, sensible, pragmatic, in control; the other, a woman out of control, careless of the physical intimacy she was enjoying with this couple, defiantly raising two fingers at her former self.

Slowly, reluctantly, the old Sheela regained control. Gently, she nudged away the palm resting on her shoulder, and, as if that small gesture had sent telepathic waves forwards and backwards, Clarissa withdrew her arm and Max moved towards the trolley.

"Some more coffee?" Max's voice sounded slightly hoarse.

"Yes please," she said.

Her throat felt swollen, overcome by a sort of yearning - in the first instant for Cyrus, for a return to her nights with him, now so distant they felt unreal; then very quickly for something more immediate. She glanced sideways, but, to her relief, Clarissa's head was turned away.

"Here you are." As Max offered the cup of coffee, his hand touched hers. Like a knee reflex, a current coursed through her, impossible to control, as if the imperative of the other Sheela, the new Sheela, was too strong to resist.

Clarissa walked through an open door to get some water.

Sheela stared at her cup, as though intent on not letting any more coffee spill onto the saucer.

"Not too strong?"

"What? Oh no, it's perfect." Sheela looked up only when Clarissa returned with a glass of water in her hand.

"Clarissa, what about Johannes?"

"What about him, darling? Oh look, there's a blackbird just outside our window!" She spoke lightly, but Sheela noticed that Clarissa's gaze remained fixed on the window and her smile was clamped into her jaw.

"Shouldn't you - do you want to visit him?"

The bird burst into song, its round flutey notes occasionally lapsing into a frayed trill.

Clarissa's face had assumed a rapt expression. The bird fell silent, then, with a whir of flapping wings, it flew towards Gibson Square.

"Why should I want to visit him?" she asked softly, without turning her head.

"Well, he's just tried to - he's just had an accident, hasn't he?"

"It wasn't an accident. It was a deliberate act of - of self-destruction." She swung round to look at Max. In her face Sheela saw not the callousness of the words she had just uttered but the vulnerability of a girl pleading to be excused from a task she knew she had to perform.

Max walked over to Clarissa and wordlessly wrapped his arms around her. Clarissa let her body slump, her head nestling against his chest. The two of them stood there, inert, seemingly lost in a world of their own. A few minutes earlier, sitting on the settee with Clarissa's arm round her waist and Max's hand on her shoulder, Sheela had imagined herself central to their lives. Now she remembered what it had felt like to watch from the periphery as people swarmed round Cyrus like bees drawn to a calendula; notwithstanding all his efforts to draw her into the conversation, they had left her on the side lines, ending up with their backs towards her.

"Well, I think it's time to go," Sheela said, trying to suppress a grimace as she gulped down the dregs of her coffee.

"Oh, please stay." Clarissa wriggled out of Max's embrace and gripped Sheela's arm. "We want to know what you think."

"Think about what?"

"Well, you know, about what Max has just said. About visiting - him - in hospital."

"But that's entirely up to you, isn't it?" The words were sharp; *good, let them know I can tell when I'm being used*. But when she looked up at Clarissa's face, wide-eyed and uncertain, she decided immediately to offer an escape route.

"Well," she said, turning to Max, who had started busying himself collecting the cups and saucers, "he might not want any visitors, and" - she tried to formulate her next statement - "if the two of you have anything to do with what he did, a visit from Clarissa might not be -"

"Welcome." It was Max who had offered the word.

"And you can always phone the hospital if you're worried about how he's doing."

Clarissa turned to her, held her hands, and said something so quietly that it took Sheela a moment to piece together the two words she had spoken.

"Nothing to thank me for, Clarissa."

She heard a clearing of the throat. "Tell you what, why don't we have a bite of lunch together?"

"Oh yes, Sheela do stay. Max has made the most scrumptious cheese and aubergine quiche - you must sample it, otherwise he will be very hurt!"

"Oh well, if you insist - I wouldn't forgive myself if he was hurt!"

Max left for the kitchen.

"Shall I put a CD on while we're waiting?"
"Yes, why not?"

They sat informally round the dining table. Max filled Sheela's plate with a generous slice of the quiche and a heap of avocado salad. This couple managed to get things right, she thought. No boring lettuce and a mouth-watering quiche.

Clarissa got up suddenly. "Clean forgot about the music."

She walked over to a shelf of CD's and placed a disk into the CD player.

"You'll find this quite jolly, I think," she said, as she settled into her chair.

The CD started with the strings of an orchestra playing a tune which was anything but jolly - extended legato lines with dotted notes stretching even further, wistfully evoking some kind of longing, perhaps for a lost love.

"Oh no, how silly of me, I've put the wrong record on - Bellini instead of Corelli."

"Now that it's on, Clarissa, leave it on. Just listen and tell me what you think of her." The last remark was directed at Sheela.

Sheela needed no introduction to the voice. "*Qui la voce*" it started, after the orchestral prelude.

She felt as though her neck was impaled against the back of her chair, the voice piercing through her gullet.

"Isn't she amazing," Max said softly, eyes shining the way Cyrus's shone when he put the same record on.

"Max adores Callas," Clarissa whispered.

Now, with its climactic cries of *"mai piu"*, the voice commanded total attention: the sad mad Elvira bewailing the loss of the love she would find no more.

As if fighting against some uncontrollable force of nature, Sheela strained to curb the sob rising up her throat and the tears sneaking down her cheeks.

Clarissa got up from her chair and wordlessly pressed Sheela's head against her waist. Sheela let out a croak, guttural and intrusive - or so it seemed because the music had come to a sudden halt. She couldn't understand the person sitting in her chair, a person so unlike the Sheela who had been the dependable head girl of the Cathedral School, the Sheela who had assumed the role of the sensible if slightly dull wife of the talented doctor whose presence cast a bright light on every corner of every room he entered.

"I'm so sorry."

She was expecting Clarissa to say "There is nothing to be sorry for", or something similarly predictable. Instead, she felt herself being helped to the settee, her head placed face down on to Clarissa's right shoulder as if to protect her from the pitying gaze of her companions. She felt her hand being squeezed.

"Here, here's some water." From the corner of her left eye, she saw the blur of a glass held close to her face. She blinked to clear her eyes. The hand that held the glass reminded her of Cyrus's, long fingered, with perfectly groomed nails, although Cyrus's had been slightly more slender.

She raised herself, sat upright, and turned to reach for the glass.

"Thank you," she said, after a few sips. "I'm fine. Really I am." There was no response, but the silence was comforting.

"Can you put that record on?"

"You mean the Corelli?"

"No, Clarissa. I mean can you put that one on again. The Callas bel canto arias. But could you start with the first CD, the one that starts with Norma - *Casta Diva*. The *I Puritani* starts the second CD, I think."

"Are you sure? I mean, please don't feel we ought to listen to it just because I like it."

"No, Max. I would really like to listen to it. I - we - used to play that music a lot. It was one of my husband's favourite records. But I hadn't played it for over a year, so hearing it suddenly came as a bit of a - a shock. Somehow it's easier with the two of you here. And it feels right that I should listen to it again with people who love her singing as much as -"

She stopped abruptly, her voice obstructed by a lump rising in her throat.

"He did. And you too?" Max said softly.

Sheela nodded. She took another sip of water.

"You're sure you want to listen to it?"

She nodded again.

With the first arpeggios followed by the entry of the flute, Sheela felt herself return to the evenings when she and Cyrus would spend hours listening to this and the other bel canto arias that Callas had made her own. Initially she had resisted Cyrus's tutelage - communicated with the boyish enthusiasm of somebody speaking to an equal - but it didn't take long for the hypnotic effect of the voice to take hold of her.

The lump, still stuck in her throat, was about to swell dangerously when the voice took up the melody begun by the flute. She couldn't blink back the tears welling in her eyes, but this time the sadness felt more contained.

They sat in silence listening to the first CD. When it was over, Max got up and gave Sheela and Clarissa an enquiring glance, to which they both responded with a nod.

This time she was able to pay attention to Elvira's lament with something approaching objectivity, marvelling at how Bellini, like Schubert, managed to tug at the heart strings with the simplest of melodies. When the second CD had come to its end, she was completely dry-eyed; it was as if the earlier bout of emotion had leached away all the feelings of loss that she had so dreaded facing, and had instead allowed the memory of that loss to return without the pain that came with it.

"I really must be going now."

"Oh no! Why so soon - we can listen to some more music."

"Really, I've got things to do. It's been so nice to be with you. Although," she managed a light laugh, "I don't know how nice it's been for you to have me."

"Sheela, we needed you to be with us."

She wanted to stay on, but Max had used the past tense, so she had no alternative but to say thank you, they had been very kind, but it was time to go.

As she walked back home along Upper Street, a question that had been niggling her came to the fore: it was clear that the couple were actively seeking her approval of the actions they proposed to take; but why? Why on earth should they have wanted *her* approval?

Her mind leapt back to her very first encounter with the Alexanders. There at Kate's Point this couple had witnessed a woman on the edge, embarking on her own "self-destruction", and they had saved her from it. It was as though their involvement in the drama to which, by pure happenstance, they had become a party, had somehow given them the right, and perhaps the obligation, to involve her in their own drama; to feel free to reveal intimacies otherwise kept hidden. As survivors in the same boat, without fear of judgement, they were able to bail one another out.

As she switched the hallway light on, she felt not the oppressive silence of the house, as she had expected, but instead a curious elation. She was not alone, not any more.

She walked slowly up the stairs, stumbled into her room and fell on to her bed.

When she woke up, it was already approaching 9.30. Extracting her mobile from her handbag, she sent a text message to the Alexanders:

Don't think I thanked you both properly. Sorry for making such a fool of myself.
Love
Sheela

Barely two minutes had passed when she heard the buzz of an incoming text message.

Hi Sheela

It is we who should be giving thanks. If, as you say, you made "a fool" of yourself, that surely is the greatest compliment you could possibly have given to us. (In any case, you didn't make a fool of yourself!)

We must meet again - soon.

With all our love

Clarissa

She re-read the message.

With all our love.

She felt the impulse to respond with something foolish but the old Sheela held her back.

26

The following morning she was woken by the jangle of her mobile phone. It was Max, phoning to inform her that Clarissa and he had found out that Johannes was recovering well.

"When I said I was a close friend, the nurse at the hospital said that the patient had become delirious shortly after the 'accident' and kept on asking for a Claire."

"Wasn't that what he called her when he came to your flat?"

"Yes, he would have done - Claire was Clarissa's name before she left Australia. She changed it to Clarissa when she arrived here. To leave behind her old identity. I know it sounds a bit bizarre."

"I recall a man shouting after us when we left Wigmore Hall. At the time I couldn't quite make out what he was saying - of course it was Johannes shouting for Claire."

"Yes, and he followed us in a taxi."

Which explains how he managed to trace me to Highbury Fields, Sheela thought.

"Sheela, it's so good to talk to you. You -" He broke off abruptly.

"Anyway," he continued, "Clarissa's going to visit Johannes. She's pretty apprehensive, but now agrees it's the right thing to do."

She thought she heard an intake of breath. "Can we meet again some time?" His voice had dropped.

"Yes of course!" she exclaimed. "I would love to meet the two of you again, but can we touch base about this a bit later - I can't remember whether I'd mentioned that my daughter's visiting."

"Yes, any time you like."

Her heart was pounding as she put the phone down and lay back on the bed. He knew that she had deliberately misunderstood his question - that was for sure.

She forced herself to go down to the kitchen and made herself a cup of black coffee. She didn't know what she wanted to do, yet she felt a sense of anticipation, and when the phone rang again it came as no surprise.

But this time the caller was unexpected. It was Bachoo, ringing from the Oriental Club in London.

"Oh Bachoo, I'm so glad you've rung! Wonderful to know you're in London."

"What's the matter, darling? Come on, tell me at once!"

"No, nothing specific. In any case, whatever mood I'm in you're bound to lift it."

"I say, you really *are* my sweetie - oops, that's what your mother calls your delightful brother!"

"How is she?"

"Your mother is always well - doing mischief keeps her fighting fit. Anyway, what about coming over this evening - say around 7.30 - for dinner at the Oriental?"

The phone rang again.

"Mum!" yelled the voice at the other end of the line.

"Darling, what a lovely surprise!"

"Surely not a surprise, Mum. I was phoning about tomorrow's arrangements - you know, to catch our plane in the evening."

"You never said anything about going back tomorrow."

"Mum, I could swear I did. Anyway, we can take the Heathrow Express like we did last time."

"As we did last time."

"The only thing is there'll be much more to carry than when we arrived here."

"Oh well, I can take you both to the airport."

"Are you sure? That would be really fab, Mum - thanks *so* much!"

Are all the young as manipulative as my daughter, Sheela wondered. Notwithstanding her exposure to America, she certainly hadn't lost her English ability to demand something without actually asking for it.

"Could we turn up around 3? Our flight's around 8pm. We just need to pack some of the things we left with you."

"We would need to leave here 4pm latest, so if you insist on arriving no earlier than 3 that will leave hardly any time for us together before your departure."

"Oh Mum, you're so cool being so flexible about everything - don't worry, we'll have a whole hour of quality time to talk on the way to the airport."

What had they left behind that they needed to pack up? Sheela went up to her bedroom, feeling she needed to look for something she couldn't remember. Perhaps it was in Nina's room?

The room was in a mess, as she had half expected it to be: bed hardly done, with the bedspread hurriedly rolled back; knickers and stockings on the floor; a toiletry bag lying on a chair, with some of its contents threatening to spill over on to the floor.

Despite the untidiness, there was evidently very little packing for Nina to do, thank goodness. So whatever Sheela was looking for might be in the boy's room.

At first, Sheela was impressed by the state of the room: almost as pristine as she had left it before his arrival. Then her eyes fell on a packet on the bedside table: condoms offering 'the pleasure you want, the protection you trust'. No bloody wonder the room was as neat as a pin! He hadn't used it at all, having spent the whole night violating her daughter!

She picked up the packet and placed it on the landing just outside the door of the guest bedroom. That would teach him a lesson. And her.

She went back to her bedroom, trying to convince herself that she was not being spiteful: after all, they had seen fit to treat her place like a boarding house, spending most of their holiday with his parents, using her as little more than a glorified chauffeur. This would never have happened if Cyrus had been around.

27

"On the dot! Once again so different from that mother of yours."

Bachoo was waiting at reception, resplendent in a shot silk sari which alternated purple and maroon with the angle of its folds. She enveloped Sheela in her arms and squeezed her so hard that the pressure of her lizard brooch made the younger woman wince. The familiar rose water perfume had drenched the whole of the reception area with its cloying scent.

"In case anybody should ask, we will be in the dining room," Bachoo announced to the man at the reception desk, as if expecting half the West End to seek an audience with her.

"Yes, madam."

A blonde girl with an East European accent beckoned them to a table next to a large sash window draped with plush gold-coloured curtains. "We've got your favourite table, Lady Dhondhy." As she sat down, Sheela noticed that the other guests were mostly Commonwealth types, some British, others from the former colonies.

"*Lady* Dhondhy?" Sheela tried to suppress her smile.

"Well, if you must know, the moment I stepped into this place they decided to call me Lady Dhondhy. Clearly it's this air of aristocracy I exude."

Unsure whether Bachoo was being facetious, Sheela gave a non-committal smile.

After they decided what to order, Bachoo turned to the blonde waitress: "The young lady will have the broth with chanterelles, followed by the halibut with trompettes. And I will have your foie gras, followed by the venison with girolles."

Sheela wondered whether the guests at the nearby table were impressed by the flourish with which the 'r's' of 'chanterelles', 'trompettes' and 'girolles' had been gargled the French way.

After ordering drinks, Bachoo asked for the latest news.

"Well, the other evening I was invited by the Alexanders." Almost immediately Sheela regretted the words spilling from her mouth. It was too late now to stop the battery of questions with which she was to be bombarded throughout the meal: how *were* the Alexanders - *such* a nice couple; how did the evening go; inviting a doddery old composer - what strange company to keep; oh, they invited you to a concert as well, did they - I say, they *are* very friendly, aren't they; I presume you've had them over to yours - no? really? why not? yes, of course, you've been busy, but no doubt you'll be inviting them sometime soon - well, count me in when you do.

"Well, that was good," Bachoo said, finishing the last morsel of venison. "Now, enough of the London news. Tell me, what's the latest on your ma-in-law?"

"The latest?"

"Oh darling, haven't you heard? I'm so sorry to be the bringer of not too good news - Khorshed was rushed to the Parsee General."

Sheela placed her hand on her mouth.

Bachoo reached out to squeeze Sheela's arm. "Look, as far as I understand, it was just the usual old age thing. Feeling unwell, suspected a heart problem, underwent various tests. Sorry to be vague - I thought *you* might be able to fill *me* in with the details."

Sheela stared at her wine glass, imagining the worst.

"Look, just before I left, I was told that she was on the mend. But why don't you give her a buzz tomorrow morning? I bet you'll find her almost back to normal."

"That's exactly what I was thinking of doing." Sheela bent over to pick her handbag up. "Thank you so much for the lovely dinner."

"I'm afraid I've rather spoilt it for you."

Five minutes later Sheela was hugging Bachoo goodbye in the reception area.

When she went to bed, she had to try hard to fight off images of Khorshed lying toothless on her deathbed, ready to be pecked at by birds of prey swarming over the Towers of Silence. She finally fell asleep, waking every few hours to go to the bathroom. She got up at 7 o'clock, having had a vivid dream of Bachoo taking pot shots at vultures eager to gouge out Khorshed's eyes, shouting "Hurrah!" as each bird plummeted with a resounding plonk.

28

Since she was up she decided that she might as well face the ordeal of phoning Bombay.

A breathless voice answered in a high pitched squeak.

"Philomena, Khorshed*bai kaisé hain*?"

"Khorshed*bai bohut achha hai.*"

Sheela registered with some satisfaction that Philomena's Hindi was even worse than hers. But she could hardly believe the girl's assurance that Khorshed was well.

"Oh Mummy!" She wanted to continue, but the words were choked by the tightness in her chest.

"Sheela my darling, what's happened?"

Sheela was alarmed to hear the voice at the end of the line, high-pitched and wispy, like a strand of horsehair about to snap from its violin bow.

"Oh nothing at my end, Mummy. Only I learned last night from Bachoo Dhondhy - who's just arrived in London - that you'd been to hospital."

"So tiresome. They rush you to hospital and subject you to a battery of tests which land up revealing nothing. Now tell me, how's life treating you?"

"Oh fine, fine - I was just concerned that -"

"So very sweet of you, but there's really nothing to worry about. Now, darling, you'll make me feel very guilty if this becomes a long and expensive call, so -"

"OK, but I'll ring you again to find out -"

"Goodbye, darling. Keep well."

Goodbye; the finality of that word upset Sheela. And if she was feeling all right, why was she so keen to end the conversation?

She dragged herself up the stairs and lay on her bed, staring at the ceiling: if her mother-in-law doesn't die, she could well suffer from a stroke and become a cabbage for the rest of her life. Who would look after her then?

Reluctantly, she came to the conclusion to which her train of thought was leading her: she would have to return to Bombay to assess the situation on the spot; then she would be able to decide how long she would need to stay in Bombay. She dreaded the disruption of returning to India after having been in London for such a short time. She felt even worse at the prospect of leaving the Alexanders; a feeling of unfinished business niggled at the back of her mind. But the needs of her mother-in-law pushed these considerations aside. Yes, she must return to Bombay. And with that uncomfortable thought she drifted into a fitful sleep.

She was back at Kate's Point, on a desperate quest to save someone - a woman - although she couldn't place her identity. That she would only be able to do once she spotted her. She wandered to the furthest end of the point. It was getting dark. She stumbled and felt a void under a foot. Her arms flailed in the air, frantic to hold on to something. But why was she so frightened? Wasn't this the very fate she had planned for herself? Then she felt her right hand gripped by something, but as this happened she heard a faint voice from somewhere below her. "Sheela, Sheela," it cried. The voice was her mother-in-law's, although somewhat fractured by the echoing chambers of the valley below.

She had to jump down to save the old lady. She dared to look up, and in the deepening dusk she could decipher the contours of a face. "Max!" she shouted. There was no response, save a tightening of the grip on her hand. She was frantic, ripped apart by the need to save her mother-in-law and the desire to be lifted into the arms of her rescuer. She made her choice, but, just as she was about to heave herself up to safety, the shadow of a figure emerged behind the man, the figure of the most beautiful woman she had ever known, a woman she had grown to love. She pulled herself away, the grip was slowly released, and she fell...

Sheela woke up with a jerk of her foot and the feeling of having left her stomach somewhere behind the headboard. She couldn't shake off the thought that there was reality in the dream, that she did face a choice between her mother-in-law - and Bombay - and the couple whose entry into her life had begun to bring back to her the sense of purpose she had lost over the past year or so.

She looked at her watch and jumped out of bed. It was already 12.20. If Nina was to be believed, she and that beefy friend of hers would turn up around 3pm, but they were quite liable to arrive much earlier. And no doubt both of them would expect to be fed.

She went out to buy some provisions for a simple salad. If she had to make something for these ingrates, she would make damn sure that it was as basic as possible.

It was only as she walked home that she let herself admit that Nina had never asked for lunch.

As she laid the table, she remembered that there might not be enough petrol in the car. It was 2.15. She stuck a scribbled note on the entrance door, saying she would be back shortly.

By the time she put the key into her front door it was already past three. She had had to endure long queues at the petrol station and a traffic jam on the approach to the Highbury roundabout. No sign of Nina and her boyfriend, though.

Just as she was about to go up to her bedroom, she heard a ring at the door and the sound of muffled laughter.

"Darling!" she said with a carefully arranged smile.

Glancing at her watch, she said, "Goodness, it's well past three. I'm afraid we'll have to take the food I prepared for you in the car."

"Thanks, Mum, but we've already eaten. Jake, let's go and pick up the stuff we left behind."

Waiting in the dining area, she heard some creaking of floor boards, the pull of a toilet flush, and a flurry of whispering which seemed to go on for a while. Then silence. What on earth were they doing? Oh God, they weren't taking the opportunity to have one last rutting session before the long journey back to New York, were they? You could never tell with these young stallion types. At long last she heard the sound of footsteps tiptoeing down the stairs, slowly and carefully. From the corner of her eye she saw them bend over to shove a few small items into the rucksacks which they had left near the front door. Then they stood at the entrance to the dining area, Nina slightly in front of the boy.

"OK, Mum, we're ready whenever you are." The smile on Nina's face quivered, and she looked away from her mother. Sheela caught the boy's face starting to flush from a slightly bronzed pink to something closer to English lobster. Why all the awkward tension? Had her worst fears, unbelievably, come true?

"Come, can I help with any of your things?"

"No, Mum - why should we need any help? We're absolutely fine."

It was exactly 3.45 when they set off from Calabria Road, Nina sitting in the front passenger seat, Jake at the back. Neither said a word. The occasional exclamation from Sheela, usually about the traffic, punctured the silence, but the two passengers made no attempt to break the tension. Could they be angry with her? Bloody cheek, she told herself, but her indignation felt forced.

"So did you have a good time in the country?" she finally managed to ask.

"Yes, it was awesome. Jake's mum and dad are lovely. They took us around everywhere. And Jake's mum is an amazing cook. Where did she learn to cook, Jake?"

Jake grunted something about cordon bleu.

"Goodness, she must be an expert in that case. Would put me to shame with my cold cuts and salads."

Again, no response. Are today's youngsters really incapable of engaging in the conversational niceties that lubricate social intercourse?

She heard the boy lean forward towards Nina's window. "Huh?" said Nina, turning round to her left.

Whatever passed between the couple was clearly not meant for her ears.

"Mum," Nina finally said, "Jake needs to go to the loo. Can you stop somewhere?"

"Now let me think. Wigmore Hall isn't too much of a detour. The loos there are down the stairs - very easy to find." Sheela tried to hide her irritation at the thought that she would now have to pay the congestion charge.

Sheela parked the car just outside Wigmore Hall. The boy mumbled his thanks and bounded out of the car.

In the car, there was a taut silence, waiting to be broken.

"What is it?" she said finally.

"What is what?" The girl's voice was sharp, accusing.

"I thought you wanted to say something."

"Well, if you must know, yes, I do. Why were you so horrible to Jake?"

Both of them stared straight ahead, as if fearful that eye contact would inflame the hostility that had sparked between them.

"What are you talking about?"

"You know bloody well what I'm talking about - it's about condoms, c-o-n-d-o-m-s! Leaving them like that outside his bedroom. It was so - like - so bloody *cheap*!"

"Look, when you said you were bringing your friend along, contraceptives were never meant to be part of the baggage."

"Mum, we have like a *relationship* - understand? And, whatever happened in your time, a relationship in the 21st century means having sex - f-u-c-k-i-n-g, if you prefer."

"This really is no way to talk. You wouldn't have dared to speak like that in front of your father."

"My father was far - was a far more understanding person." Sheela thought the girl was going to cry. She was on the point of turning to give her a hug when she was stopped in her tracks by what Nina said next.

"Mummy, what actually happened - I mean with Daddy? I've felt for quite a while that you've never really been open about how he - how he went." The girl sounded as though she had suddenly lost ten of her nineteen years.

"Oh my darling!" Sheela leant over and squashed Nina's slim young frame against her bosom. She loved her daughter most when she became the vulnerable child into which she had suddenly metamorphosed. "Darling, I have told you every -"

"It all seemed to happen so suddenly, almost like mysteriously. And even before that there seemed to be things about Daddy that were like a closed book - I felt I knew him so well, like he was the best dad in the world, yet - oh, I don't know, sometimes he would go all quiet and shut himself away. As if he was depressed or really stressed out or something. I could never work out what it was all about, and I felt too - too, like, scared - to ask, like there was some silent demon stopping any of us from talking about it. And then he would re-emerge his usual smiley self, as if nothing had happened. It just didn't feel quite, like, normal -"

The rear left-hand door clicked open. Sheela and Nina immediately withdrew from each other and looked into the distance.

"Wow, Jake, that was quick! Now we still have plenty of time."

The warmth in Sheela's voice appeared to have taken the boy by surprise. "Oh, that's a relief!" he laughed, and then, as though aware of the weakness of his response, he added, "It's really good of you to drop us all the way there."

"No problem at all - in fact, a pleasure." Sheela felt Nina give her a sideways glance. She squeezed her daughter's hand, and Nina returned the squeeze, although less whole-heartedly: clearly the girl thought her outburst about the condoms lay behind her mother's new-found friendliness towards Jake. Sheela was relieved that her daughter, for all her manifest manipulativeness, remained naive and straightforward enough to have missed the real reason behind the change in her behaviour.

Soon they were on the Westway. There was silence in the car. Sheela saw her daughter sleeping, lips slightly parted, lashes nestling against her cheeks: a modern day Madonna. Through the rear view mirror she saw, to her relief, the head of the young man lolling forward.

It was only as they approached Terminal 5 that signs of life returned in the car. Nina gave a deep sigh and the boy rubbed his eyes with his knuckles as he might have done as a toddler.

When they entered the departure terminal, Jake and Nina scanned the information boards announcing the check-in zones for their flight.

"Mum, you don't need to wait in the queue with us."

"No - I want to see you off at the departure point."

"Oh Mum, what's the use of waiting unnecessarily?"

What's the use, she could have retorted, of getting to an empty home half an hour earlier?

"OK, if that's what you want." Then, turning to the boy, Sheela said, "Nice to have met you."

"Thank you very much for your hospitality," he said. He bent forward hesitantly. Seized by a feeling of regret, Sheela pulled his arm towards her and kissed him on the cheek. The boy's face turned slightly pink and the smile he gave, almost grateful, made her regret feel more acute.

"I'm sorry I couldn't be - I wasn't - more hospitable," she said, trying to give a light laugh.

She turned to Nina and put her arms round her, first tentatively, then, sensing her daughter's response, very tightly. "Look after yourself," she said, "and give me a ring on your arrival." Nina was crying and Sheela pursed her lips to dam the surge in her throat.

She knew now the reason behind her daughter's wish to part company as soon as possible: she wanted to be spared the pain of a prolonged farewell.

"Oh Mummy," the girl said between sobs that sounded like hiccups. She still cried as she did when she was ten.

"My darling, just be happy. God bless."

Nina looked up at her mother, a hint of memory lurking inside the tear-drenched eyes. God bless: that was what her father had always said when saying bye, and Sheela had, after years of listening, developed the same habit.

Walking to the exit of the airport building, she turned back and exchanged one last wave with the young couple. She was not far from them, and saw in her daughter's face an expression of - she couldn't make out exactly what. Pity? Gentle reproach? Whatever it was, that exchange of glances felt like a mute recognition that Nina's question, the question she had asked while they were waiting for Jake outside Wigmore Hall, still remained to be answered.

29

On reaching home after a two-hour nightmare of traffic jams, Sheela helped herself to the cold cuts and salad she had bought for lunch. She tried to remember something she had resolved to do while caught in the traffic. Oh yes, she needed to phone the Alexanders to inform them about her plan to visit Khorshed.

"Hello. Is that Max?"

"Yes - hello, Sheela."

"Sorry, your voice sounded different. I do normally recognise it!"

For some reason she wanted Clarissa to be the first to know about her plan. "Is Clarissa there?"

"Er, can she call later? She's not feeling too great - her visit to Johannes seems to have set her back somewhat. Apparently he was very loving to her and asked for her forgiveness. Quite the opposite of what she'd expected."

"Oh I understand," she said. "Please ask her to call me any time she feels up to it."

She replaced the receiver and sat on the stairs, staring at the front door. Max had sounded like another person, distrait, even distant.

The clanging of the telephone jolted her to her feet.

"Hello Sheela, it's Max again. I just wanted to say I wasn't being totally truthful with you. Clarissa is in hospital."

"What?"

She heard what sounded like a wheeze at the end of the line. She wanted him to continue, however much she dreaded what he was going to say.

"You see," he paused and took a deep breath, "she's been very ill." The voice broke on the last word. "She's had cancer for a long time, and it's suddenly become worse." He was almost shouting down the phone now; shouting down, it seemed to her, the grief that was threatening to engulf him.

As if he had just read her thoughts, Max continued in a softer voice, "I'm sorry, I should've told you earlier. But Clarissa wasn't sure - she felt that talking about it would somehow bring things to a head."

She wanted to say something, something to reassure him, to reassure herself, but she felt as though a gag had been shoved down her gullet. The new life that had begun with the arrival of this couple was beginning to unravel.

"Don't cry, Sheela, please don't cry." The words were so tenderly spoken that they had the opposite effect, opening the floodgates that the shock of the news had so far held back.

"Sheela, Sheela." Somehow his soft voice managed to break through her sobbing. "She's OK, you know. All she's concerned about is that" - the voice was struggling not to break - "that we should be happy."

Be happy? How can we - I - be happy? This is a sick joke version of the stiff upper lip.

"I'm so sorry to give you this news."

"You're so sorry?" she finally heard herself whispering between the sobs. "Surely it is *I* who should say sorry to *you*!" And as she spoke she saw how, caught in her own emotions, it hadn't occurred to her to think about Clarissa's suffering or Max's grief.

Now the words spilt out. "But think of all the medical advances in the treatment of cancer. I know of many people given a - a disturbing prognosis who are now as right as rain." She hoped she didn't sound too false.

"Oh yes, that's always possible, in principle." His words were kindly, but empty of conviction. He went on, "We've done everything we can do." The last remark might have been intended to reassure her, but it had the opposite effect.

"Is it possible to see her?"

"That's just what I was going to suggest. She should still be at UCH tomorrow morning, although at some point soon she'll be returning home."

Sheela felt a dead weight sinking in her belly. Returning home to die, that's what the terminally ill do, don't they?

"But - I mean - don't they have the equipment and everything in hospital, to do whatever is necessary?"

"I think she wants to come home. You see, she isn't suffering - no pain, no need for drugs or anything. When we were in India, we met a guy there who gave her - actually, that's a long story I'll need to tell you some other time. Let's just say she feels pretty good." Then, after a silence, he added, "You must believe me."

"Of course, I believe you." She cleared her throat and said in a matter-of-fact way, "I'll visit her as soon as possible tomorrow morning."

When she put the phone down, she reflected for a moment on the business-like manner in which the conversation had ended, each of them trying to suppress their real feelings, each trying to raise the spirits of the other.

That night she went into a deep sleep, or so she thought because when she woke up she couldn't remember any dreams. She lay in bed, unwilling to face the day. She had to return to Bombay as soon as possible to be with Khorshed. At the same time she wanted to remain in London to be with Clarissa and Max. She was wrestling with these conflicting demands when she heard the grandfather clock chime eight o'clock.

30

When she arrived at Warren Street tube station, a force pulling her in opposite directions made the walk to UCH longer than the three minutes it should have taken.

At the information desk of the hospital a woman told her, after much consultation of computer screens, that Ms Alexander had discharged herself that very morning.

"Hello, Max. I've just been told by the hospital that Clarissa has returned home."

"So sorry, Sheela - I was going to call you to let you know." Then, with a lowered voice: "They've confirmed there isn't much that they can do except keep her as comfortable as possible. And since she's already comfortable she couldn't see the point of remaining there."

"So when can I come to see her?"

"Why don't you come straightaway? I know Clarissa would love to see you. And of course so would I."

"There isn't much that they can do." The ten minutes to Highbury and Islington tube station and the fifteen minutes to Theberton Street felt like twenty-five hours filled with nightmare visions - of Clarissa thrashing around hot and cold, with Max by her side, pressing her forehead with compresses, watching helplessly as his wife slips into oblivion.

Max came to the door almost immediately after she pressed the bell to the flat.

Wordlessly he wrapped his arms round her, so tight that she couldn't tell whose heart she felt hammering her chest. Then, very gently, she wriggled herself free. Placing a hand softly on each of his cheeks, she dared to look straight into his face. His eyes were shining and his lips were fixed in a pursed smile.

He cleared his throat and said, "She's in our bedroom. I'll leave you with her - I think she'd like to be alone with you."

When they reached the bedroom door he knocked quietly and stepped aside to let her in.

The first thing Sheela noticed was a wall hanging of a cart drawn by a bullock in some archetypal Indian village scene. Below it, against the wall, was a circular cane armchair on which were strewn a couple of cushions; she recognised the covers bought at Fabindia. Against the light colour of the cane they looked elegantly subdued, no longer drab as they had appeared in the shop. Although it didn't take more than a few seconds to take these images in, she felt she needed this time to brace herself for what was to come next.

"Hello Sheela."

The voice was clear, almost jaunty - instantly recognisable as Clarissa's. Sheela turned to her left to find a figure lying in the shadows of the bed. She rushed over to it and held out her hands to grip an outstretched arm; but she stopped herself from bending over and hugging her friend, as she would have wanted to do. The person she saw lying in front of her was so delicate, so emaciated, that some irrational fear - of passing on an infection, of breaking her bones - stopped her from giving physical expression to the feeling that was overwhelming her. Clarissa's rake-like arms were the only fully exposed part of her body, but from the outline of the form under her nightdress she looked even thinner than she was the last time they had met. Sheela's eyes moved slowly up, towards Clarissa's face. It took her breath away - quite literally so - and she had to make a conscious effort to suppress a sob. Clarissa had never looked more beautiful, but there was a mask-like quality to the face; it was as though the skin, so fine that it was almost translucent, had been stretched tight over the chin, the jaw line, the mouth, the nose, the cheek bones, the temples, up towards the hairline: Nefertiti come alive, or on the point of death.

She had been shocked when Max had given her the news, but she realised now that she had not been surprised. Everything fell into place: Clarissa with the sunken eyes at Wigmore Hall, Clarissa with the skeletal frame, Clarissa like a porcelain figurine about to crack under pressure.

"Sheela, I'm so happy to see you."

Sheela nodded, clasped Clarissa's right hand and kissed it, trying desperately to blink back the wetness in her eyes.

"Now listen, Sheela, we all need to be happy." After a pause, she said gently yet forcefully, "You know, I have faith, so there is no place for fear or grieving."

Her voice was remarkably strong. Sheela was suddenly reminded of Kathleen Ferrier's last performance; of how, notwithstanding a body ravaged by cancer, her contralto remained as rich and luminescent as ever. That, at least, was the story told by Cyrus - and Cyrus was seldom wrong.

"That's wonderful," Sheela managed to blurt out. Then, having found her voice, she added, "Are you comfortable?"

"Do I look as though I'm in pain? And I haven't taken any drugs, at least not the kind prescribed by hospitals. All I do is take some herbal medicine. If you want to know more about that, Max will tell you some time. You don't realise how much we owe to India."

What on earth was she rambling on about, Sheela wondered. *They say this can happen when the end approaches.*

As if she had just read her mind, Clarissa continued, "We met a wonderful man in India. He is the reason why I feel so well."

Then, to Sheela's dismay, Clarissa raised her head and heaved herself upright. Sheela quickly propped a pillow behind her head.

"Thank you." Clarissa then turned to Sheela and gripped her arm with a force hardly believable coming from such a broken frame.

"Please promise me that you will lo - keep an eye on Max. I know you think I'm sounding strange." She gave a quick laugh, and the image flashed by of the 21st century Botticelli Sheela had first noticed at the Mahabaleshwar Club. The tears she had been trying so hard to contain spilled out, not, it seemed, just from her eyes but from the wellspring of grief she had been carrying inside her for over a year.

"There's nothing to cry about," Clarissa whispered, holding Sheela's face next to hers. Sheela felt the wetness on the pillow and realised that the tears were not just hers. She wrapped her arms around Clarissa's meagre frame, and for what seemed like a precious interlude the two women remained still, as if, having drawn strength from each other, they were making their peace with the reality facing them.

Then Sheela stirred. Max. Poor Max. Waiting outside, wondering what was happening. She raised her head, and said, "You wanted me to promise I would - keep an eye on Max."

"And I've asked him to promise that he'll keep an eye on you."

The lump in Sheela's throat took time to subside. Finally she managed to say, "I don't fully understand everything because - because it's all very sudden - but" - she tried to stop her voice breaking - "I'll do my very best as long as it makes you happy."

Clarissa's body relaxed. "Oh yes. Definitely - it will make me happy."

Sheela felt her heart twist with the radiance of the face smiling at her.

"I'll come over again. Very soon."

"Yes, of course. Of course." Clarissa gave a half-wave.

As she closed the door behind her, she found Max sitting on a dining chair. He moved quickly towards her. She held his hands but didn't come closer. She wouldn't be able to cope with any more emotion, and being calm, even if it was a pretence, was at this point the only way to behave.

"She's very strong and positive."

He nodded, and attempted a smile.

By trying to comfort him she was also seeking to convince herself. But those last words of Clarissa's, that repeated "of course", had not sounded at all convincing, and as she walked into the silence of the staircase outside the Alexanders' flat she felt the darkness closing in on her.

31

She couldn't remember the walk back to Calabria Road. She had relapsed into the emotional auto-pilot that had been her crutch for much of the past year.

When she was in the hallway, the first thing her eyes fell on was the telephone. She needed to phone somebody. She had been planning to contact the people at her language school to let them know she was back in London; but, with Khorshed on the one hand and Clarissa on the other, she was too unsettled to make a commitment.

There was still somebody to call. Oh yes of course - Nina. It was now 2.30pm, 9.30am New York time. Even Nina should be up by now.

"Huh?" The voice sounded drowsy, slightly tetchy.

"Nina! Darling! How are you?"

There was a sound of scuffling at the other end.

"Hello? Mom?"

"Yes. Did you arrive safely?"

"Oh Mom, of course I arrived safely. Mom, can I call you back? I've got to rush to a lecture right now."

"Funny, I could've sworn I'd woken you up. Your voice was so groggy it was barely recognisable."

"OK, OK - it was Jake who answered the phone. We were both asleep when you rang."

Nina's reply was clearly meant to be a challenge, but right now she could muster neither the energy nor the imagination to make an appropriate response. Finally she managed to say, "Sorry to have disturbed you then - glad to know you're safely back in New York."

She put the phone down, wondering whether it would ring with a contrite Nina at the other end of the line. But even after she removed her scarf and hung it on the coat stand, the phone remained silent.

She had no appetite to eat, even though she hadn't had any food since her morning cup of coffee. She didn't want to do anything, yet the prospect of having nothing to do was depressing. "When you feel paralysed just do something - anything," she recalled her father saying. So without letting herself think too much, she got out her car keys and drove to Hampstead Heath.

It was almost six by the time she returned home. She was tired but at the same time energised by the long walk and the visit to Kenwood. She wrapped a piece of mackerel in foil, sprinkled it with crushed spices, and placed it on a baking tray in the oven. She used to make this fish dish for Cyrus, but this was the first time in over a year that she felt able to cook it for herself.

As she finished her meal, she realised that all this activity was nothing more than a futile attempt to ward off the desolation - of loss - that was threatening to overwhelm her: the loss that was imminent - of Clarissa - forcing back on her the loss that was past and remained present - of Cyrus. Even though it was barely eight, sleep was the only escape.

Fifteen minutes later she was in her bedsheets. But sleep, when it came, was fitful. She was conscious of turning in her bed, and the movement reminded her that she needed to go to the loo. As she left the bathroom to return to her bed, she was aware of lightning flashing through a chink in the curtains. When she reached the bed, an explosion shook the house. She clutched on to the bedside table. *It must be a terrorist bomb.* Miraculously the house had escaped annihilation - but for how long? She waited, heart pounding, for the next blast. There was a repeat roar, but more distant, and only then did she realise that she had heard the loudest crack of thunder that she could remember. Sheela looked at her watch. It was now approaching 3.15am. A sense of foreboding kept her wide awake, but she was unable to locate its source. Gradually she slipped into an uneasy sleep.

She was woken by the distant sound of the landline ringing downstairs. She tried to ignore it, but like a fretful child it didn't let go.

She swung out of bed. Something terrible had happened to Khorshed. She fumbled her way down the staircase. In the grey shafts of early morning light she could just make out the time in her watch. It was 7.35.

"Sheela." The voice sounded like a copy of Max's, recognisable but blurred.

"Yes Max." She was trying to sound matter-of-fact. Her response was met with silence - but it was not an empty silence. She could almost hear the crack in that soundless voice wrestling to say the unsayable. She had to take control. This was no time to break down.

"Are you at home?" She heard a grunt which she took to mean "Yes".

"I'm coming straightaway."

As she rang the doorbell, her teeth chattered slightly with the effort to keep calm.

The door opened to a lank figure with a pronounced stoop. As she fixed her arms around his waist, she could feel his ribs and the protrusion of the shoulder blades on which she momentarily placed her cheek. The side of her head bumped lightly against something hard, and, moving her face slightly, she noticed he was wearing dark glasses.

"Come," she managed to say. When they walked to the bedroom, it was not clear who was leading the way.

Clarissa was lying in her bed, much as Sheela had seen her when she was last here. The face was still exquisite in its mask-like beauty, but this time there was something shocking about the mannequin stillness of the figure lying in front of her.

There were two chairs by the side of the bed. Sheela sat on one and pulled Max on to the other. There they sat for some minutes in silence. She stretched her left arm to lay her hand gently on the sheets covering Clarissa's chest. But she couldn't get herself to lean over and kiss the person lying in front of her. Death seemed to have broken a connection; she was conscious only of a numbness, as though the stupor of the body resting lifeless had petrified all feeling.

Finally she managed to find words. "Does anybody know? Your doctor, I mean."

Max shook his head. She felt there was an appeal behind his glasses.

"We will have to inform your doctor sometime soon. She can't remain like this. You understand, don't you?" She meant to sound gentle, but she feared that the words came across as cold and unfeeling.

"Do you have any idea when she - when this happened?"

Max took his glasses off. His eyes were bloodshot, as though he had spent the night drinking. He was trying to articulate something, but all he could manage was a roll of his Adam's apple.

"Don't worry. Take your time." But she didn't feel patient. There was something morbid about a corpse - horrible word - lying in the bed (for God knows how long?), and the authorities would surely need to be informed soon. Clearly she would have to take charge.

"She died in the middle of the night." He spoke distinctly and loudly, like a novice actor trying hard to project his voice to the farthest members of his audience. "I'd gone to the loo and returned just in time to hear a kind of - a sort of gurgling - and then she just went limp. I realised that was the moment she'd gone. I know the exact time, because I'd just looked at my watch when I left the bathroom. It was precisely thirteen minutes past three."

"You mean when we had that terrible clap of thunder?"

"What clap of thunder? There was no clap of thunder. I remember thinking how quiet everything was, because the sound she made - I'll never forget that sound - it felt so raucous in all the silence."

32

The next week passed in a haze of distractions.

Max had regained some of his strength, in response, she hoped, to her sturdy practicality. Together they arranged everything - the doctor's visit, the registration of the death, the funeral arrangements and all the other diversionary details that help to suspend the full onslaught of grief.

Bachoo had rung and, before Sheela could say anything, had launched into a tirade about a rude waiter at a restaurant in Dukes Street. When finally there was a pause Sheela burst out crying about Clarissa's death. After an initial "how terrible" Bachoo asked about the details of the funeral. "OK, look forward to seeing you at the Golders Green crematorium," she said with the animation of someone excited about a dinner party.

While she was not busying herself with funeral arrangements, Sheela spent some of her time calling Khorshed (who insisted she was fine), Shireen (who assured her that Khorshed was indeed fine), and Nina (who snapped at her mother for "stressing like non-stop"). But most of her time was spent with Max. He had plunged himself into rehearsals for another chamber music concert, but he seemed only too glad to be with Sheela the rest of his time. She wondered yet again why *she* had become so important to the Alexanders (and now to him). Surely there were other friends to give support? There was an unspoken understanding that it was appropriate only to meet in public places like the South Bank, Regents Park and Hampstead Heath. Besides, they felt cheered by the bustle of strangers going about their everyday lives.

Most of the time was spent in silence, but it was a comfortable silence. In any case, apart from plans for the funeral, no other topic seemed to merit discussion.

Not even the circumstances leading to Clarissa's death; she never probed and he made only sporadic references to the subject. It was only when she was alone that she pieced together the chain of events: Clarissa had ignored a cyst on her breast; she had finally gone to the doctor on Max's insistence; the referral to the hospital was delayed by a miscommunication between the doctor's surgery and the hospital; the cyst was initially diagnosed as benign; later it was found not to be; further examination showed that the cancer had begun to spread; the holiday to India had already been booked and Clarissa refused to cancel it; on the return from India, she began to feel worse; she was losing weight; a hospital visit had shown that the cancer had spread to the vital organs; Clarissa refused further treatment.

Yes, silence felt comfortable, but it also felt respectful. And when they walked together in the Rose Garden or near Kenwood House they kept a slight distance from each other. That too felt respectful.

Sheela got up early on the morning of the funeral. She was anxious about how Max would cope and nervous at the thought of meeting people who had probably known the Alexanders far longer than she had. To assuage the sense of phoniness that had taken hold of her, she tried to remind herself that she had really cared for Clarissa, even loved her. But right now she wished she was in Bombay looking after Khorshed.

As she approached the crematorium she decided that she would sidle into the chapel unnoticed and slip away when the funeral was over. She dreaded the thought of joining the after-funeral queue of people offering their condolences to Max, and she certainly had no desire to attend the wake to be held in a café at the crematorium.

Entering the East Chapel she sat in the first empty space available. She imagined a few prying eyes scanning the back of her neck, but she looked straight ahead and caught sight of the rear of Max's head. He was in the front row, half hidden by somebody in the row behind him. As if he had felt her gaze, he looked round and their eyes met. She didn't know whether to smile. He jerked his head towards the space next to him, but she shook her head. The service hadn't started, but she didn't want to draw attention to herself.

Although the East Chapel was the smaller of the two in the crematorium, it wasn't full. She recognised Jolyon and Gladys a few rows ahead of her on her left, and she thought she saw the annoying second violinist she had met at Wigmore Hall.

The door next to her swung open with a loud creak, and she felt the full bulk of a brocade-clad Bachoo squeezing against her side. "The bloody taxi driver lost his way," she spat out. A few faces turned briefly, wearing frowns of disapproval intended, thought Sheela, to cloak their curiosity. Sheela gave Bachoo the briefest of smiles, then buried her face in the booklet describing the order of service. To her relief, Bachoo appeared to have taken the hint. She settled into her seat, shifting her bottom from side to side with much jangling of bangles and swishing of sari material. Her behaviour threatened to be embarrassing, but Sheela was grateful for the older woman's presence.

The service proceeded as she had anticipated. She couldn't help feeling slightly self-conscious as she went through the motions of the Christian ritual. For all her exposure to St Thomas Cathedral in Bombay, she remained an outsider in a place like this. Such feelings of alienation didn't bother Bachoo: she sang the hymns lustily in a quavering soprano which plunged into a contralto when the notes became too high for comfort. But Sheela remained mute even when it was time to sing *Dear Lord and Father of Mankind*, one of her favourite hymns from Cathedral School days; it was one of Cyrus's favourite hymns as well, and when the congregation sang "Let sense be dumb, let flesh retire" she felt a constriction in her throat that would have throttled the words even if she had wanted to sing.

A portly preacher of indeterminate years began the service with an air of studied solemnity. She sat there wanting to be moved as he spoke in ever more reverential cadences about our dearly beloved Clarissa, how she had lit up every room she had entered, how her fragrance had permeated everything she had touched. But Sheela felt nothing; it was as though her heart was encased in a carapace of flint that hardened with every exhortation to remember how the grace of God had given us the good fortune of having known our dear departed one. Even when it was time for the coffin to glide into the opening into which all such coffins disappear, she felt nothing, although she sensed a collective intake of breath as realisation dawned on the people sitting around her that Clarissa was finally, irrevocably gone, that there was no way in which she could miraculously lift the lid of the coffin and step out wearing the numinous smile that the preacher's ode might have led them to imagine.

Later she recalled filing forwards to pay her respects, together with Bachoo and the rest of the mourners. What struck her most was the weight of conformity which had squeezed out of her any sense of the sadness of the moment. Still later, it occurred to her that ever since Cyrus had gone she had been trying to embalm herself against the grief, against the rage, always threatening to engulf her. Perhaps it was her fear of what lay buried inside her, not the banality of the service, that had deadened her to the poignancy of the occasion.

Finally, it was time to leave the chapel and meet Max in the arcade overlooking the gardens of the cemetery. He was already surrounded by people offering their sympathies. Sheela and Bachoo (who had managed to maintain a respectful silence), joined the queue creeping towards him. She noticed that he was dry-eyed and controlled, as the etiquette of the occasion demanded.

As they approached him, Sheela caught sight of a man standing on his own under an arch. At first glance, he looked very old - head bent down, hunched shoulders heaving and jerking, a shaky hand leaning precariously on a stick. Then, as if drawn by a sixth sense, he looked straight up at her. His face and neck were partially bandaged and in the bright sunlight she could see that the bandage was wet. It took her a few seconds to process the individual features of the face into a recognisable form. It was Johannes. He didn't try to hide the tears, and as he looked at her she felt that he was making an appeal to her, or perhaps to anyone who would understand. Bachoo was now a short distance away, separated by a couple immediately in front of her. Sheela left the queue and walked towards Johannes. Then, as if it were the most natural thing in the world, she wrapped her arms round him, wanting to give him strength but instead weeping together with him, this man who just a while ago had been such a figure of fear.

"Come," she heard herself say, and she led him to Max. As they came closer, she noticed that Max was struggling to maintain his composure. When they were together they held one another, each wanting to comfort, each moved by the others' comfort. But with Max's arm clasped round her waist, she felt like a fraud locked in the two men's embrace. How could her sorrow compare with theirs? She gave Max a squeeze so light that she didn't expect him to notice it. But he looked her straight in the face, his grey-green eyes soft and his generous mouth trembling as if on the brink of saying something. The eyes came closer and she felt the fullness of his lips on her lower cheek, brushing her mouth. She wished that the older man, still sniffling, was no longer there. She wished that everybody around them was no longer there.

The wake was a simple affair held in a tea room at the crematorium. She couldn't get over the absence of gravity as people ate their Bakewell tarts and drank their beverages as they might have done in the tea room of a sports club. She caught snatches of conversation as she looked around the room: Bachoo loudly explaining the finer points of bridge to Gladys; Max saying something about the sonata form to the preacher; the second violinist talking about Monet to a blonde woman with blue eyes – probably one of Clarissa's fellow artists.

She noticed Max casting a glance at her every now and then, but she avoided eye contact. She wanted to stem the commotion aroused by the meeting under the arches. Thinking about which, she noticed that Johannes was nowhere to be seen. Perhaps he had been repelled by the prospect of all this English revelry - the only mourner, this sinister Daily Mail reader, who had appeared genuinely bereaved. For Sheela, this thought was another reason to dislike herself: as the morning had progressed, all consciousness of Clarissa had faded from her mind, as if erased by the babble around her and the chatter inside her.

She slid along the edge of the room, careful to avoid bumping into a couple wolfing down doughnuts as though they had never eaten before. Funeral Dunkin Donuts, H G Wells might have said if he had been living in the early 21st century. She reached the door and, casting a final glance in Max's direction, slipped away, avoiding the gaze of the kindly tea lady in case she should insist on another cuppa before she departed.

As she walked towards the tube station, she realised that Bachoo didn't know she had left the wake. She would have to call her when she arrived home to explain what had happened.

"Hello Bachoo, I'm so sorry -"

"What happened to you, leaving me in the lurch! In any case, you've got that young man of yours quite worried."

"What young man?"

"You know perfectly well who I mean - the host at the funeral!"

"Sorry - I just felt I needed to slip away."

"Hmph. *You* needed to slip away. At least you weren't in the clutches of that composer female - she just wouldn't let go of me, asking me questions non-stop about bloody *Mum-bye*!"

"Look, let me make amends by taking you out to tea. There's a really nice Italian patisserie place on Wardour Street."

"Patisserie? After all those doughnuts at the funeral festivities? OK, since I'm so kind and forgiving, I shall say yes - but don't expect me to have more than a cup of tea."

They arranged to meet at around 5pm outside Haagen Dazs in Leicester Square.

33

As she put the mobile away, she saw the landline flashing. She pressed the button for voice mail.

"Darling, it's me. Nothing to worry about really. It's just that Ramu had to be rushed to hospital. But he's much better now, so please don't worry. God bless, darling. Lots of love."

Sheela felt the familiar stirring in the pit of her stomach. Nothing to worry about *really*. And Khorshed's voice sounded so tremulous. She must call back immediately.

It turned out that Ramu had developed appendicitis; it was only because Khorshed got his nephew to rush him to the best hospital in Poona that a burst appendix was avoided. He was much better now and was on his way back to Mahabaleshwar.

"Thank God. He's probably alive thanks to your quick thinking, Mummy. But if he's so much better -"

"Why did I bother to call you? You see, ever since he's had the operation he's been saying he wants to see you. I tried to check with his nephew whether he was suffering from some sort of delirium, but he was adamant he was his normal self - mentally, that is. The doctor at the Poona hospital confirmed this. So I'm at a loss as to why he wants you. Perhaps he's convinced himself he's going to kick the bucket."

Sheela's mind was made up. She needed to be with Ramu. But, more important, she wanted to be with Khorshed.

"Mummy, I'm taking the earliest possible flight to Bombay." Expecting her mother-in-law to object, she added, "I do really want to come. And, Mummy, could you please let Shireen know I'm coming?"

"Yes of course, darling."

Sheela was struck by the ease with which she had convinced her mother-in-law about the need for her to return to India; normally Khorshed would have protested about expenditure and carbon emissions.

There was no reason to delay her return. In fact there was every reason to leave as soon as possible. For Mummy and Ramu's sake, she told herself.

As she booked the night flight for the following day, she had to admit that all this urgency had to do less with Khorshed or Ramu than with the need to escape. But she tried to avoid thinking about the reason for that need.

She went upstairs to take a shower and dress. As she stepped into the shower, images of Max kept intruding: Max dutifully receiving the mourners, his lanky stoop both solicitous and vulnerable; Max earnestly explaining the sonata form; Max bending over her, with his salty cheeks, his caressing eyes, his lips hovering close. She felt a stream of soapy water run down her neck, turning into beady rivulets reaching below her belly, teasing the inside of her thighs. She switched the shower off, grabbed the towel and scrubbed her body hard, every nook of it. It really was time she returned to herself, to the Sheela she had always known.

When she arrived at the front entrance of Haagen Dazs, the air was chilly and yellow with a late afternoon drizzle. It was a little before 5pm. No sign of Bachoo. She sought distraction in a bowler-hatted street entertainer who was surrounded by a crowd spurring him on with hoots of laughter and rounds of applause.

It was five past the hour. *Oh dear, hope she hasn't lost her way.* Just then she caught sight of Bachoo, hips swaying side to side as she came puffing towards her.

"Oh Bachoo, I was getting really worried."

"For goodness sake, sweetheart - such a nervous wreck." Bachoo squinted at her silver diamante watch. "It's barely seven minutes past five."

As they made their way to the tea place, she spoke more or less non-stop about how the good old Blighty of her youth had turned into a "blooming multicultural hodge podge", going to pot with the infiltration of unsuitable types who bred like rabbits and couldn't be bothered to offer her a seat in the tube.

"Bachoo, you're beginning to sound like Enoch Powell!" Sheela said, as they arrived at their destination.

Soon after they placed their orders at the counter and settled into their seats, a waiter approached their table, pushing a trolley rattling with cutlery.

"And you see what's happening now," Bachoo added darkly, "bombings, terrorist attacks, you name it. This is what all this bally political correctness does to a country."

"Well, Bachoo, on this occasion we'll have to agree to disagree. How do you like your goodies?"

There followed a discussion about the sourdough toast with Italian jam and the Makaibari Darjeeling tea they had ordered ("far superior," pronounced Bachoo, "to the mediocre fare at the funeral tea party").

"OK - now let's get back to brass tacks. Why did you leave the funeral without letting me know? And your young man looked so lost when he couldn't find you."

"The way you keep calling him a young man reminds me of my mother."

"How is she? Tried calling her before I left for London."

"I don't know. I really should call her myself. I did speak, though, to -"

"What?"

The place had suddenly become noisier. A group of young Italians squeezed past their table, calling out to one another as if they owned the place. Instead of being annoyed, Bachoo gave them an indulgent smile. Like most of the upper middle class Parsis Sheela knew, Bachoo had a soft spot for "the country of Leonardo and Michelangelo".

"I was saying," Sheela said when the room had quietened down, "that I did speak to my mother-in-law."

"Oh how is she?"

"Apparently better. But she said our *mali* in Mahabaleshwar had an emergency operation - appendicitis - so I'm planning to go to Bombay very soon. In fact, tomorrow evening."

"What? You've just *been* to Bombay - and I've just arrived in London, only to be abandoned by you. Really!"

"Oh Bachoo," Sheela said, clasping the older woman's arm, "returning to Bombay so quickly is the last thing I want to do. Especially now that you're here."

The look in Bachoo's eyes told Sheela that she was ready to be mollified. "Anyway," she glanced mischievously at Sheela, "does your young man know you're planning to return to Bombay?"

"Oh for goodness sake, Bachoo, do I really need to tell everybody about my travel plans?"

"He's not everybody."

"What d'you mean?" Sheela said, then quickly added, "Anyway, it's not like I'm going to be away for ages. It's just that, unless I check things out myself, I will never be quite sure if my ma-in-law is really OK. I suppose I'm just being neurotic, but I've already booked the ticket."

She clasped Bachoo's wrist. "I don't know what's got over me of late."

"Hey, hey, what's happened to you, darling?" Bachoo held Sheela's outstretched hand and squeezed it gently. "Have I said something to upset you?"

Sheela shook her head.

"Then why the tears, sweetheart? It breaks my heart to see you like this."

Sheela dabbed her nose with the paper napkin on her lap.

"I know it sounds ridiculous, but I was just thinking of Clarissa."

"What's happened to Clarissa has just hit you."

Sheela nodded. She felt her chest stretch to bursting point. Bachoo's comfortable voice and the chatter of the revellers sitting nearby had blended and faded into white noise. Now what she saw in front of her was not Bachoo's kindly gaze but a montage of Clarissa: at the Mahabaleshwar Club, at the Tea Centre in Bombay, at Wigmore Hall, in her bed fully alive to the end awaiting her; Clarissa, whose absent presence at Golders Green she had sought to blank out of her mind. And all those images, so disparate in mood and circumstance, were bound together by one thing: a transcendent beauty in which spirit and form had blended so completely that it was impossible to distinguish the one from the other. And as those images floated through her mind, she felt heartsick as she had felt only once before: she was back at university, talking to a friend who introduced her to this impossibly perfect man - handsome, gracious, a gentleman; just her type, she had thought, and it wasn't long before she was in love with him; and as the weeks had passed into months, and he had shown little sign of reciprocating her feelings, she had in the lonely hours of the night tortured herself by reliving every evasive glance in her direction as proof of his indifference towards her. It had turned out that she had misread him: his apparent aloofness had come from shyness, and it wasn't much later that Cyrus had proposed to her. So, happily, she had been wrong all along to think that her love wasn't returned. With Clarissa (and in the end, as it turned out, with him as well) any love that was returned was fated not to last.

"Look, sweetheart, I think we should make a move."

When she returned home, Sheela couldn't remember the walk back to Leicester Square station, the journey to Highbury and Islington, or even where and how she had parted company with Bachoo. She was aware only of the older woman's firm hold around her waist as, through a blur of tears and rain, she had stumbled across Shaftesbury Avenue to turn left on Gerrard Street.

34

Now that she was at home, exhaustion took over. As she pulled herself up the stairs, her legs felt like somebody else's luggage. When she finally made it to her bedroom, she didn't switch the light on. Instead she slipped off her shoes and lay down fully clothed, determined to lose herself in sleep and blank out everything that had happened earlier in the day. She fumbled in her pocket and extracted her mobile phone to place it on her side table. Her eye fell upon the beginning of a message.

"Are you OK?" it said. "Nobody knew where you'd..."

She would have had to open the message to read the rest of the note. She turned away from the table. There was no way she was going to be disturbed, not even by Max; most of all by Max.

Sleep came only after a purgatory of half-wakefulness infested by black thoughts too many and too frightening in the loneliness of the dark to trace back to their source.

She woke up the next morning, groggy and out of sorts, to find the sheets damp with perspiration. She leapt out of bed and pulled off her clothes, tearing her dress where the zip had caught the fabric. She turned on the hot water tap of the shower and stepped into the cubicle. "Bloody hell," she cried as she leapt back to avoid the steaming jet of water.

From a little corner of her ear she heard her mobile ring. *I'm darned if I'm going to interrupt my shower for that bloody phone.* Her would-be American brother called it a cell phone. And her mother, trying to out-American her Chweetie when the mood took her, also called it a cell phone. *Stupid bitch of an empty-headed Mumsie darling, always making herself look like a pathetic imitation of Joan Crawford at her most vampish.*

The mobile stopped ringing. Then, from an even more distant crevice in her ear she heard the landline ring. *Oh God, suppose it's bad news from India?* It took her barely two minutes to dry herself and return to her bedroom.

Her eyes fell upon the mobile. There was a second text message.

"Been trying to contact you. Please call. Max." Then, as if to make amends for its abruptness, the message continued, "PS Been quite concerned. Xxx."

She scrolled back to find the text sent the previous night: "Are you OK? Nobody knew where you'd gone. Your friend Bachoo was in quite a tizzy. I'll try again if I don't hear from you. Love, Max."

So Bachoo was in a tizzy. And Bachoo had spoken about that young man of hers looking so lost. Each of them saying that the other was concerned, both unwilling to admit to their own concern.

These people - Bachoo, Max, Clarissa if she had been alive - they really cared for her. She, not the most likeable of people, was the object of their affections. Nothing seemed to fit. She had to reciprocate in some way - that was the least she could do.

"Max - I owe you an apology."

"For what?" he said with a slight laugh. If only he wouldn't be so infuriatingly English.

"For leaving the wake without telling you, and then not contacting you."

"Well, all is forgiven now that you've rung." He could have chosen to take umbrage, but instead he seemed genuinely pleased to hear her voice. "So when can we meet?"

"I'm sorry, Max, but that won't be possible."

"What won't be possible?" She could tell that he was trying not to let his voice snap.

"Meeting." She heard an intake of breath, but before he could say anything, she added, "You see, I'm going to Bombay."

"But you've just returned from Bombay! Why? I mean, why so soon?"

He sounded more dismayed than angry, and for a moment she was tempted to suggest that they meet straightaway. Instead, she told him about Khorshed and Ramu.

"I'm leaving for Bombay today - in an hour, in fact." Before he had the time to detect the lie, she hurried on, "I feel an urgent need to go. I feel responsible for them, now that my husband -"

"Yes of course, I understand." Ever the gentleman, especially since he knew she was concealing something from him; of that she was convinced.

"Can I take you to the airport?"

"How sweet of you. No thank you, I've booked a taxi - and I wouldn't dream of putting you out like that."

"You know you wouldn't be putting me out, Sheela. You know that, don't you?"

His voice sounded as though it was trying hard to contain itself.

Oh Max, I want to remain here with you, I hate the thought of leaving. The force of the feeling inside her was so strong that for a moment she feared she might have actually uttered those words.

"I know, Max - but really, everything's been organised."

She added that she didn't expect to be away for less than a month.

"And presumably you'll be staying at the same place - not too far from Marine Drive?"

"Yes, in Bombay I'll be with my mother-in-law. And in Mahabaleshwar I'll be staying at the family bungalow."

"Your place in Bombay is called Tower View, isn't it – I remember because it faces the clock tower near the law courts. But let me see, doesn't your Mahabaleshwar place have something to do with an old novel?"

"Yes, it's called Lammermoor Lodge. Mahabaleshwar is full of Sir Walter Scott!"

"Yes, I remember Bachoo's bungalow also having some connection with Scott." It was so nice to hear him laugh.

A pause followed, as if each of them was waiting for the other to speak.

"I - I really don't know what to make of everything. Life has gone quite topsy-turvy. I mean with Clarissa gone. And now you returning to Bombay."

"It shouldn't be for too long, I'm sure."

"That doesn't sound entirely convincing. You see, Sheela -"

"Yes?" Sheela heard a pulse drumming in her head.

"I really - I'm going to miss you."

"I'll miss you too, Max." Then, trying to sound as brisk as possible, she added, "Well, I've got to do all the boring last-minute packing, so I'll need to ring off."

"Yes of course. Have a safe flight. Will you text me to let me know you've arrived OK?"

"Sure I will." Then, remembering that he was expecting her departure to be earlier than the time she was scheduled to leave, she added, "But don't worry if you don't hear from me straightaway - it may take me a few days to settle down."

When she put the phone down, she flopped down onto the bed and let her body shake with the release of the tension that had built up during the call.

When she calmed down, something she had found vaguely troublesome swam into focus: why had he wanted to confirm the locations in Bombay and Mahabaleshwar? Nothing particularly untoward about such curiosity, for sure, but somehow it took her aback.

She got up and bent over to drag her suitcase from under her bed. There weren't that many hours before the taxi came to fetch her, so she really did need to focus on her packing. With an effort of will, she tried to banish all thoughts of Max and Clarissa. She extracted the packing list from the drawer where it was always kept, and started the process of ticking off each item as she stuffed it into the case.

Return

35

"Darling, lovely to see you again - and so soon!"

When she had stepped out of the car at Tower View, Sheela had felt happy to be back. The commotion and chaos of the city was a comforting antidote to the silent sorrow of the last few weeks.

But the change she saw in her mother-in-law, after such a short space of time, disturbed her. Everything about her signalled the course of decline, particularly the heavier gait, with the sideways swaying of her body causing her feet to drag. But her mental faculties were as sharp as ever - and there was such a thing as mind over matter, wasn't there?

"How am I?" Khorshed responded to her enquiry. "Oh, feeling a bit creaky, but we have so much to be grateful for, don't we?"

Behind the bravado of those words could have lain a plea for reassurance.

"You're marvellous, Mummy - an example to us all."

"Well, I feel quite - quite fraudulent." Khorshed paused for a moment, then held Sheela's hands. "But I know what will make me feel less guilty, even though it means more trouble for you."

"You mean go and see Ramu, don't you?"

"Clever girl, reading my mind like that. But it's really selfish of me making demands like this when we haven't even eaten."

Khorshed turned towards the kitchen. "Philomena, please *jaldi khana lav.*" Like many Parsis, Khorshed decorated her Hindi with sprinklings of Gujarati.

"So why did you have to go to hospital?"

"The truth is the doctors themselves are quite clueless. They hum and haw with serious frowns on their faces, then put it down to this mysterious disease called old age."

Sheela let out a loud laugh. "Mummy, you looked just like Dr Batliwala - you remember Nina's paediatrician - whenever he couldn't work out what the problem was with Nina."

"Well, there you are. Anyway, enough of this boring talk about me."

Sheela felt the conversation come to an abrupt halt. It was as though both women had suddenly been reminded of another doctor - the man who had brought them together.

Philomena walked in with a steaming bowl of prawn curry.

"So, what are your plans?"

"Well, my main objective was to see you - and of course Ramu - but before that I'd like to get in touch with Shireen. And I suppose I'll have to contact my mother."

"Oh yes, you should. Your mother is your mother, you know."

"Peculiar way she has of being motherly - but I suppose you're right."

"She knows you're here presumably?"

"I'm afraid everything happened so quickly that I never got round to telling her."

Khorshed's mouth was trembling, as if struggling to hold back a smile. *Funny how competitive old people can be.*

"And how is Nina?"

The rest of the lunch passed quickly with Sheela's account of Nina and her boyfriend's trip to England. She said nothing about Clarissa, Max or the Daily Mail man. And she didn't mention Bachoo's visit: it was too closely linked with the events surrounding the funeral.

"Hello." Saroj's voice was thick with querulousness.

"Hello, Mumsie."

"So, Lovely, to what do I owe the honour of this surprise long distance call?"

"Mumsie, I'm in Bombay."

"What? So soon, and you don't bother to tell me in advance? I bet you informed your saintly mother-in-law."

"Anyway, when can I see you?"

"Come for supper - tonight. I have a nice surprise for you." There was something ominous in the deadpan announcement of the nice surprise.

"Lovely, thanks. But if she's free, can I bring Shireen Kapadia along?"

"So you can't stand my company all by yourself! Yes yes, bring whoever you wish to bring. Just make sure you're here by 8."

"Sheels! How funny - I was just thinking of you, wondering whether you'd arrived."

"So how is my darling friend?"

"Your darling friend is fantastically fine!"

"Shireen, you sound really happy."

"As a matter of fact, I am. I've met the nicest guy you can imagine."

"Oh Shireen, I'm so happy for you!"

"The only thing is he's a Parsi."

"So?"

"Well, you know how I've always been - quote unquote - the unconventional one, shunning the idea of settling down with somebody from my parochial little community. But Dorab is sweet and crazy and says he wants to marry me."

"Wow, that's quick!" Sheela worried that her friend might be in for another disappointment.

"The only thing is that he lives in San Francisco, which means that if this really goes the way it seems to be going I'll need to up sticks and join him there."

Curious, thought Sheela, how even in this day and age, it was the woman who was expected to fit in with the man.

"But surely the most important thing is that he's the right man for you."

"I think he is, Sheels. He's not a heartthrob type at all, but he's - oh Sheels, you'll understand when you meet him."

"So he's in Bombay? You see, I was hoping you might accompany me to my mother's place for dinner tonight."

"I'd love to come. Today's the one day Dory's away - in Poona for some work of his."

"Great - I'll pick you up around 7.45."

When she put the phone down, she noticed an incoming text message on her mobile.

Have you got there OK? Please let me know asap. Love, Max PS Miss you.

She started unpacking her suitcase, but found it difficult to concentrate. Picking up her mobile, she responded to Max:

Dear Max, So sorry not to have texted you earlier. I'm fine. With my mother-in-law, who isn't too bad. Love, Sheela PS

She paused. She was tempted to repeat his PS, but then thought the better of it.

Hope all's well with you.

36

"Hi Sheels!" Getting into the car, Shireen gave Sheela a kiss moist with gloss.

"What exciting news, Shireen - your young man sounds so nice."

"Well, darling, he must be in his fifties. But, hell, you're right - fifties is hardly old nowadays."

There followed a long debate about the pros and cons of a late marriage. As they spoke, Sheela felt the conversation come uncomfortably close to the relative merits of an early marriage. She was relieved when Shireen changed the subject and asked her for the reasons behind her hasty return to India.

Gopal swerved at breakneck speed into the driveway of Beethoven. Sheela had to curb her instinct to lecture him: a reckless Gopal in good humour was preferable to a cautious Gopal in a permanent sulk.

They were greeted at the door by Saroj herself. Sheela was pleased to find her mother looking well: she would have no reason to indulge in pity-seeking.

Saroj gave her daughter a kiss on both cheeks and held her at arm's length. "My, *again* you look so pulled down! What have you been doing to yourself?"

Before Sheela could respond, Shireen said, "Hello Aunty, it's very kind of you to have invited me over."

"Well, that's not exactly the way it happened, but never mind. Oh, and please don't call me 'aunty'. That was OK when you were at school, but now we're all *femmes d'un certain age*, as they say, aren't we."

"Speak for yourself, Mumsie!" Turning to Shireen, Sheela said, "My mother hates being reminded of her age - so please call her Saroj."

"My, you certainly haven't lost the gift of the bitchy gab, have you! Anyway, as I said, I have a wonderful surprise for you." Saroj swung her arm with a flourish towards the figure approaching Sheela, arms wide open, mouth stretched into a yellow-stained smile.

"My lovely Lovely! How *are* you? Mwah, mwah!"

"Mohan, you remember Shireen, don't you."

"Lovely, how could I forget any of your friends? And, talking about friends, look who's here!" Mohan pointed to a tubby figure peering closely at the homage to Khajuraho displayed on the far wall.

"Plizzed to mit you", said the maharajah, turning round momentarily. "*Yaar*, Mohan *sahib*," he continued, "this painting is *hot, pretty pretty hot*. Send the artist to me. I would like to - how do you say, commit? - him to do another one for me. Even more bigger and better - for my peliss."

"How about a drink, ladies?" From the fixed grin on his face Sheela could tell that Mohan had already had a drink too many.

Shireen asked for a whisky with water and ice.

"A not-so-*chhota* peg is coming your way, madam! All the better to make you drunk! And you, Lovely, do you want to get drunk too?" Shaking with the hilarity of his own joke, Mohan spilt some of the drink he was pouring for Shireen.

"I'll just stick to water."

"What news of your British friend?" The maharajah was still leering at the painting as he spoke.

"Which 'British friend'?" Sheela glared at the maharajah.

"The British woman interested to see my picocks."

"Really? I don't recall any interest in your 'picocks'."

With a flick of a finger the maharajah beckoned Mohan to sit beside him.

Mohan, still giggling, ambled towards his friend and collapsed on to the sofa. The maharajah whispered into Mohan's ear. Sheela thought she caught three words: "Bitwin her legs". This was followed by a bout of belly-clutching that resulted in more drink being spilt, this time on Mohan's lap.

Sheela got up, a glass of water in her hand, strode towards her brother, jerked his trousers out at the waist, and poured the contents of the glass down the resultant gap.

"The British woman 'interested' in your friend's 'picocks' is dead. Do you understand? DEAD!"

She turned back quickly, determined not to let the two men see that she was holding back her tears.

Shireen rushed to Sheela, gripped her arm, and turned towards Saroj: "Where is your bathroom, Aunty?"

"First room on the left. Can I come and help?"

Sheela bent over the basin. Shireen locked the bathroom door and stroked Sheela's back to help draw out whatever she wanted to regurgitate, but all that Sheela managed was a coughing fit that turned into hiccups.

There was a soft tapping on the door.

"Sheela *beti* - are you OK?"

"Shall I let her in?" Shireen whispered.

Sheela shook her head so vigorously that she was overcome by another bout of coughing.

"It's all right, Aunty - I mean Saroj - we'll be out in a minute."

"OK, let me know if there's anything I can do."

Sheela blew her nose, looked at herself in the mirror and nodded to Shireen. "I'm fine now. Let's go."

When they returned to the sitting room, she ignored the two men and walked straight to her mother, who got up to greet her with outstretched arms.

"Mumsie, I'm not feeling too good, so if you don't mind, I'm going home."

"Are you sure, Lovely - the food has all been prepared for you."

"I'm sure, thanks. Besides which, mine was a surprise visit, so the food had been prepared for your guests of honour."

While Sheela and Shireen waited for the lift, muffled voices could be heard from inside the flat. Then Saroj's voice rang out loud and clear: "Oh you're a nautchy nautchy boy putting your Mumshie through all this!" This was followed by a male voice, soft and emollient.

As they descended to the ground floor, Sheela visualised her mother weeping profusely, her Chweetie trying to pacify her, and the maharajah looking on wondering what all the fuss was about.

Sheela reluctantly agreed to Shireen's suggestion that they have a bite at the Willingdon Club.

Once they were settled in the ground floor restaurant she felt obliged to outline the events leading up to Clarissa's death.

"Her other half must've taken it badly. It was obvious they were devoted to each other when we met at Bachoo's place."

"Yes."

"It's funny, though," Shireen continued, "that you've said very little about him."

"About whom?"

Shireen raised an eyebrow. "The other half, of course. What was his name - Martin or something?"

"Max," said Sheela, peering down at her chocolate rum praline ice cream.

37

"Good morning, darling."

Sheela hadn't noticed her mother-in-law joining her at the breakfast table.

"I'm sorry to say Ramu has apparently taken a bit of a turn for the worse. Somehow Gopal found out he was refusing to get out of bed."

Philomena came in with a soft boiled egg for Khorshed. Without asking, she topped up Sheela's cup of tea.

"By the way, how's Saroj?"

Under Khorshed's searching gaze, Sheela felt compelled to tell her the gist of what had happened the previous evening - which also meant telling her about Clarissa. Khorshed listened without interruption. When the story was finished, she stretched out her arm to give Sheela's hand a squeeze.

They sat in silence, Sheela finishing her toast with strawberry jam, Khorshed gulping down the last morsel of the *mosambi* Philomena had cut for her into quarters. Sheela remembered Cyrus talking about how his mother would buy *mosambis*, which she preferred to oranges, from her favourite fruit seller in Crawford Market.

"Mummy, coming back to Ramu, I really think I need to check on him as soon as possible."

"Oh I'd be so grateful if you did - as you say, the earlier the better. I've already taken the liberty to tell Gopal that he might be needed to drive you to Mahabaleshwar. And Amoli has also been told."

"Great - if it's OK I'll leave as early as possible this afternoon."

Sheela returned to her bedroom to start her packing.

She heard a faint buzzing and turned to find an incoming message on her mobile.

Getting quite worried. Haven't heard a thing from you. Have you arrived safely? Please respond asap. Love, Max PS I really miss you.

Oh these bloody mobile phones - so unreliable. How come he never received my message?

It was then that she noticed she had forgotten to press the 'send' arrow after typing her message to Max.

Oh Max, she wrote, *I did respond to your earlier message but stupidly forgot to send it. I'm so sorry. Yes, I'm here safe and sound. In fact, about to set off for Mahabaleshwar this afternoon. Expect to be there for some days. How are you?* She paused, then continued, *Hope you're taking care of yourself. Love, S*

She hesitated, paralysed by indecision. She went back to her packing, hoping that doing something would clear her mind, but quickly returned to the mobile, fearing that she might again forget to send the message. *PS*, she added, *I miss you too*, and, without letting herself double-check what she had written, she touched the 'send' arrow.

She found it difficult to concentrate on the rest of the packing.

After finishing the packing she took her case into the sitting room. She found her mother-in-law engrossed in a crossword puzzle.

Khorshed turned to Sheela: "Well, that was good, getting ready so quickly. By the way, darling, I've asked Gopal to make sure he goes easy climbing up the ghat - I remember Cyrus - I remember you telling me how car sick you got."

"Thanks, Mummy - hopefully I'm past my car sickness days."

The sunshine of Bombay no longer felt like an escape from the gloom of London. Sheela might have got over her car sickness, but the other, deeper nausea began to stir inside her as she walked out of Tower View to find Gopal waiting at the gate.

38

The car journey got off to a bad start. A problem with the air conditioning system meant that she had to choose between a cold blast and the heat and fumes of the outside air. She decided to brave the April sun. To make matters worse, Gopal had switched on a radio station blaring out a Bollywood number about a man captivated by the coquettish fluting of his sweetheart.

"Gopal, radio *bundh karo*," Sheela said, then added, "please."

Gopal didn't respond for some seconds, then, as though weighed down by sandbags, an arm stretched out slowly to turn the music off.

As Sheela had surmised, the rest of the journey was spent in sulky silence - although the silence was interrupted by comfort stops so frequent and so prolonged that an onlooker unaware of the radio conflict might have put them down to acute diarrhoea.

As you climb the ghats, you arrive at a bend where the air turns fresh and scented. At that precise point you know that you are approaching Mahabaleshwar, that you have finally left the swelter and squalor of the urban sprawl radiating in ever-lengthening trails from the megalopolis that is modern-day Mumbai. For the moment at least, Sheela's anxieties - about how she would find Ramu, about how she could avoid the dark memories brought on by the hill station - were swept away by the whiff of the breeze caressing her hair. This mood, of something approaching elation, continued through the final twilit drive that brought her to the bungalow.

When the car came to a halt, Gopal took his time to open his door. She pretended not to notice, and pulled the passenger door handle to step out.

The first person to greet her was Amoli, who gave a shy *namasté* before stooping to touch Sheela's feet.

"*Nahi, nahi,*" Sheela protested, bending over to pull the old lady back to her upright position. As she gave Amoli a hug, Sheela remembered that, for the first time, she had forgotten to get anything from Bombay for her or for Ramu. She would have to make amends by scouting the bazaar for something that was not made locally.

Hobbling behind Amoli was Ramu, looking frailer than he had been, but thankfully showing no sign of a serious illness.

Sheela chided him about venturing out in the cold the way she might have chided Nina when she was little.

Ramu beamed, protesting with several shakings of the head that he was feeling very well.

When she got into the house, she found everything spruce and orderly, a comforting return to normality: the dining table had been laid, her bed made, the bathroom fully equipped with fresh towels, soap and shampoo.

Where had Ramu and Amoli got the money to pay for these provisions? What about the food? In the dining room she had smelt something cooking. She must remember to reimburse them. First things first, though: she needed to phone Khorshed to tell her that she had arrived safely and that, all things considered, Ramu looked quite well.

Dinner was a full three-course affair, the centrepiece of which was *dhandar* and *patia*, the Parsi dish served on celebratory occasions. Sheela thanked the couple for the trouble they had taken, and ended up eating far more than she had wanted to.

At the dining table the next morning, Amoli asked what Baby would like for breakfast. A vague unease took hold of Sheela: normally, it would have been Ramu taking her breakfast order.

As if he had been eavesdropping on her thoughts, Ramu shuffled in, stumbling as he tripped over the edge of the Persian rug spread across the dining room floor.

When Sheela asked whether he was really back to normal, his insistence that he was gave her the reassurance she wanted, although she felt slightly guilty for not probing further.

Some thirty-five minutes later, she was ready to go to the bazaar. The crunch of tyre against pebble signalled the arrival of the car at the main gate.

"Good morning", said Gopal, opening the passenger door for her.

"Good morning, Gopal," she said. Had he slept well? Yes indeed he had, he answered brightly, and had she? She thanked him for asking, but then remembered her mother pronouncing that, "with these people", you never knew how a show of friendliness today might be regarded as a licence for impertinence tomorrow. So she rested her head against the back of the car seat, eyes determinedly shut.

After greeting her friends, the *chikkiwala* and the *chanawala*, she went to a shop displaying sari pieces draped from a slat. She remembered Ramu and Amoli the previous evening, arms crossed against their chests as if to ward off the cold. She checked the labels of a grey sweater and a green and marigold shawl: thankfully, no reference to any of the local places. After a half-hearted attempt at bargaining, she bought the two items at five percent less than the asking price.

As she continued towards the other end of the bazaar, a whiff of something savoury drew her to a little shack. On an impulse she went in and ordered a plain *dosa* with *sambar* and chutney. The food arrived at her table served on a greasy metal dish, but it was piping hot and exceeded her expectations: the *dosa* was crispy brown and feathery, the *sambar* swelled her salivary glands, and the green chutney had a minty zest which felt just right. She ordered a plain *lassi*, the perfect antidote to the spicy food.

When she walked back to the car she felt satisfyingly bloated and decided that the only way to digest the meal would be to sleep it off.

Back at the bungalow, she drew the curtains, changed into her nightie and went straight to bed. The presents to Ramu and Amoli could wait.

She was woken by a sinking feeling in the pit of her stomach. Shivering, she reached out for her blanket. When she raised her head, she felt the room swirling around her. It was the same sensation she had experienced when, for the first and last time, she had ridden a wooden horse on a merry-go-round. But at least on that occasion she had had her father to kiss away the fright, puke and tears.

She fell back on the bed, but the prone position made her panic: she couldn't possibly throw up all over her nightdress. Clutching the bedstead, she got up and staggered to the bathroom. In the end only the bathroom floor and basin bore the brunt of the day's lunch.

It was the chutney that had probably caused the stomach upset. But this felt more like food poisoning. The giddiness was unrelenting and the nausea lingered on, although without the ferocity of the initial bout.

She lurched back to her bed, swaying like a drunkard, gripping whatever her hands could reach. Lying flat on her back, she tried to will away the sickness and lightheadedness by following her father's advice: "Think of beautiful things, *beti*," he would say when unsure what medicine to give to his ailing daughter. But she could think only of roses in the Chelsea Flower Show, which reminded her of the sickly sweet scent of Bachoo's rose water.

She knew that she needed to drink something - water, or preferably Electral - but how was she to get it? Every part of her body seemed to be working against every other in wilful disharmony: the slightest movement of her head caused the room to spin around; her gullet was battling against the threat of another eruption from the pit of her stomach; her torso jerked with spasms of shivering, yet her body burned and sweat poured down her brow.

Then everything drifted. She felt she was losing herself, floating away into some black hole. There was no alternative but to let go. *This is what dying must be like.* It was not unpleasant, this slipping into nothingness. As if there was no room for a separate identity she felt herself melding into the darkness.

There followed a blank. Oblivion.

Voices emerged from somewhere, voices that felt distant yet sounded close. Then came a more immediate sound, the sound of moaning. Only after a while did she realise it was coming from her.

Her eyes, sticky with sleep, struggled to open a chink. Everything was a haze, but she was conscious of figures hovering near her bed. *They are coming to get me.* She tried to scream, but managed a croak.

"Baby, Baby!" The voice was familiar and vaguely comforting.

She dared to try opening her eyes wider.

"Ramu," she murmured, and moved her hand slightly to lay it on the old man's extended arm.

What happened, she asked.

She had been very ill, came the answer.

Slowly the memory of the snack in the bazaar and its gruelling aftermath returned to her.

For how long? For quite a few hours, she expected Ramu to reply.

For two days.

Surely not? These country folk had no concept of time, she thought to herself.

But Ramu's gentle assertiveness was convincing. "Doctor *aya tha aur* medicine *diya tha.*"

So the Mahabaleshwar doctor - the blackmailer - had come to administer medicine.

What medicine, she asked, trying to hide her alarm.

It was then that she noticed another figure on the far side of the bed. Amoli went to the bathroom and returned with a sachet of Electral and two strips of Crocin. Electrolyte powder and paracetamol - at least the doctor hadn't tried to bump her off. But then why should he have wanted to do that? You can't blackmail the dead.

She wanted to return to her sleep. This time she knew it would be undisturbed.

As she drifted off, her mind was now clear enough to recognise the irony of the situation in which she found herself: here she was, weak and helpless, being cared for by the very people she had come to look after.

39

She was woken up by slats of light trickling through the half open shutters of the bedroom windows. Noticing a shifting towards her left, she turned to find Amoli sitting on a small upright chair at the foot of her bed. Her hair looked more dishevelled than usual and for once the smiling *namasté* couldn't hide the toll that her hard life - or perhaps the all-night vigil - had taken on her.

Will Baby have some breakfast, she asked.

Some forty minutes later, Sheela was seated at the dining table, greeted by a boiled egg, perched slightly askew in an egg cup, and a large slice of white toast.

Ramu entered the room with a pot of tea and a jar of milk, his bent figure shuffling briskly towards her. She rose from her chair and gave the old man a hug which would have toppled him backwards if he hadn't had the presence of mind to hold on to the edge of the dining table. For him, she knew, such an open display of affection was embarrassing in the extreme, flouting as it did the norms of behaviour determined by station and sex. But, while Ramu's hand gripped the table even tighter, his mouth widened into a beaming smile and his eyes glistened with gratification or, Sheela feared, tears of gratitude.

It was 11.15 when she finished breakfast. Ramu and Amoli accompanied her back to the bedroom and insisted on tucking her in.

As the couple moved to leave the room, Ramu turned round and cleared his throat. The doctor had come again.

When, Sheela asked sharply.

Almost two hours ago.

And what did he say?

He had come only to ask after her. So said Ramu, but she was sure that the old man was trying to shield her from the whole truth. She demanded, more abruptly than she had intended, that the doctor should under no circumstance be allowed into the house, let alone the bedroom.

She wanted to doze off, but her mind was buzzing with images of Peter Lorre. Dragging herself towards the bedroom door, she headed for the living room.

In a hidden corner of the room was an alcove big enough to accommodate a settee. The settee backed a wall at right angles to a small window. It was here that Cyrus and she would sit wordlessly, reading a book or staring out of the window at the distant plateaus of the Western Ghats. Sometimes Cyrus would regale her with stories about his childhood visits to Mahabaleshwar. He spoke a lot about his mother, very little about his father, and least of all about himself. Throughout their marriage, if he did offer information about himself, it was only after she pressed him hard. The behaviour of a man with no ego, she had believed at the time, but now, thinking of that fateful day a year ago, she knew that modesty wasn't the only explanation.

Willing herself into a state of forgetfulness, she rested her head against the cushion behind her and drifted into sleep.

She was back with Cyrus on the landing stage of Lake Venna, waiting for a rowing boat.

The boat arrived, and they were off, Cyrus taking the oars while she sat at the opposite end, giving a silent prayer, as usual, that the boat shouldn't develop a leak. But she didn't need to worry as long as Cyrus was in control. His wiry forearms glided the boat forward so smoothly that only the lapping of the water reminded her that they were not on solid ground.

Daring to look round, she saw the landing stage taper into a barely recognisable blob.

A thrill of excitement, not altogether pleasant, made her turn to Cyrus for reassurance. But the figure opposite her was now nothing more than a blur, still moving back and forth, but veiled by a mist that had descended over the lake.

"Cyrus!" she called out, "Cyrus, what's happening?" No response save the plashing of the oars. "Cyrus?" she cried out once more, "Why aren't you answering me?" and the more she repeated her cry the more she frightened herself with the silence that followed.

She tried to reach out to him, but now he was like some phantom oarsman, almost totally shrouded by the grey-white fog that had settled over them.

Then she felt the grip of his hand. She expected to scream, but the hand was firm and strong yet gentle and warm.

She realised it wasn't his.

"Sheela!" She woke up with a start, and let out a gasp as her eyes registered the person sitting by her side, cupping her hands in his.

"Oh Max," she whimpered. There was no time for second thoughts to take over: she found herself clutching on to his shirt. He drew her closer to him, wrapping an arm around her. She closed her eyes, letting herself succumb to the protection of his embrace.

Then, remembering that there were other people in the bungalow, she pulled away. "How did you get here?"

The people at the club had given him very clear instructions. "Then this sweet old guy opened the door and let me in when I mentioned your name."

"But - why are you here?"

"I had to be with you."

Why, she was tempted to ask but didn't dare to.

As if he had heard her silent question, he said, "I just didn't know what might happen to you." Very softly, he added, "Thinking about the first time we saw you."

She could hear voices approaching. Ramu emerged from the bend of the living room. There was agitation in his gait.

The doctor had arrived, he said. He sounded supplicatory, as though seeking forgiveness for having failed to follow her instructions.

Never mind, she said to allay his concern. Let the odious doctor come in; this time she had an ally by her side.

"Oh, good day," said the doctor, "how nice you have made such a wonderful recovery, Madame!" The smile dropped for an instant as he took in the presence of the man sitting next to madame.

"I understand you had a hand in it."

"Madame, how can you say such thing? As doctor, I am believing in Hypocrasy Oath. I am not believing in monkey business putting hand in anything, not your pocket, not your purse, not nothing." On the last word, the voice rose in tremulous self-righteousness. "However, madame," he continued, "you might recall our last conversation?"

"You mean your last attempt to blackmail me?"

"Now, madame, this is no way to speak to humble village doctor." His nostrils had widened and he was twisting the lapel of his jacket.

"He has come here to blackmail me," she said, turning to Max.

"Madame, you are taking big risk talking about me like that."

"What risk?" The words were spoken softly, but there was a steely smile on Max's face.

"Madame, you have to speak to me privately," the doctor said, extracting a crumpled handkerchief to wipe off the shine on the folds of his neck.

"Madame doesn't *have* to do anything." Max stood up and advanced towards the doctor. "Now you'd be doing yourself a favour if you left this place and never came back. So kindly beat it."

At the mention of the word 'beat' there was a flicker of alarm in the doctor's eyes. But quickly recovering, he opened his palms out and said, "I am only talking about next instalment, that is all. These small-small instalments - they are *nuth-thing* for you. In Mumbai they would not buy you cup of coffee."

His beady eyes widened and his voice choked on the last sentence.

"I owe you nothing more than the fee for your last consultation."

"Oh, but madame, I do not charge you for saving your life! I am following Hypocrasy Oath."

"Here, take this for the last consultation." Max extracted five 100-rupee notes from his trouser pocket.

"Madame," the doctor pulled his hand away, "I am insulted -"

"No, you're not." Max shoved the notes into the doctor's palm. "Now off you go."

The doctor held on to the money, but refused to budge.

Grabbing his arm, Max pulled him towards the front door.

"You have not right to attack me!" the doctor screeched, trying to wriggle away. "I will call police!" he shouted even louder.

Sheela saw Ramu and Amoli looking on from a safe distance, their faces expressing what looked like approval.

The doctor's free arm was pummelling Max in futile fury. As the door closed behind the two men, Sheela rushed to the main verandah. It offered the best view of the garden, the parapet encircling it, and the valley beyond.

Max was dragging the doctor towards the parapet. Sheela heard something that sounded like a tirade against fucking imperialists.

The doctor screamed "No, no!" as he was lifted by the shoulders on to the parapet. He was now clinging on to Max, his head looking down at the clumps of bushes and stumpy trees cascading steeply towards the distant valley.

What ensued could have been a scene from a silent film. The screaming had stopped. The doctor was nodding his head frantically, and even from the verandah Sheela thought she could see his body shaking.

This was going too far: suppose the man let go of Max and lost his balance? She brushed past Ramu and Amoli to get out of the house. But by the time she was outside, the man could be seen scuttling down the driveway.

Max walked towards her. His face was tense.

"I felt like some Flashman from Tom Brown's School Days. But there was no alternative. He won't bother you again."

She didn't know what to say. Relieved that the doctor wouldn't return, she felt phoney disapproving of what Max had done. Instead, she thanked him, and the conversation turned to the Mahabaleshwar Club, where Max had managed to book a room.

"Oh Max, I don't know what to say. Coming back to Mahabaleshwar and all that."

"I promised to keep an eye on you, didn't I?" His smile was bright, but the voice was pensive.

As they entered the living room, she turned to him: "You'll have lunch with me, won't you." It was an assertion more than a question.

"That would be lovely - thank you."

She saw it as a compliment that he had dispensed with the usual "Are you sure?".

40

Lunch had been confined, on her part, to an account of her food poisoning; and, on his, the usual expressions of concern, followed by niceties about the excellence of the food being served. A strained formality had set in. How precisely this came about Sheela couldn't work out. What she did feel was the pressure of questions - on both sides - to be raised; questions risky to ask and even riskier to answer.

She suggested a walk. Not having to meet each other's direct gaze might allow them the freedom to let go.

"You can get a lovely view about a quarter of the way along the path we need to take."

"Sounds great. Is it steep? I'm not very good with heights, I'm afraid."

For the first time since they had gone in for lunch, Sheela looked at him with a smile that wasn't forced. That last admission was so typical of the Max she had thought she had got to know and like; no macho posturing. Just like Cyrus in that respect (although Cyrus, a more confident person, would have had less need for posturing).

Sheela held on to the parapet to lower herself on to a path a metre below. She turned round to find Max gripping a crevice in the parapet, his eyes fixed on the red earth bordering the bottom of the ledge. She extended her hand, which he gripped for somewhat longer, she thought, than his nervousness warranted.

They walked together in silence.

The thought crossed her mind that being alone with him she would be at his mercy if he seized the moment to take advantage of her. But she knew that if anything should 'happen', it would be only because she let it happen. How liberating it would be just to let go, blaming whatever followed on the opiate of this sleepy afternoon.

Finally they arrived at a promontory which allowed them a 240-degree panorama of a mountainous landscape so placid and one-dimensional that you could fool yourself into thinking it was nothing more than a massive water colour painting. Yet in the silence, broken only by the buzz of unseen insects, you could never escape the sense of something dangerous lurking nearby.

After pausing for a short while to take in the view, she pointed to a fork in the path that would lead them back to the bungalow.

After walking a few metres, she turned to him. "Tell me, what did you really think when you first saw me at Kate's Point?" The voice she heard sounded sharp and demanding. "I've had the impression that somehow you had a gut feeling about why I was there."

"Well, there's no short answer to your question because there's a sort of back story to all this."

They turned a corner, to be confronted by steps too high and pebbly for anyone to mount without support. This time it was Max who went first, gripping an overhanging branch to heave himself up. Then he turned round and pulled Sheela towards him. He was clearly more comfortable climbing up slopes than clambering down them. She was half a step behind him, towards his left. He hadn't let go of his grip on her right hand. Her eyes traced his broad shoulders, his back, his boyish hips swaying sideways with the upward stride of each leg following the other; she noticed how snugly they fit into his trousers, brown corduroys just like those she had once bought Cyrus from Marks and Spencer. How snugly they fit...a fleeting vision of a shiny black outfit skimmed over her eyes, but she scotched it by turning her attention to the path in front of her.

They were now walking side by side. She tried to free her hand from his clasp, but he seemed not to notice this.

"I need to do up my shoe laces."

When she got up from her crouching position, he extended his left arm sideways, but this time it was her turn to appear not to notice. Hands tucked firmly in her trouser pockets, she looked straight ahead and tried to stop the chattering of her teeth. If he noticed her agitation, he might put his arm round her waist; and if he did that, her hands might free themselves to do something against her better judgement.

"So, what about the back story, as you called it?"

"You see, when Clarissa's cancer got worse, the consultant said that now was the time to do everything we'd ever wanted to do together."

Sheela glanced sideways. Max was frowning straight ahead, as though trying to piece together the details of a story he would rather forget.

"She'd always wanted to go to India, so that's how we landed up here. Well, doing the Golden Triangle stuff, we met this guy on the Jaipur-Agra train, very old and wizened, but there was something in his eyes, a child-like sparkle, a joy, quite at odds with the rest of his mole-ridden face and his general demeanour

– he looked like a retired bank clerk, wearing a shirt and trousers with a fountain pen sticking out of his shirt pocket.

"After chatting for a while - mainly about our travels around India - he suddenly asked Clarissa to hold out her hand, because 'Good lady' - I won't forget that quaint phrase - 'I think I might be able to help you.' 'How can you help me?' Clarissa asked. I remember her nervous laughter.

"His reply was totally unexpected: 'I don't know whether you have long to live on this earth, but I do know there is nothing to fear.' Clarissa burst into tears."

With the last sentence Max's voice faltered. Sheela had to resist the impulse to grasp his hand.

After a pause he turned to Sheela and spoke about how the man rambled on about the ills of the world – ills like cancer – and how they could be overcome, if not in this world then in the next.

"It was clear to both of us that he was a thoroughly good person, but whereas I wasn't at all sure where all this was leading to, Clarissa seemed to be convinced - or perhaps wanted to be convinced - that the man knew everything about her."

"But did you feel he was making sense?"

"Let's just say that we both *wanted* to believe him, but I have a natural scepticism about this sort of thing. Anyway, the guru - for want of a better way of describing him - asked us about the rest of our itinerary. We told him that Bombay was our last stop.

"Again he started meandering on about some hill stations not far from Bombay which offered amazing views of the surrounding mountains and valleys. We should go to one of them, he said, because who knows what chance encounter there might change our lives for the better. He went on somewhat bizarrely about how strangers can 'rescue' one another. I was wondering whether the guy might be a bit gaga, but Clarissa was certain that he was obliquely telling us that a hill station was where we would find some sort of redemption. I didn't have the heart to say what I really thought - instead I promised we'd go to a hill station if that was what she wanted."

"That's how you landed up in Mahabaleshwar."

"That's it. Well, the first day we arrived, somebody at the club told us that Kate's Point was a must. So we set off with some sandwiches late morning so that Clarissa would have time to do a little painting. Arriving there we decided to avoid the crowds by moving to an isolated area that nobody seemed to be aware of."

"Nobody, that is, except for me. So that's when you saw me."

"Yes. We saw your figure from a height. We noticed you were walking as if dead to the rest of the world, towards what looked like a cliff edge. We weren't too concerned, though, thinking it was probably someone enjoying their solitude. Then - I remember so clearly - Clarissa cried out, 'Max, remember what the guru said about people rescuing one another! That's the person we need to rescue, I'm convinced of it.' Whatever I thought, it was clear enough that the figure in the distance was, unwittingly or otherwise, going to do something pretty dramatic. We quickened our pace and managed to catch up quite a bit, but we weren't able to reach you - remember you were below us."

"So that's when Clarissa called out to me and you came to my rescue - even though I resented you for that.

Oh look, we're almost there now - you can spot a corner of the bungalow." Sheela pointed ahead.

"Actually," she continued, turning to Max, "I say I resented being rescued, but I do wonder whether your 'rescue' was something I really resisted - or in fact something I welcomed, even though I mightn't have realised it at the time. In any case, you said the guru had spoken about people rescuing *one another* - so, whether or not the two of you rescued me, how on earth did *I* 'rescue' the two of *you*?"

"Clarissa's no longer with us - that's what you mean, don't you. But," he paused as they approached the front door of Lammermoor Lodge, "thinking about how you came into our lives, perhaps it's not too fanciful to say that in a way you did rescue us."

41

The shrivelled figure of Ramu was waiting for them near the entrance. How long had he been watching them, Sheela wondered. Because of his discretion - and his modest station - he was always circumspect in revealing what he could see. She realised this from the part he had played in this very place over a year ago. He had never taken advantage of his knowledge of what had happened then; if anything, he had become even more protective of her.

Tea was ready for them on the dining table – a pot of Darjeeling and a plate of Amoli's homemade *bhajias*.

"So I rescued you!" She tried to sound playful but felt like some foolish Hitchcock heroine blundering into dark alleys no sensible person would ever dream of entering.

"Well, it all goes back to the guru." Max gulped his tea and looked up. "He handed us the address of a man in Bombay who would give Clarissa some powders to make her feel much better. So we arrived at this shabby street stall where a craggy old guy handed Clarissa some phials filled with white powder. He must have somehow got to know about us from the guru. This was not a cure, he said, but he promised 'no suffering'. He said something about this being Unani medicine."

"A traditional Muslim branch of medicine. But, going back to the guru, what happened with him?"

Max looked down, apparently drawn by something floating on the surface of his tea.

"When he gave us the medicine man's address, the guru turned to me and said - he said that, although we hadn't known each other for long (how he sussed that out I haven't a clue), he knew how much - how much I loved Clarissa, but that there was no need for tears."

Sheela stretched her arm out and placed a hand lightly on Max's wrist, then quickly withdrew it as Amoli entered the room.

The presence of the old woman seemed to help Max recover. "He said Clarissa would be at peace, and one day we'd be reunited. One side of me felt angry - how could he possibly know what I was feeling - but the other side was grateful, seeing how comforting Clarissa found his words."

There was a pause; then, with a tentative smile, Max looked directly at Sheela. "There was something else the guru said: while, in this earthly existence, I would lose the soulmate sitting next to me, I would find another to share my life with."

Ramu hobbled into the room and asked Sheela whether he could clear the table.

"Let's move to the sitting room," Sheela said, averting her gaze.

Having settled themselves opposite each other, she on a sofa, he on a matching armchair, Max continued as though there had been no interruption: "My new soulmate, the guru said, could be a person we were going to rescue, a person who in turn would rescue the two of us from the anguish of our separation. At the time it felt like a load of rubbish, to put it politely. But," Max looked up with a quizzical smile, "funny how things seem to have turned out…"

Sheela picked up the cushion cover beside her and pressed it against her chest. Then she blurted out, "The guru said you hadn't known each other for that long. So how long did you know each other?"

A shaft of light entered the room. Gopal was standing at the main entrance door. He asked if the car was needed.

Although the question was addressed to Sheela, his gaze was fixed on Max.

When Max said he would be walking back to the club, Sheela insisted that Gopal take him in the car. Turning to Gopal, she instructed him to wait until the *sahib* was ready to leave for the club. Gopal ignored Sheela and beamed at Max before leaving the room.

They sat in silence. Female voices were calling in the distance; Sheela imagined local women returning home, heavy bundles balanced on their heads.

"Returning to your question," Max broke the silence, "as you know, Clarissa was born and brought up as Claire in Sydney. She had a brother two years older than her. The parents split up when she was about eleven. Her mother decided to leave for England - she had inherited quite a lot of money from a rich uncle in London. Anyway, she took the boy with her, and Clarissa - Claire - was left in the care of her father. After school, she studied art history at the University of Sydney. On graduation, she joined an atelier and started to make a name for herself as an artist. It was there that she met Johannes Becker - he was the art teacher who became her mentor. She adored him, but only the way a student hero-worships a father figure. He mistook this for love, and it wasn't long before he fell in love with her. Flattered by his attention, she managed to convince herself that she would be able to love him. So they got married. She was 32, he 52."

"This is the sort of story that doesn't end happily."

"Well, of course it didn't. After seven unhappy years, she packed her bags and flew to London, ostensibly to look for her long lost brother. Her father had died some months earlier, so there was nothing to tie her down."

"And that's how you met each other."

"We met at a Festival Hall concert."

"So you just bumped into each other and fell in love."

"When we set eyes on each other, it felt like - like some force had lifted us somewhere beyond ourselves, way beyond our control."

"How romantic! Goodness, just realised what time it is. I'd better call Gopal."

"Really, I can easily walk back."

"Are you sure?"

"Yes, definitely." He made for the door, then turned round and said, "Sorry, I feel I've upset you. But," he continued before she could speak, "I was only answering your question as accurately as I could."

She heard the crunch of his footsteps receding down the driveway. She sat still, then on impulse rushed to the verandah to check that he had taken the correct turning for the club. She imagined a figure walking in the opposite direction but wasn't sure whether it was him.

Her eyes fell on an old Mahabaleshwar guide book resting on the coffee table in the middle of the room. She flicked through the pages, so ravaged by white ants that they looked as if a maniac had gone to town with a hole punch. The pages were illustrated with yellowing photographs - of leopard hunts, of the club in the old days, of the much more genteel bazaar of the early half of the 20th century - all interspersed with a typewritten history of the hill station.

But her mind couldn't shake off the image of Max venturing in the wrong direction.

She called for Gopal and told him the car was needed straightaway; the *sahib* might have lost his way.

Getting into the front passenger seat, she instructed Gopal to drive slowly in the direction of the club.

Every passing second seemed to confirm her worst fears. She was about to risk Gopal's annoyance by asking him to try the opposite direction when, just as they approached a bend, she saw a slightly stooped figure walking briskly in the dark. She told Gopal to halt the car. Jumping out, she ran towards Max. He turned round only when she had almost caught up with him.

"Max!" She tried to disguise her breathlessness by coughing.

"Sheela! Hey, are you OK?"

"Yes, yes. Just a little tickle." Then, clearing her throat, she said, "I'm sorry. I shouldn't have let you return on your own."

"Oh don't be sorry. I was enjoying the walk." His face was only half-visible under the light of the street lamp, but he sounded genuinely pleased to see her.

"I *do* feel sorry. But we can't be talking here all night. Look, why not stay at the bungalow tonight?"

Oh my God, what am I saying?

There was a pause before he responded. He was probably as stunned by her proposal as she was. Then, as though carefully choosing his words, he said, "But I couldn't possibly impose on you like that."

"You wouldn't be imposing on me." He was inviting her to insist, and she complied. "We have a number of spare rooms - and saying 'yes' would give me the chance to make amends."

Another pause; then, "I'll need to get my things, though, from the club."

"No problem - we're barely five minutes' drive away."

They walked to the car. Gopal jumped out to hold the door open for Max. Under the street lamp his eyes could be seen darting towards her, then returning slyly to Max; but the puzzlement on his face reassured her that he hadn't worked out what was going on.

But then, for that matter, neither had she.

This time she sat behind Gopal, and Max sat at the other end of the back seat. In silence, they peered out at the jungle shadows speeding past them. Retracing what had just happened, she convinced herself that the only reason why he had accepted her invitation was to spare her feelings of guilt. But it was too late to withdraw her offer.

The car arrived at the club.

"I'll be back in a minute."

Almost true to his word, he returned remarkably quickly, with a small overnight case which he placed between them.

"That was fast!"

"Oh, I had very little to pack."

There was nothing more to say and, like the drive to the club, the journey back to the bungalow was marked by a jagged silence.

42

Sheela went to her room and switched the light on.

She sat on the bed and crossed her arms to protect her from the chill of the evening air. Yes, her feelings must be reciprocated - after all, he had returned to India to be with her. But Clarissa was irreplaceable, and she would be foolish to believe otherwise.

Her shoulders slumped. It was as though her errant mind had squeezed all the energy out of her. She glanced at her watch. Half an hour had almost elapsed. On returning to Lammermoor Lodge she had suggested that Max meet her in the dining room in thirty minutes - enough time for him to settle in his room and freshen up before the *akoori* on toast meal she had asked Ramu to prepare.

She really must pull herself together. She got up to go to the dressing room. The figure staring at her in the full length mirror could, at least on a good day, pass muster as a reasonably handsome woman. As she applied her lipstick, she peered into the mirror to avoid smudging her mouth; she certainly wouldn't wish Max to be reminded of her mother.

The meal passed pleasantly enough with chatter about the old Mahabaleshwar guide book, about panther shoots, about *akoori, papeta pur eeda* and other Parsi egg dishes - all subjects innocuous enough to ensure that the conversation would not veer into emotional cul-de-sacs from which it might be difficult to escape.

By the time they had finished the caramel custard prepared by Amoli, Sheela felt that they were running out of topics; a change of scene was necessary if they were to avoid awkward silences. So she asked Ramu to serve coffee in the sitting room.

They settled themselves, she again on the sofa, he on the armchair.

As Ramu came in with a trolley rattling with crockery, Max got up to take the trolley off the old man.

"Oh let him do it," Sheela said. "It makes him feel important." But she recognised that she was only trying to cover up for the fact that she hadn't thought of helping Ramu herself.

To her surprise and shame, after a half-hearted protest Ramu let go of the trolley and tottered back to the dining room.

Max poured the coffee and milk into the cups on the trolley, then handed a cup and saucer to Sheela.

Staring into his coffee, he continued stirring it well after the milk had blended in.

"Is there something -?"

Max bent over the side of the armchair and picked up a packet wrapped in paper decorated with a pink and cream Paisley motif.

"This is for you," he said quietly.

"What beautiful wrapping paper. It seems a shame to tear it."

The object was rectangular, possibly eight by six inches, but not yet clearly visible under the layer of bubble wrap stretched over it.

When she removed the bubble wrap she saw a charcoal portrait of a woman of indeterminate age -

anything between thirty-five and fifty. She had a strong aquiline nose, offset by flashing eyes, a generous mouth and luxuriant black hair. Sheela was reminded of somebody. Somebody perhaps from the golden age of cinema. Ah yes, it was Anna Magnani - the way she looked in the DVD of *The Rose Tattoo* she had watched with Cyrus. She moved the portrait further away and peered at it with half-closed eyes. Now she looked less like the handsome Italian actress, more like a younger, more classically beautiful woman. Could it be Ava Gardner?

But why on earth was he presenting her with this picture?

"She looks so familiar," she finally said, "like some famous actress. I can see the individual features clearly but somehow can't put them together to form an impression of the person as a whole."

As she spoke, the features suddenly came together like the pieces of a jigsaw clicking into place. She looked at Max with a lightly smiling gasp of disbelief.

"Oh gosh, it can't be -"

"Yes, it is. It's you."

Sheela sank slowly into the sofa, clutching the portrait's dark wooden frame.

"You might want to look at the back of the picture."

She turned the picture over on her lap. She read,

Sheela, my dear friend,

I thought you might like this little memento. I hope that you approve of it, and that it brings back happy memories of our times together. It certainly does for me.

All my love, Clarissa

Sheela felt her stomach tighten. She opened her mouth, trying to let something out, but all she could manage was a silent cry.

"She really wanted to do this for you," Max said. The words were spoken softly but their effect was to puncture the obstruction in her throat.

He came to the sofa and put an arm round her shoulders. Slowly her sobbing subsided. Only then did it occur to her that her sorrow, perhaps no more than a sentimental outburst sparked by the picture, couldn't possibly compare with the heartbreak felt by Max on losing the love of his life.

She drew away from him.

"I'm sorry, Max. How much you have had to go through." She didn't know what she was apologising for. The selfishness of her outburst? Her earlier coldness towards him? It didn't matter.

She looked at the picture again. "That's an extremely flattering portrait."

"No, it captures everything about you. You did recognise yourself in the end, didn't you?"

"Yes, sort of - in the end."

"You would have recognised yourself immediately had you been prepared for it."

"You're very sweet, Max," she said, mustering a smile. He was still close to her, his hands resting lightly on the back of the sofa.

"I could tell from the paintings in your flat that Clarissa was an extremely talented artist - but how did she draw this portrait? I mean, I never sat for her or anything."

"Clarissa had an amazingly photographic memory which enabled her to capture the truth of the original. That's why I think she's got you just right."

"But when did she do it?"

"Some time after our return from India. One day, she just handed it to me, out of the blue, saying I should pass it on to you after - after she was gone. I'm sorry, but with the funeral and everything it slipped my mind to give it to you earlier. So I brought it with me on this trip to India."

"I must keep this picture in a very safe place. It will be one of my most treasured possessions."

She read the message again. Then she saw a scribble at the bottom. For some reason she hadn't noticed it earlier. It was difficult to decipher, as though hurriedly written as an afterthought: *PS Please remember my wish*. She looked up sharply at Max. It was difficult to tell whether he had seen her read the PS.

Max returned to the armchair. "You know after we first met you, Clarissa said she was convinced that you were the other soulmate the guru had been referring to."

He cleared his throat loudly, as if by doing so he would be able to ease the flow of thoughts he still needed to express.

"She kept on insisting that we - as a couple - needed to get to know you better, so that in the end I - as an individual - would know you better. She told me one night that I should be happy with you, that I shouldn't feel guilty. 'That's the only way I'll be able to go in peace.' Those were her exact words."

Sheela couldn't sit there impassively any more. She got up, sat on the left-hand arm of his chair, resting her hand gently on his shoulder. He remained still, his head slumped - for so long that she wondered if he had fallen asleep. Then he shifted slightly, put his right hand into his side trouser pocket and extracted some tissue paper with which he wiped his face.

Slowly he raised his head and sat upright, but his face was turned away, towards the window, as if drawn by the sequins of stars embroidering the Mahabaleshwar night sky with their ornamental sparkle.

Feeling the need to break the silence, Sheela blurted out the first thing that came to her mouth: "But switching one's lo - one's affections - is not like turning a tap, is it?"

"Of course it isn't."

He turned round and fixed his gaze on her with an expression she couldn't quite decipher. Of incredulity, perhaps, that she should say something so crass; of anger, even.

"Oh that sounded so shabby - I didn't mean it that way."

His face softened instantly. "There's something I need to explain. It's true I'll never stop loving Clarissa. But," he looked away again, "a point had come in our relationship when the original intensity waned - at least for me. I had begun to feel stifled. Sounds horrible, but I felt that she was clinging on to me like a drowning person clutching on to her rescuer so hard that she threatens to drag him down with her."

Sheela pursed her lips. His eyes darted towards her. "You must think me such a jerk talking like this."

But he was wrong if he thought it was disapproval that had triggered her reaction: what was flashing through her mind was the image of Clarissa's upturned face, desperate and fragile, as she clung on to Max in that glade on the way to Bombay Point. Later, the same Clarissa, now reconciled to the inevitable, was able to find the generosity to urge the man of her life to seek solace in another woman. If only Clarissa were with them now: Sheela would be able to tell her that she was the most precious friend she had ever known, that somehow in the end all would turn out well. Instead, Clarissa had left before her time, thinking only of those she was leaving behind when it was she who should have been given the succour she needed and deserved.

"Oh no - you're far from being a jerk. I just feel so sad. In the midst of everything she was going through, she put herself last. I wish she knew how much I felt for her, what a star she was."

But as she spoke she had to admit to herself that, however remorseful she felt, right now the person uppermost in her mind was not Clarissa but the man sitting next to her, gazing at her with a tenderness so immense that she had to resist the urge to return it with a full-mouthed kiss.

She tried to switch her train of thought by getting up and collecting the coffee cups and saucers on to the tray. But remorse had turned to guilt - and now not only on Clarissa's account: here she was with another man she had invited to stay at Lammermoor Lodge - Cyrus's beloved Lammermoor Lodge. It came as a shock to her that all these days Cyrus had faded far enough for the thought of his reaction not to have occurred to her. But the truth was that Cyrus, being Cyrus, would have given his seal of approval. Clarissa had encouraged Max to come closer to her. Similarly Cyrus would have surely been happy to see her coming closer to Max. Now the guilt was displaced by sadness; sadness and confusion: a disapproving Cyrus would be easier to cope with than the kind and open-hearted husband who had become the centre of her life. Then further confusion: what about the darkness that her husband had kept concealed for so long?

She sat down at one end of the sofa. Max got up and sat at the other end.

"Are you OK?" He touched her arm lightly.

"Yes. Thanks." She gave a deep sigh. "I was thinking of my husband."

"That evening at Kate's Point - it had something to do with your husband, didn't it?"

She moved her arm away from him.

"Sorry - I shouldn't have asked."

"No, it's only natural to ask. After all, both of you played a major role in how everything turned out."

She noticed that the silver chain round her neck was no longer hidden inside her top. She looked down and tucked the delicate *farohar* hanging from the chain back into her top. Cyrus had bought the little pendant for her because she was a more fervent Zoroastrian, he had said half-teasingly, than most of those born into the faith.

The *farohar* had fallen out: was that a signal of something? was this winged talisman of Zoroastrianism telling her maybe now was the time to reveal the truth? This was nonsensical, she told herself, she was in a heightened state. But somehow, however absurdly, the sight of the *farohar* gave her the courage to contemplate the unthinkable: to break down the fortress of secrecy she had built around her ever since that terrible event over a year ago. Looking at the man sitting next to her, she felt that if she didn't seize the moment and put her faith in him she would never be able to trust anyone, and her life would continue its arid course until she shrivelled into half the person she had been before that fateful day.

She clenched her teeth in a determined effort to control their chattering. Finally she managed to find her voice.

43

"Yes, Kate's Point had something - everything - to do with my husband."

She was about to expose herself as she had never done before. And the exposure revolved around Cyrus, the person she had trusted more than any other - and, in the end, the person who had abused her trust in a way she could never have imagined. Was she mad baring her soul to a man she had just come to know? But then, what had she really known about Cyrus?

"The thing is, I'm not at all sure whether I want to talk about this."

She looked him straight in the face as if searching for guidance. He was sitting still, a few feet away from her, engaged yet relaxed. She knew that at this moment she was highly suggestible, responsive to any trigger, however tenuous. But she also knew that somewhere embedded in her apprehension was a sense of something true and tender that needed to be harvested.

"But," she continued, "I'm going to tell you anyway."

Her heart skipped a beat, then she opened her mouth and let the words spill out.

It had all started, she told him, some fifteen months ago. Cyrus, her husband, and she had come to Mahabaleshwar for a five-day holiday. They had settled down into the usual happy routine, pottering around the bazaar, going for walks, visiting the club. On the third day she received an unexpected call from an old friend. Having somehow found out that she was in Mahabaleshwar, the friend invited her for lunch to her place in Panchgani.

"Isn't that the place with the plateau - not too far from here?"

"That's right. So we fixed the lunch for one o'clock the next day."

Sheela left at 11.30 - to give herself about an hour to potter around Panchgani. Cyrus wasn't around when Gopal drove her off because he had gone for a long walk.

"At exactly 12.43 - the time is imprinted in my head - I heard my mobile ring. I thought it might be my friend. Instead, it was Ramu."

Sheela shut her eyes and clutched her diaphragm. The sofa creaked softly as Max shifted his position to come closer to her. But she kept her eyes shut.

She took a deep breath as she continued the story. Ramu had been quite hysterical, barely coherent, but through his gibbering she had managed to make out three words which frightened the life out of her: Baba, *kharab*, accident. Cyrus had had a bad accident.

When she returned to the bungalow, Ramu was waiting at the entrance door, babbling away about how he could have prevented the whole thing, and how he needed not only God's forgiveness but also Baby's.

"Something that Ramu did, a gesture perhaps, told me that it was to our bedroom that I had to go."

Sheela's throat felt as though it was going into rigor mortis. She sat still, looking straight ahead of her. Then, with a painful gulp, she found her voice again. Walking into the bedroom, she found Cyrus lying on his side of their bed. From the entrance to the room he looked as though he was sleeping peacefully, but as she approached she sensed an air of disarray: Cyrus was in his pyjamas, but the pyjamas looked as though they had been clumsily put on. She called out his name three times, but there was no answer.

"I felt my legs about to give way, but there was nobody there to take control - certainly not Ramu, who had subsided into a sort of whimpering - so I just had to get a grip on myself. I came closer to the bed. Cyrus was lying totally still, on his back, his normally pale face paler than usual. But it was his eyes that -"

Sheela was aware of a slight movement near her, but she continued to look straight ahead.

"His eyes, half open, were without any focus. I knew immediately he was dead." Then she had noticed a figure emerge from a dark corner of the room: it was the local doctor. At the time she hardly knew him, aware only that he tended to the less well-off people in Mahabaleshwar. Ramu must have called him when he discovered Cyrus in this state. The doctor murmured his condolences. Ramu continued with his whimpering. She asked them to leave the room.

"Funny, on the surface I was calm. I must have been in shock. You could say that was the way I coped for most of the year that followed, just blanking my mind. I drew a chair and sat next to Cyrus. Although he looked dishevelled he was still as handsome as ever. I sat there for what seemed a long time; and throughout I felt nothing. The only thing I found disturbing were those half open eyes, so I lowered his upper lids."

Some survival instinct pushed her into action. Learning that there was a Parsi burial ground in Mahabaleshwar, she made all the funeral arrangements and called for a Parsi priest from Panchgani.

"The worst thing was having to ring my mother-in-law. When I broke the news, the phone just went dead. Later I learned that she had collapsed when I told her what had happened. Anyway, she called me back. Bless her, she tried to make things easy for me. I told her that Cyrus had died suddenly; mentioned a heart attack because that was the only plausible reason, and she said she would come to Mahabaleshwar immediately. I arranged a taxi to transport her here.

"I survived the three days of prayers by operating on auto-pilot. Besides, I had to think of my mother-in-law. God knows what she was feeling underneath that sphinx-like exterior of hers, her only child dying so suddenly."

"Probably a coping mechanism for her as well."

"Yes, no doubt each of us was trying to be strong for the other's sake."

"Did you establish that it was actually a -"

"A heart attack? Well, that's what I'm coming to."

She patted the empty seat cushion on her right, and Max slid leftwards to occupy it. He seemed to sense that the most difficult part of the story was about to be recounted.

"After the funeral prayers were over, my mother-in-law returned to Bombay with Gopal. I told her I needed an extra day or two to finalise things, after which I would return by taxi. The truth was I didn't know what we'd say to each other during the long journey back. She agreed very readily, quite possibly thinking on the same lines."

Shortly after Gopal's departure Sheela received an unexpected visit - from the local doctor. He had attended a small part of the funeral, which had vaguely struck her as being surprisingly kind. He said he had come to offer his condolences, but Sheela suspected straightaway that he had another agenda.

"Thanking him, I said I had only five minutes to spare because I had to attend to a number of things before returning to Bombay. 'Ah,' he said, 'five minutes will be enough to tell you about my –' I think he used the word 'concern'. 'What concern?' I asked him. I could swear that he licked his lips and smiled. He made a great show of hesitancy, saying that the shock might be too much for me. In the end I was screaming at him. Whatever I said, he was startled enough to stop the cat and mouse game and come to the point."

Sheela looked into the distance as if to ward off any distractions that might deflect her from telling the next part of the story. Between the bungalow and the servants' quarters, she continued in a flat voice, was an overgrown area hidden from view. As a child Cyrus used to play there on a swing, but over years of neglect, with Ramu's increasing infirmity, the swing had become rusty and was almost completely concealed by foliage. The day Sheela went to Panchgani, Ramu took it into his head to do some clearing up and started cutting down some of the overgrowth.

"The doctor told me that when Ramu had gone to clear up the mess around the old swing, he found Cyrus..."

Sheela sprang to her feet and opened the window wide enough to stick her neck out.

She felt a firm but gentle grip on her waist. "It's OK, it's OK," she heard Max whisper. Her natural inclination to preserve her amour propre yielded to the feelings of the moment: she didn't care that he could hear her whimpering like a small child.

"Just stay there for a minute," he said quietly.

He returned with a glass of water.

"Have a sip." With one hand he supported her neck and with the other he placed the glass gently against her lips. "Look, don't you think we should call it a day? We can continue tomorrow if you like."

"No, now that I've gone this far I must finish." The voice she heard was somebody else's. People had often commented on her chocolatey contralto, but now it had mutated into something robotic, robbed of animation by the effort to master her emotions.

Sheela returned to the sofa, sitting upright as she readied herself to resume her narrative. Max sat next to her.

"He - the doctor - told me that Ramu had found my husband - he'd found him there... hanging... hanging from the beam of the swing."

She gripped her chest to still the shaking of her body.

"When the doctor arrived, the two of them managed somehow to ease him - the body - down.

The words that followed came hurtling out.

"He then pointed to a black rubber-like garment - like a diving suit - which had been laid neatly on a chair near the bed. Apparently he and Ramu had found Cyrus in this outfit, which they somehow managed to remove before dressing him in his pyjamas and laying him on the bed."

She paused again, this time in anticipation of a reaction. There was a response, but not one of shock or disgust. She felt a weight shifting fractionally closer to her. For a moment she braced herself for a hand to be placed on her arm, and when it didn't come she was relieved.

"He then went on to say that although my husband had clearly died in unnatural circumstances he'd be prepared to certify that heart attack was the cause of death. But giving the authorities a plausible cause of death would require some toing and froing between Mahabaleshwar and Satara. This would of course involve expenditure - so discretion would come at a price. I was so dazed that I just gave him some money to stop him bothering me - not thinking through what this could lead to. That is how the blackmailing began.

"The diving suit thing was evidence of sorts to support what he'd said, but there were other reasons why I believed him. A few years ago I discovered that Cyrus had ordered some diving gear through Amazon. I thought nothing of it at the time - he said that Amazon had got the order wrong, they should've sent swimming trunks - but now when I look back on what happened... Anyway, there were some other things I discovered after Cyrus's death that confirmed the truth of what the wretched man had said. And that's how the blackmailing continued."

Sheela let out a deep sigh. Suddenly she felt exhausted, her energy drained by the telling of the story. But she managed to summon the will to rise from the sofa and make her way towards the corridor.

"Are you all right? Can I get -"

"No, you stay there, Max."

She returned with a pile of old newspaper cuttings and magazine articles held together by a piece of string.

"I discovered these behind a chest of drawers in a sort of prayer room at the back of the bungalow. I hardly ever went there, but the day before my return to Bombay I thought I'd do a clear-out - to be precise, something told me to look for anything that might be pertinent to Cyrus. That's when I found these. Go on - please have a look."

For over a year she had kept the press cuttings hidden in a locked cupboard. Now, having unburdened herself, she felt liberated, able to reveal everything to this man sitting by her side - a stranger to Cyrus and, not too long ago, to herself as well. That surely was the point: her freedom to tell Max the truth stemmed precisely from the fact that the two men had never met.

She heard the rustle of paper as Max placed each cutting on his lap, skimmed through it and laid it on the rug before reaching out for the next one. He didn't dwell on any of the items. There was no need: in most cases the headlines said it all.

She stole a glance at his lowered head. Then, against her will, her eyes turned towards the titles: *Accidental Autoerotic Death: a review on the lethal paraphiliac syndrome; Kristian Digby, the BBC presenter, may have died in sex game gone wrong; Autoerotic asphyxiation kills 600 people annually*. In a printout from a Wikipedia entry about the death of David Carradine, one sentence was marked with a yellow highlight pen: *The cause of death became widely accepted as 'accidental asphyxiation'*. Another highlighted extract from BBC News cited Paula Yates maintaining that her husband Michael Hutchence would never have committed suicide and that *he died attempting autoerotic asphyxiation*.

Sheela scanned Max's face for the slightest hint of revulsion. She found none. He had a look of thoughtful concentration, as if he were studying a Beethoven score.

He laid the last cutting on the floor. Slowly he turned towards her. His mouth, slightly open, appeared to be hovering between the compulsion to say something and the awareness of the futility of doing so. Then he leaned forward and wrapped his arms around her, first tentatively, then more confidently as she slumped into them. He gave her a kiss, chaste and tight-lipped, on the forehead. Then he kissed her again, this time on the cheek; then yet again, near the corner of her mouth. She did not respond, but neither did she resist. Instead, the shell behind which she had tried to protect herself began to crumble, and his lips were now wet with the tears trickling down her cheeks. He moved away slightly and extracted from his trouser pocket a clean tissue with which he stroked her face.

"You know," she said, her voice thick with sadness, "ever since that day I've been living like a zombie. Pretending to lead a normal life. Desperately trying to blot out what happened – not only because the thought of it was unbearable but also because I feared blurting the whole thing out to the wrong person."

She looked him in the face. "And I somehow succeeded. I didn't let on to anybody about the real reason for his death - not until now. Sometimes I felt my mother-in-law had an inkling that it was more than a heart attack. The only other people who know are Ramu - who is totally trustworthy - and the doctor guy, but when I realised he couldn't prove anything, I stopped paying him on my return to London. Besides which, you gave him a fright he won't forget."

Turning away from Max, she continued, "The problem wasn't other people. I cannot tell you how many times I've racked my brain for things I might have said or done that could've triggered all this. I couldn't forgive myself; and I couldn't forgive him for what he did - to himself, to his mother, to his daughter. To me. To think that this man I adored as the most flawless human being on earth - that he could be some perverted charlatan hoodwinking me for God knows how many years of marriage. Everything I thought I knew about him turned out to have been one big sham. If you'd met him, you'd have thought him the kindest, wisest - quite simply the best - person you'd ever met."

"*Everything I thought I knew about him turned out to have been one big sham.*" Max moved away slightly. "But is there anybody we ever know *everything* about?"

"It's true that sometimes I used to find him hard to figure out. And looking back I can see there were signals of what was to come - the way he sometimes cloistered himself, the way he would suddenly go quiet. So perhaps I was naïve to have felt so shocked. I could go a step further and say that perhaps I did suspect something, perhaps I could have known the truth if I had wanted to – if I hadn't been so terrified of finding out that he wasn't the paragon of virtue I had needed him to be.

"As they say, when something horrible happens, you are alone, because only *you* know what you're going through." Sheela's voice was gentle now, as though she was trying to comfort her bereaved self. "The thing is, nobody else can possibly understand." She turned to him. "Not even you, Max, for all your kindness."

Her last comment gave him the cue to speak, but she put a finger against his mouth and continued, "I feel alone, yes, but not quite as alone as I've been all these months. So thank you."

"I've done nothing."

"But you want to say something."

"Just that - can you really discard everything you knew about him? I mean is it conceivable that throughout your marriage he was just play-acting? That he wasn't genuinely loving and kind?"

She did not respond; she did not know how to respond. All she was aware of was a stirring inside her - a feeling she couldn't quite grasp, but it was not unpleasant: a feeling of relief perhaps, even hope. A feeling she hadn't experienced for a long time.

"So -" he broke off suddenly "- are you OK for me to continue?"

She nodded.

"So, it's possible, isn't it," - she could sense him formulating his words - "that everything you knew about Cyrus was *not* a sham, that he *was* quite simply the best person you'd ever met, but that there was another side to him - call it a darker side - which you weren't aware of. A side which made him less flawless than you thought he was - but which hardly invalidated all the good things you felt about him."

"But all those cuttings show that he realised the risk of doing what he did - that it could all end horribly. And why didn't he tell me that he had this - this problem?"

"Maybe he thought telling you could do more harm than good."

"That's just it - that's why I've been racked by this awful guilt. He couldn't trust me to stand by him."

"But the fact that he didn't say anything doesn't necessarily signify anything about *you*. He probably saw this as something to be kept private because it would do no good telling anyone, however understanding they were."

"You're sweet, Max, trying to console me like this. But I've never been able to rid myself of this feeling that, if I'd had more courage, I could've done something about it. And when the anniversary of that day approached -"

"You decided you could take no more."

"Yes. I was totally single-minded, so much so that I blanked everything and everyone else out of my mind - including, I'm ashamed to admit, my own daughter; although, in fairness to myself, it was only because of her that I hung on for the best part of a year. She just went to pieces when I told her that her beloved Daddy had died - of a heart attack, as I'd told everybody else.

"The approach of the anniversary - it plunged me into a state of total darkness, not the faintest glimmer of light anywhere to be seen. Anyway, I decided that Kate's Point would look like a tragic accident. I knew a godforsaken part of the point that the tourist hordes never approached."

"But you didn't reckon on us."

"No, I didn't reckon on you. Yet I sometimes think that deep down I knew somebody could discover me. And, if that were the case," she smiled at Max, "did I become a sort of active participant in your guru's take on how things were going to pan out?"

"We were meant to be there to rescue someone. And you were that someone waiting to be rescued."

"Something like that."

"As you've probably gathered, I'm not sure I believe in that sort of - what's the word I want? - serendipity. But the way things have worked out, who am I to say?"

Sheela looked at her watch. "Goodness, it's late. I think I'm ready to crash out. I'm sorry for having unburdened myself on you like this."

"And by doing so you've paid me the biggest possible compliment." He touched her arm lightly and added, "And I promise I'll never betray your trust."

"I know."

But his promise teased out a question that took her by surprise. "And now that I've revealed all, I don't suppose you have any dark secrets to hide from me, do you?" She wondered whether he had caught the unease that lay behind the frivolous tone of the question.

"Well," he said slowly, "as I said, can we ever know everything - even about the people we know and love the most? Don't we all have secrets? I suppose it all depends on what you mean by 'dark'." He gave her a gentle smile, but she couldn't help noticing the slightly awkward twist of his mouth.

"Sorry, that was silly of me. Look, I'm just going to do a little clearing up before going to bed, so don't wait for me. Good night, Max."

"Good night, Sheela. Sleep well." He bent forward slightly, then stopped himself.

As he walked away, there was something in his gait that made her want to give him a consoling hug. But she didn't want them to leave the sitting room together. She didn't want them to say good night in the veranda and retire to their rooms at the same time.

44

Sheela lay in bed and closed her eyes to will herself into unconsciousness. Instead, half-formed thoughts jumbled through her mind, each strand champing at the one that had just raced past: she was becoming too close to Max; she had betrayed Clarissa, yet it was Clarissa who had wanted her to come closer to Max. And she had betrayed Cyrus. She wanted to convince herself that this betrayal paled beside that of Cyrus himself - but Max's intervention had broken the habit of thinking developed over the past year: the sense of betrayal gave way to remorse as she recalled how Cyrus had pleaded with her to recognise that he had needs and flaws like everyone else. A sad acceptance of her own role in the events that had played out lulled her into an uneasy sleep.

The sleep was crowded with mini-nightmares she could barely remember during the moments of half-wakefulness - barring one, in which Ramu, shaking his head in sorrowful admonition, refused to countenance the excuses she gave for having committed some terrible wrong.

Now she heard a knocking. Oh no, it was Ramu returning to reprimand her. She heard the knocking again, hesitant but clear. She wanted to keep her eyes shut, but they had a will of their own. She imagined a shadow hovering behind the curtain covering the glass of her bedroom door. She blinked and saw the shadow again, this time more distinct; she noticed that a verandah light was on.

She heard a voice. *Oh God, I'm getting delirious.* Then she heard the voice again and she wanted to scream for Ramu. The call, repeated once more, finally took shape: "Sheela, Sheela! Are you OK?"

Without letting herself think, she swung out of bed, and forgetting that she had only a flimsy nightie to cover her against the cold, she walked barefoot to open the door. Max was standing there in pyjamas and a light knee-length dressing gown.

"I couldn't sleep. I was worried about you, so I thought I'd check that things were OK."

She nodded.

"Everything is fine" was what she wanted to say, but the words were blocked by a torrent of tears which felt like a final cleansing of the anger, guilt and sense of betrayal that had shut her out from the reality of her grief.

"Oh Sheela, my darling Sheela." She succumbed to the breath of his lips, the touch of his fingers, the strength of his arms around her. She didn't know how she had got back into her bed, but now she was not alone, and when he felt under the nightdress she didn't turn away but clung to him even more closely. His dressing gown had come loose, and her hands were now under his pyjama top, clenched against his bare back. And when he came inside her she felt a joy so piercingly immediate that all memory yielded itself to the quickening of the moment.

When it was over, he rested his face close to hers. She could barely see it in the dark, but she knew that he was smiling at her.

He leaned over, wrapped an arm around her waist and kissed her gently on the mouth. He lay his head on the pillow and she buried her face in his chest.

I should be feeling guilty - but I don't. For the first time since Cyrus's death she was happy.

Their arms and legs entwined, she snuggled closer to him. If only this moment could last forever.

She couldn't remember when she fell asleep. It must have been a deep sleep. Waking up to Ramu's early morning call - "Hey, Amoli!" - she found that Max was no longer by her side. *Oh God, he's left!*

She hurried to the bathroom, gargled with mouthwash, splashed her face with water and brushed her hair. Looking briefly in the mirror, she slipped her dressing gown on and rushed towards the bedroom door.

When she entered the sitting room she found Max gazing out of the window. He turned round and came towards her. She could tell from the dampness of his hair that he had already showered. She had never seen him look more handsome. He gave her a broad smile, open and warm, and there was a spring in his gait which carried with it a dynamism she had noticed only once before – when he was first violinist at the Wigmore Hall concert: the boyish carom player had mutated into somebody more adult, more confident, more manly. Or so it seemed to her: perhaps there had been no change and the difference she saw in him lay in the fact that by taking control last night he had altered the terms of their relationship.

"I thought you'd left me."

"Left you? Why would I ever do that?"

"You weren't there when I woke up."

"You were fast asleep, so I slipped away. Besides, I heard some activity outside - probably Ramu - and I thought that finding me with you -"

"Talk of the devil," she mumbled.

Ramu came in to ask what Baby and the *sahib* would like for breakfast.

Exactly half an hour later she was back in the dining room, having showered and dressed.

"I feel more presentable now."

"You look beautiful."

As they were settling into their chairs, Ramu and Amoli brought in their breakfast – two poached eggs for Max and a scrambled egg for Sheela. Max turned to the elderly couple and somehow managed to converse with them about the excellence of their eggs - using hand gestures, English words that they recognised and the few Hindi words he and Clarissa had picked up in the course of their previous trip to India. Sheela was delighted that Max met with the approval of the couple and was particularly happy to see Ramu beaming at this *sahib* who thought nothing of getting up to help Amoli bring in tea, toast and marmalade. Ramu's blessings meant more to Sheela than her own mother's.

When Max returned to his chair, he said, "You know, I haven't felt so happy for a long time."

"And I -" she paused "- I think I can truly say the same."

The smile on his face made her want to blurt out "I love you". To stop herself she shovelled a mouthful of the scrambled egg.

"You know," she said instead, "I really know so little about you. You have this quartet, but I don't know much else - what happened before the quartet, and so on."

There followed a potted history of how Max's mother brought him up as a single parent in London. Having come into some money, she was able to give Max a comfortable life: she bought a house, had many friends and sent Max to a good school. After school, Max did music at Oxford and then returned to London to study at the Guildhall School of Music.

"And then my world was turned upside down - my mother died suddenly."

"I'm sorry to hear that. She can't have been that old."

"In her fifties. Cancer."

He paused. The room fell very quiet.

"I *am* very sorry," she said, extending her arm across the table to squeeze his left hand. As he held on to her, she felt he understood why her sympathy was more heartfelt this time.

"Living alone, trying to focus on my music, wasn't easy."

"You had no other family members at the time?"

There was another pause. "No," he said finally, "not at the time."

She withdrew her hand and gathered the plates and cutlery.

"Anyway, after Guildhall I struggled for some years as a sort of jobbing musician. Then a friend - Jolyon, the one at our dinner party - suggested I set up a music group of my own. Which is what I did."

"And that's how Caracalla came into being. You should feel very proud of yourself."

"Look, I've spoken enough about myself. Come to think of it, I don't know all that much about you - how you landed up in London, for example."

"Shall we go outside for a bit? It will be nice to take a breath of fresh air."

She led him to a pockmarked bench set against a wall extending to the entrance gate.

"I thought you already knew quite a lot about me. But maybe I'd told Clarissa - when we'd spent time together in Bombay."

She skirted over her family life - she had had a doting father, a Sikh called Jagdeep Singh, who had died prematurely of a heart attack; as for her mother and brother, having met them Max could draw his own conclusions. She dwelt instead on the Cathedral School, where she learned by heart the poems of Keats and Shelley; where she took part in elocution competitions; where she was taught about relative clauses, syntax and parsing by Mr Browning, the Anglo-Indian Head of English. Poor Mr Browning, tittered the girls, so much more *Indian* than *Anglo* on account of a skin colour that seemed to get *browner* by the day.

"You read English at university, didn't you?"

"Yes, first at Elphinstone College in Bombay, then at UCL. Then I became a freelance writer - but in addition I got an English teaching qualification. I also did some art courses at Morley College. So that took me to writing about fine arts."

"And it was at UCL that you met -"

"Cyrus. Yes, that's right. He was studying medicine there."

She rubbed her hands. "Gosh, it's become quite chilly. Maybe we should go in."

As they proceeded back to the bungalow, she said, "After UCL I worked for a multinational in Bombay, but that didn't suit me, so I went back to London to start a master's course at UCL - but I suppose the real reason for returning to London was to -"

"Be with Cyrus."

She smiled. "How did you guess? Anyway, I just sort of drifted - doing the writing, the teaching - but that flexibility suited me well, especially when our daughter arrived."

They had just entered the sitting room. "So now you know everything about my boring life."

"Not boring at all," he shook his head. "Look, I think I should go back to the club. I need to check out."

"So you're returning to Bombay today?"

"Yes, I'd ordered a taxi for this afternoon. Sorry, hadn't I told you?"

"I don't think so. But why the hurry?"

"Well, I've achieved my objective here."

"Which was?" She knew the answer, but she wanted to hear him give it.

"To make sure you were OK - the reason why I flew to India."

"When you say that, Max, I just don't know what to think."

"Come back with me, Sheela. You've found both Ramu and his wife well enough - so there isn't any reason for you to stay on here, is there?"

She shook her head. "OK - I'll leave for Bombay today, but" - she turned to him with a smile - "only on one condition - that you return with me in the car."

The quirky grin he gave her made her wonder how many hearts he had broken before he met Clarissa.

"I'll drop you at the club, then return here to pack my things. That will give you enough time to get ready and settle with the club. I'll get a pack lunch organised for the journey and then come back to fetch you from the club."

Before he could respond she turned to Ramu, who had just entered the room, to inform him that she needed to return to Bombay that afternoon, earlier than planned, and that Gopal would have to get himself ready. The *sahib* would be going back to Bombay with her, so could Gopal come immediately to drive him to the club. Ramu took the sudden announcement with his usual sangfroid - that was to be expected, but she never anticipated the warmth of the smile he gave Max when she told him that they were returning to Bombay together.

"Good morning, Madam," Gopal said, holding the left-hand passenger car door for her.

"Good morning, Gopal," she said, flashing him a smile which, for once, didn't feel forced.

After Sheela settled into her seat, Gopal rushed round the front of the car to open the other passenger door, but Max had already got in beside her.

"Today going to Bombay." Gopal was smiling, clearly pleased with the change of plan. Only now did it dawn on her that he was an urbanite, impervious to - if not at home in - the garbage, congestion and stench of modern-day Mumbai. Not for him the world of bird song, fragrant earth and sweeping vistas into which Ramu and Amoli had been born. But Sheela wondered whether the grin on his face was also down to the opportunity he had to impress Max with his command of English.

She glanced sideways at Max. He was looking out of the window, softly whistling a tune; it took a few seconds for her to recognise *The Trout*. Cyrus used to sing the song, but today it wasn't the heroic husband with impeccable taste in music - and in everything else - who came to mind, nor the man with the secret that had caused her to recoil in disgust. Instead, for the first time, she felt compassion: my poor Cyrus, she thought, what he must have gone through, all on his own, with nobody he felt able to confide in - not even his own wife. She turned again towards Max. It was thanks to him that she could allow herself to feel for Cyrus in a way she had never felt before - in a way she would never have imagined feeling.

She was seized by a minor panic: she mustn't lose this man sitting next to her; she mustn't look back on this moment as something she had carelessly allowed to slip from her grasp.

She slid her hand along the seat until it rested gently on his. He turned round and gripped it as if he was never going to let it go. With her free hand she placed her cardigan over the interlocking fingers. Thankfully, Gopal hadn't noticed anything.

"I'm so happy we're returning to Bombay together," he whispered.

She smiled. "I get into a panic sometimes. It's as if everything's too good to last."

The car slowed down as it approached the side of the club.

"But it *will* last - remember what the guru said."

She wanted his reassurance, but a worm of doubt continued to wriggle inside her, a doubt she couldn't quite put her finger on.

"I thought you'd taken what the guru said with a massive pinch of salt! True, Clarissa gave her blessing, but what about that mysterious brother of hers - what would he think about his sister's husband being involved with someone else? So quickly, I mean." She paused, then added, "I'm assuming of course that he knows you."

Max withdrew his hand and turned to her, looking straight into her eyes as if striving not to avert her gaze.

Before he could speak, she knew the answer to her own question. It was as though his gaze had lifted a veil: Claire and her brother; Clarissa and Max.

45

Dear Sheela

I just want to say how sorry I am for the shock I gave you in Mahabaleshwar. You must be wondering whether you can trust anybody. That really troubles me - the feeling that I had somehow led you up the garden path, the same way you felt when you learnt about Cyrus's death.

The truth, though, is that I have no excuses to give: what happened - our love for each other - swept everything else aside. What we felt and did is not acceptable to most people, I know. But in my heart of hearts I believe there was no other way for us.

What happened to us probably explains my reaction to the Cyrus story. I genuinely cannot get myself to feel that he did anything 'wrong'.

But then - as I'd already told you - this overwhelming feeling had become too all-consuming, at least for me. That's not to say I stopped loving Clarissa; I'll never stop loving her. But when you came along I felt a sense of release - I could feel, but in a way that didn't make me a slave to the feeling.

I'm probably coming across as supremely self-centred - talking about feelings overwhelming me and then about a sense of release, as though Clarissa's own feelings didn't matter. And (at the risk of sounding presumptuous) you might ask 'What about my feelings?' The point is it's not as though I don't care - it's just that I had to tell you the truth as best I could. You might well be thinking 'what a joke to speak of truth when he's been deceiving me all along'. But when I think about it I cannot see any way I could have handled things differently. Would baring my soul at some earlier point in time have done any good? Would you have welcomed being told?

As I write I feel myself more and more confused. I don't know any more what's right or wrong. What I can say is I don't <u>feel</u> I've done anything wrong.

Thinking about the future, there's only one way forward: I must go away. If, as you think, I've betrayed you, it's not fair to expect you to accept me in your life. You are strong; you'll be able to pick up the pieces and move on.

With love
Max

Sheela read the note carefully a second time. The first skim-through had yielded nothing more than a vague sense of panic: the pieces of her life she had recently begun to re-assemble were now threatening to fall apart.

She returned to the top of the page, driven by a compulsion to work out, and thereby somehow exorcise, the real meaning of the words scrawled out in Max's spidery handwriting. But it was the last paragraph that stayed with her: he had decided to leave her.

Her attention was caught by the last two words of the note: *With love*. The 'with' looked smudged. As she held the paper against the light, she saw that the word had been written over something else. She strained to decipher the original writing: the first letter started with something like a capital 'h' and the next two letters were both 'l'; there followed a letter that looked like an 'n' or maybe an 'm'. Then it all came together: 'All my' - that was it - 'All my love'. That was what he had written first.

She was grateful that her bedroom door was shut. She wouldn't want her mother-in-law to see her crying.

"*Bai*, dinner *taiyar hai*."

"*Achha*, Philomena."

She went into the bathroom and splashed her face with cold water. Thankfully, her eyes didn't look puffy.

She was about to leave her room when a thought struck her: why the handwritten note? Why not an email? Perhaps because an email invites an easy response; it leaves the door open a chink. She stepped into the sitting room convinced that the note signified the end of their relationship.

"Oh darling, you look so much better. It's amazing what even an hour can do. Was it a really gruelling journey?"

Khorshed was already seated at the dining table. Sheela sat next to her and clasped her hand.

Philomena came in with a dish of lightly battered pomfret slices, reddish-brown with chilli powder, and a bowl of ladies' fingers.

"Come, you must tuck in. Mahabaleshwar seems to have made you lose weight. So did you really find Ramu much better?"

"He certainly looked far better than I'd expected."

"Well, you know what a bunch of frauds we oldies can be!"

After a short pause, Khorshed continued, "Is something the matter?"

"Oh why would you think that?"

"I don't know. Ever since your return earlier this evening you've been looking somewhat - somewhat bothered."

"No, Mummy, I'm quite fine. Now what's the latest Bombay news?"

Back in her room, Sheela was determined to have an early night. But the thoughts haranguing her throughout the return trip to Bombay kept on intruding. Seated on her bed, she revisited what had happened over and over again, as if by doing so she could somehow reach a resolution. Instead she succeeded only in torturing herself with recriminations: when Max had told her the truth about his relationship with Clarissa, why had she been so cold and dismissive? "I think you'd better take the taxi to Bombay after all." What madness had triggered that cheap parting short, culminating in a "goodbye" so heavily loaded with finality? How could she have hardened herself against the look of shock on his face, against the apology, almost tearful, that he had made for having upset her? Was it surprising that he had decided to "go away"? She had been horrified by what Cyrus had done, until Max had shown how horror could be transmuted into compassion. And now she had turned against Max. Would she never learn?

46

Sheela rose from her bed. With a growing sense of panic, she felt that if she didn't take action now - immediately - she would lose him forever. And then? No doubt she would struggle to carry on, for Nina's sake, until the futility of her existence would finally draw her to its faltering end.

She had to trace him. He had returned to Bombay the previous day. She looked up her contact list in the vain hope of finding an Indian mobile number, but, as she had expected, all she could locate was Max's UK mobile - which he would have certainly switched off.

The only option was to look for him. With luck he would be staying in the same apartment building he and Clarissa had occupied when they were together in Bombay, the one on the corner of Marine Drive and a side road. What was it called? Sunbeam - no, Sunset - Villas.

It was 9.45 - not too late to meet him. No need to disturb Gopal. She could walk there - it wouldn't take more than fifteen minutes.

She hadn't changed from the shirt and trousers she had worn on the journey back to Bombay, so she slipped away from the flat five minutes later, and reached Sunset Villas by a little past ten.

Watchman, she called to the *chowkidar* dozing on a stool by the entrance gate, has an *angrezi sahib* been staying in the building, the one who had been here not long ago with his wife? He yawned and informed her that the same English gentleman had indeed occupied an apartment in the building, but had left with all his baggage that very morning without saying where he had gone. The *chowkidar* was fully awake now. "May I know your good name?" he asked. Sheela was so taken aback by his ability to speak English that without thinking she answered "Marker".

It was only after leaving him that she wondered why he had wanted her name. She walked away feeling exposed to the prying eyes and pricking ears of all the residents of Sunset Villas.

Instead of turning right to return to Tower View, she turned left on to Marine Drive. The last time she was here she had bumped into Clarissa. She was gone, never to return; and now Max had gone, nowhere to be traced.

Walking along the promenade skirting the Arabian Sea, she noticed passers-by casting curious glances at her. She realised that she wasn't moving in a straight line. She rested gingerly against the ledge lining the pavement. She felt better in this half-seated position. Her light-headedness was hardly surprising, she told herself, given the sleepless night before the gruelling journey back from Mahabaleshwar. Brother and sister - now it seemed so obvious: hadn't she noticed their physical similarity? Two beautiful peas in the same pod, separated only by gender.

She felt her phone vibrate against her thigh, but by the time she had extracted it the ringing had stopped. The call was from Shireen.

If she had to get in touch with anybody, the only person she could contemplate talking to right now was her old friend.

"Oh Sheels, I heard you'd returned from Mahabaleshwar. How was it?"

"Oh it was fine, fine."

"Methinks the lady doth protest too much. In fact I *know* she doth. Let's meet tomorrow. How about 11 o'clock at the front entrance of the CCI?"

"OK, look forward..." Sheela felt her voice dry up.

"Sweetheart, don't worry about anything - we'll sort things out. Goodnight and God bless."

47

"What was your night like, darling?"

Khorshed stretched her arm out over the toast rack to squeeze Sheela's hand. "You know how precious you are to me, don't you?"

Sheela got up from her chair and pressed the old woman's head gently against her chest. "And you, my beloved Mummy, you are my true mother."

She felt her chest heaving in the effort to stop the sobs welling up her throat.

Khorshed's arms encircled her waist; they were surprisingly steady and strong, and the shaking in her body subsided.

"You give me a lot of strength, Mummy," she said as she returned to her chair.

"As you do too, my darling. I always told Cyrus he wasn't the only lucky one to have you in our family. You are the daughter I never had."

For a moment Sheela feared that the liquid rimming Khorshed's eyes was something more than a sign of old age.

"Tell me, Mummy, when you can't sleep at night, what do you think about?"

She immediately regretted asking the question. Khorshed dabbed the sides of her mouth with her napkin.

"I think about a lot of things. My husband, my parents. But most of all I think of Cyrus."

Sheela was astonished that Khorshed had allowed herself to reveal a chink in her armour. "There's not a single day I don't think of Cyrus myself," she wanted to say. Instead, she said, "Some toast?"

"No thank you, darling. But don't let me stop you."

She's so English - at least the way the English used to be - with her stiff upper lip propriety. But it was obvious, more than ever before, that behind that self-control lay the desire to shield those she loved from her own sense of loss.

"Goodness, it's already 9.45 - I'm supposed to be meeting Shireen at 11 at the CCI."

Khorshed smiled. "Oh, that's nice. I've always liked your friend Shireen. She makes me laugh." The smile broke into a chortle that brought to mind the woman she must have been half a century earlier.

"By the way, Mummy, please don't make lunch for me - I'm not sure about my plans for the rest of the day."

Closing her bedroom door, she recalled her conversation with the *chowkidar* of Sunset Villas. *I will never see him again. I will never see him again.* However much she tried to banish those words, they kept returning like a malevolent mantra.

This is absurd, she tried to tell herself: she could always get in touch with him when she returned to London. No, that would be too late. She needed to make amends now, right now, because every passing day would distance him further, would reinforce the rightness of his decision. But how was she to get in touch without any contact details?

"Sheels!"

Unusually, Shireen had been waiting for her. She suggested a walk along the perimeter of the Brabourne Stadium, followed by a coffee in the veranda. Sheela readily agreed: a brisk walk around the lawn meant that she wouldn't need to face her friend's anxiously cheerful face.

They started the circuit in silence, their breathing settling into a rhythm as they got into their stride. But the absence of conversation began to feel oppressive.

"So how are things going with your nice Parsi gentleman?"

Shireen went on to talk about the generosity of her Dory, who so sweetly showered her with clothes and jewellery - most of which, she added with a tinkling laugh, were sadly not to her taste. Then, after a pause for breath, she placed her hands gently on Sheela's shoulders. "Now, sweetheart, enough of this charade. Tell me what's up. Come, you can unburden yourself while we're walking."

Shireen strode forward, looking straight ahead of her. Following half a step behind, Sheela decided that she might as well get over the whole thing with the minimum of information: Shireen was not going to be fobbed off easily.

"Well, you know the English couple - actually, the Australian couple."

"Yes, of course. So sad, her dying like that - such a lovely woman, I thought."

"I know. Well, her - her husband - I got involved in helping him with the funeral and everything, and we sort of got to know each other quite well -"

"So the two of you have become an item."

"Oh Shireen!"

"I know, I know - but when we were last at the Willingdon I felt something might be afoot. And you know what? I thought how lovely it would be if my Sheels, after everything she's gone through, got hitched with somebody like him - an absolute sweetheart."

They had completed two-thirds of the circuit. The figures seated in the cane chairs on the lawn were now large enough to become recognisable. Sheela kept her eyes fixed steadily on them.

"Look," she said, "that woman in the dark blue sari - I could swear I've met her somewhere."

"Well, I haven't! So what about the husband?"

"Well, it's all over. Something happened in Mahabaleshwar, and I decided that it wouldn't work out."

"In Mahabaleshwar?"

"Sorry, I didn't tell you - he came to Mahabaleshwar."

"You mean he came all the way from London to be with you in Mahabaleshwar?"

As they approached the verandah, their pace slackened.

"Look, Sheels, I don't know what happened in Mahabaleshwar - and," she raised her hand, "I don't need to know. All I want to say is this: if you still like this guy, then all is most certainly not lost. Just think of me - until I met Dory, I thought I was going to be consigned to the laundry basket of discarded spinsters. So whatever happened in Mahabaleshwar can be undone. For one thing, this guy flew five thousand miles to be with you. For another, I know that if you like a person there's a good reason for that. You have an instinct for goodness, Sheela, and that instinct won't let you down."

A gust of wind ruffled Sheela's hair, and a fleeting vision of Cyrus's smiling face brushed past her; one of the few things she used to find irritating about him was the way he tousled her hair when he was being playful.

"Oh I'm certainly not as confident about my instinct as you are! But thanks, my darling Shireen, I'll try to bear in mind what you've just said."

"That's my Sheels! Now, coffee in the veranda, or would you prefer the pool side?"

48

Sheela returned to Tower View at 4.45. She had lost track of time, as she usually did when in Shireen's company. But not far below the surface of gossip and girlish laughter, a feeling of escapism never let go of her: if she could have, she would have stretched the afternoon to late evening, but Shireen had made a five o'clock manicure appointment at Lakmé.

She entered her room, got to her bed and drifted into an uneasy nap.

She was awoken by her mobile. It was only after she pressed the answer button that she noticed the word "Mumsie", but by this time it was too late to avoid the call.

"Really, Susheela," (*signal: she's very angry with me; no, not really, she's only pretending to be, so that she can come over all rejected and wounded*), "what's this, leaving your mother in the dark - as usual! First you scoot off to Mahabaleshwar, then you sneak back to Bombay - and I only learn about it through the Bombay gossip vine! "

"Sorry, I did intend to tell you."

"Oh, go on. Anyway, I was phoning to ask if your royal highness would be so kind as to grace me with your presence over lunch tomorrow."

This, Sheela supposed, was her mother's way of making amends for the evening with Sweetie and his maharajah friend.

"Thanks, Mumsie. Can I come back to you -"

"Oh, the usual thing. Well, since it's my lot to be last in the queue, I'll just have to wait until your majesty -"

Her mother's voice came to an abrupt halt.

"Mumsie? Mumsie?"

Her mother had been cut off. She would need to call her back if she was to avoid a tantrum.

Sheela looked down at her mobile and found that the screen was blank. How annoying - now her mother was going to think she was deliberately snubbing her. Must be the battery. She plugged her battery charger into the phone, but there was no sign of life.

She asked Philomena to summon Gopal. The man's talents extended beyond reckless driving: he was a useful handyman, and if anybody could bring her phone back to life it would be him.

Gopal shook his head doubtfully, and disappeared with the phone into the kitchen area.

Sheela looked at her watch. It was almost 6.15. After barely two minutes, he returned, his headshaking having now taken an ominous turn.

"Mobile shop *koh batana paréga.*"

Oh no, how long would the mobile shop people take to solve the problem? No idea, he said; and, as the owner of the phone, she would have to come with him in case they asked questions. Was she imagining a hint of glee in his voice?

"Hello, darling." Khorshed had just emerged from her bedroom.

Sheela gave her mother-in-law a hug. "Mummy, sorry, but my mobile's gone completely dead. Is it OK if I go to the mobile shop to get it seen to right away?"

"You know what my answer is, darling. Gopal will take you, of course."

The man at the mobile shop near Flora Fountain fiddled inscrutably with the buttons of Sheela's phone. He was either an expert or, she thought more likely, quite clueless. Mobile in hand, he sauntered into a back office, returning after almost ten minutes to ask if madam would kindly come back in two hours. Two hours, are you crazy? she wanted to scream, but instead she said OK. After asking Sheela for her good name, he turned to another customer.

Sheela left the shop perturbed that the man was now attending to the other customer instead of dealing with her problem with the urgency it deserved. She glanced at her watch. It was ten minutes to seven. With time to kill she decided to walk over to Kitab Khana, one of her favourite bookshops in Bombay, to browse through the books on display.

Today, however, she was finding it difficult to concentrate, picking books at random and almost immediately returning them to their spaces. It was with relief that she heard a staff announcement reminding customers that it was almost 7.30, the store's closing time.

Back in the car she asked Gopal to take her to the Trident Hotel at Nariman Point. She would spend the remaining hour looking at the shops.

As the hour crept by she became increasingly edgy: would the mobile store really be open so late, and, even if it were, would it have solved her problem?

To her relief, the shop was still open at 8.45 and the assistant who had attended to her was standing at the counter.

"Madam," he said, with a beaming smile, "I am feeling very happy to inform you that your phone is like *pukkah* new phone - and it has guarantee of one month."

"One month?"

"Yes, one *whole* month!"

"Oh, amazing. And what do I owe you?"

"No, nothing - my manager is saying it is our kind service."

Sheela looked at her mobile, and, sure enough, it showed signs of life. She would have to buy a new phone, but the one-month guarantee ensured that at least she wouldn't be stranded while she was in Bombay.

It was already 9.15 when Gopal dropped her at the small wrought iron gate leading to the entrance of Tower View.

Once in her bedroom, she started to unbutton her top. As she did so, she felt a buzz from the bulge against her thigh. She prised her mobile out of her trouser pocket and saw that there were three new messages.

One was from her mother, no doubt complaining about having been disconnected. The next one was from Bachoo (who had presumably returned from London).

And the third was from Max.

As she touched the screen to read the last message, she felt as though all her vital organs were colliding against one another.

Went to a game reserve in Madhya Pradesh for a change of scene before my departure for London. When I returned, the building security guard said a lady had come looking for me - the name he gave sounded like Marker but I couldn't tell for sure. If it wasn't you please forget I ever sent this message. I need to stop now - I'm taking a BA flight back and I have a lot of packing etc to do before my taxi takes me to the airport later this evening.

No *Dear Sheela*, no *Love, Max*. But he did text her, didn't he? She let herself hope that he hadn't - yet - cut her off totally.

She saw that the message had been sent at 6.29, shortly after her phone had gone dead. Her chest weighed down on her as she dialled the Indian mobile number he had used to send the message.

After a short pause, she was greeted by a continuous hum. He must have switched his phone off, or returned it having acquired it only for the duration of his stay.

She located his UK mobile number and pressed lightly on it with an index finger that refused to stay still. As she had feared, she heard Max's smiling voice informing her that he wasn't available right now.

She felt the pressure on her chest sink even lower. Now that he was leaving the country, reaching him on any phone was likely to be impossible. In any case, in view of the delay of almost three hours - it was now just past 9.20 - he would have concluded that she had no intention of returning his message.

The BA flight left shortly after two in the morning. Max was the sort of person likely to report the requisite three hours ahead of the departure time. That would mean not much later than 11pm. It took about an hour to get to the airport, but he could have decided to allow a comfortable hour and a half for the journey. That would mean departure from Sunset Villas between 9.30 and 9.45.

She had sent Gopal home, so she couldn't just hop into the car to make the five-minute drive to Sunset Villas. She would just have to try hailing a taxi.

She stuffed the mobile into her pocket, grabbed her handbag and rushed down the stairs, not bothering to wait for the lift. She ran towards the corner of Dinshaw Vachha Road, hoping to find a cab, but the only taxi passing by was occupied. There was a taxi rank at the other end of the road, outside the CCI. She started to sprint down the length of the road, slowing down when she needed to catch her breath.

Finally she found a taxi near the CCI and directed the driver to head as fast as he could for Marine Drive.

They were on the wrong side of Marine Drive, the one hugging the sea, and she kept her eyes glued to the right, looking out for a gap in the central reservation as close as possible to the location of Sunset Villas.

"*Idhar* U-turn *maro*," she called out as she spotted the gap.

The driver broke sharply and swerved round. Then he pressed his foot on the accelerator and shot past the apartment block. She screamed at him to stop. He brought the taxi to a juddering halt, and a car behind crashed into the cab.

Sheela got out of the taxi just as the owner of the car - a Mercedes E-Class - swaggered out to inspect the damage. The two drivers started shouting at each other. She shoved a 50-rupee note into the hand of the taxi driver and sprinted towards the entrance of Sunset Villas.

She had no idea where the flat occupied by Max was located, the *chowkidar* was nowhere to be seen, and the names of the residents displayed on a board in the lobby area meant nothing to her.

An elderly lady with tufts of salt and pepper hair emerged from the lift.

"Excuse me, sorry to bother you, but have you by any chance seen a European gentleman anywhere around here?"

The lady smiled benignly through horn-rimmed glasses.

"A what, dear?" Her voice was as fragile as her sense of balance.

"A European gentleman - Eu-ro-pean - gentleman."

"Sorry, I'm a visitor." She tottered towards the compound and boomed out "Chauffeur!" Sheela was astonished by the transformation wrought by the exertion of authority. A man scurried from the side of the building to escort the old lady to her car. Following the chauffeur was another man who stopped to open the door for her. Sheela recognised him as the *chowkidar*.

"Watchman!" she cried out.

The *chowkidar* turned round and ambled towards her, showing no sign of recognition as he came closer.

She asked him for the number of the flat occupied by the foreign gentleman who had recently returned. Oh, he said, he left just a minute ago. Where did he go, she asked, trying to control her voice. To the airport. Did he use a private taxi firm? Yes, he did. Do you know the name of the firm?

Without responding, the *chowkidar* turned and opened a door leading to a cubicle. He entered the cubicle and leant on a small table, his back towards her.

He remained frozen in that position, and she wondered if he had chosen to forget that she was waiting for him. She was about to scream at him when he turned round, a small notebook in his hand. Here is the mobile number of the taxi firm, he said, pointing to some digits scrawled on the top page. She whipped out her mobile and dialled the number. It kept on ringing, every repeated ring reinforcing her fear that nobody intended to answer.

Just as she was about to end the call, a voice barked out the name of the taxi firm.

"Hello, a taxi came a few minutes ago to fetch a passenger from Sunset Villas near Marine Drive - to go to the international airport. Can I speak to the passenger?"

"What is your good name, madam?"

After she gave her name, there was a long pause, then a sound of rummaging at the other end.

"Oh yes," the man returned to the phone, "name of passenger is Mr Alex?"

"Yes, yes - Mr Alex. Can I speak to him please?"

"Sorry, madam, you cannot speak to passenger directly. But if you wait one minute, I can try to connect driver myself and tell him passenger call you."

"Oh, please, please - it's very urgent." She wished they were speaking in person; she could have shoved a 100-rupee note into his hand.

"No problem, madam. Kindly wait."

There was a click and the phone seemed to go dead. She looked at the second hand in her watch and followed its path as it scanned the circumference of the dial - five, ten, fifteen, twenty seconds - until a whole minute had elapsed. Some fifteen seconds later, the phone came to life with the sound of phlegm being cleared.

"Sorry for waiting you, madam. I am trying to connect to driver five times, but every time same - no sound. His mobile is switch off."

"Oh no! At least can you tell me the make and registration number of the car?"

"Yes of course, madam. It is Tata Indica. The car number - kindly wait -"

There was a shuffling of notes before he found the registration number. Sheela scribbled it down.

Just as she ended the call, the *chowkidar* approached her with the expectant smile of somebody anticipating a reward. Remembering that the man had prided himself on his English, she said, "Watchman, please call a taxi immediately," slipping a 50-rupee note into his hand.

"Yes of course, madam." Rushing towards the gate he poked two fingers into his mouth to let out a whistle shrill enough to be heard as far as Chowpatty Beach.

The whistle did the trick, and she was in a taxi within twenty seconds.

49

"Please *bohut* fast *jao*."

"*Arré* madam, *dekho kitna* traffic *hai*!"

Unhelpful bastard. True, the traffic on Marine Drive was unusually busy, but the man knew she was desperate to get to the airport as soon as possible.

She had the Tata Indica registration number on the slip of paper in her hand. Although trying to identify Max's car was almost certainly a thankless task, she felt compelled to look out for any Indica she could spot.

As the taxi approached Chowpatty Beach, the driver, to his credit, seized the opportunity to overtake the car immediately in front and, once on Babulnath Road, she saw an Indica turning left on to Hughes Road.

"*Jera* faster *nahi ja sakté hain*?" she cried out to the driver.

The driver didn't respond, but he did accelerate, and by the time they approached the Pedder Road flyover there was only one car separating them from the Indica.

Sheela craned her neck to get a better view but the Honda immediately in front blocked everything except the Indica's wing mirror.

Suddenly the Honda swerved into the left-hand lane, towards Kemps Corner. Sheela leaned forward to read the registration number of the Indica. It wasn't the one on the piece of paper. Just to make sure, she peered closer to see if there was a European-looking passenger in the back seat. The traffic slowed down and the taxi almost grazed the rear bumper of the Indica. She caught sight of a little boy gazing through the rear windshield. When the taxi passed a street lamp, the child noticed Sheela looking in his direction, gave her a broad smile, turned towards an adult seated next to him and disappeared into the depths of the car.

For a moment she wondered whether she should return to Tower View. No, she would persist: it would be well-nigh impossible to spot the Indica on the roads to the airport, especially this late in the evening, but there was a tiny chance that, if the driver put a spurt on, he would be able to catch up with the car on the approach to the terminal.

Thinking about Tower View reminded her that Khorshed had no idea where she had gone. It was only a little past ten. Khorshed was likely to be awake and might have knocked on her door to ask if she wanted a nightcap - she knew her daughter-in-law liked Horlicks. Sheela dialled the Tower View landline.

Her mother-in-law was as discreet as ever; no questions about why she was out so late at night, only a plea that she should take care of herself. So different from her mother, Sheela thought not for the first time; oh no, she owed her mother a return call - but that would have to wait.

The traffic cleared up slightly as the taxi went up Pedder Road, but slowed down again on the approach to the road's summit. When the taxi began its descent, Sheela leaned out of the window to get a better view of what lay ahead. The long line of vehicles, spangled red with rear lights, was creeping forward like some giant bejewelled centipede just roused from its slumber, only to come to a standstill in a frenzy of honking at the junction with Breach Candy. She was more than ever convinced that she had embarked on a fruitless enterprise.

Just as she was about to tell the taxi driver to take her back home, he turned round to inform her that it shouldn't take long now to get to the airport because the traffic was showing signs of clearing up. His encouragement was all she needed to cling on to the hope that this wasn't going to be a wild goose chase after all. She fell back into her seat.

After what felt like a good half hour - but was only seven minutes when Sheela checked the time in her watch - they had made the right turn towards Haji Ali. The traffic was flowing more easily now, and, once past Haji Ali, the taxi was speeding along the road at a steady 40 kilometres per hour. The driver was now swerving recklessly between lanes as he tried to overtake any other vehicle impudent enough to block his way.

It took less than half an hour to reach the approach to the airport. The road was now sprucely lined with trees which succeeded only partially in blocking the yellow lights of the slums that lay beyond.

As the taxi took the final turn towards the departure terminal, she slumped into her seat. All this effort - made so that she could tell herself that at least she tried - was never going to come to anything. The airport building looked grey, and the air smelt putrid even though the sea was nowhere near close enough to spew its stench. But something urged her on, some speck of hope, even though she knew that this was the hope of fools who see a chink of light under the door of a darkened room.

As they approached the entrance for BA passengers, she asked the taxi driver to wait at the drop-off point. But, he protested, the maximum waiting time was a minute. Sheela offered to give him more money.

He succumbed to the bribe, with the proviso that she wouldn't make him wait longer than ten minutes.

While talking to the driver, she had been keeping her eyes scanned for an Indica. She spotted one in the distance but it was too dark to see the registration number, and in any case there was no sign of anybody in the vehicle.

She alighted from the taxi and hurried towards the entrance at which departing passengers had to run the gauntlet of uniformed officers checking passports. There was a large crowd of Germans calling out to one another in a general state of confusion; apparently one of the passengers' passports was missing. Sheela stood on tiptoe to peer over the shoulders of the tourists. She spotted the back of a man, tall and slightly gangly, some way ahead of the German group. He walked into the airport building and turned left. Sheela couldn't trust her own sight or judgement, but the flicker of hope she had been harbouring became a lurch of excitement.

"Max!" she called out.

The man had disappeared from view.

"Max!" she cried louder. This time a few of the German tourists forgot about their passport problem and turned to look at her. A uniformed officer glanced in her direction and then returned his attention to the clamour of the Germans, one of whom, a brunette with streaks of straw-blonde hair, accused the officer of having mislaid the missing passport.

"Max!" This time, imagining a dozen German heads swivelling towards her, she didn't call out as loudly as she would have liked to. The officer turned to her and waved her away. His demeanour was not unkind: yes, this woman was being a nuisance creating such a *tamasha*; but, being respectable, as she clearly was, she had to be treated with deference.

She had time to spare: the driver had told her he might have to take a spin round the terminal area; so it could take him a good five minutes to return to the BA entrance. She looked straight ahead of her, willing the figure of Max to emerge from the airport building. Her gaze was glued to the entrance, as if the merest blink of an eyelid could risk her losing sight of him. But the waiting only intensified the feeling of futility.

The Germans had departed, but a few other travellers, Indians surrounded by large metal trunks and cloth-bound parcels, were casting curious glances at her. Five minutes must surely have passed. The pressure to give up was now irresistible. Reluctantly, she decided to leave and wended her way through the crowds towards the meeting point she had agreed with the taxi driver. She turned round once, twice, in the hope - forlorn, she knew - of seeing a lanky European figure emerging from the entrance. Her feet dragged behind her. Missing a step where the pavement met the road, she stumbled. As she tried to recover her balance, she imagined all the people around gazing pityingly at her, a lonely and fragile creature with nothing to show but the hopelessness that marked the stoop of her shoulders.

The taxi pulled up in front of her, juddering as the driver slammed on the brakes.

She was numb to everything whizzing past her, to the noise, pollution and bright lights of this insomniac city of her birth. She was unmoved even by the taxi driver's habit of clearing his throat with a guttural flourish and spitting the resultant phlegm on to some unsuspecting passerby. All she felt was an absence, an emptiness. She had lost him.

She was stirred by the ringing of her mobile. She took it out of her handbag, expecting a worried Khorshed to be at the other end. When she saw 'Nina' moving across the screen, she switched the phone off; she was in no condition to cope with her daughter's problems, real or imagined. Almost immediately the phone rang again. She stared at her daughter's name, hoping that Nina would give up and send her a text message instead. The ringing continued - twice, three times, four times - until she felt compelled to answer: suppose the problem was a real one, and wasn't Nina the only reason for her to carry on?

"Hi Mum, I was almost giving up on you - what took you so long to answer?"

"Sorry, Nina, but -"

"Anyway, Mum, I have the most amazing news to give you. Jake and I are getting married!"

"What? But how -"

"I know, I know, you're thinking like we're too young, must give it more time, blah blah blah - but we won't like actually get married for some years, not until we've finished our studies, started working and all the other things you'd approve of. Of course, Mummy," - now the little girl lost crept into her voice - "I - we - do want your approval. More than that, your blessing. And you're like the first person to know - Jake said we shouldn't tell his parents until we had told you."

"Oh, very sweet of Jake," and in case Nina should see irony in her remark, Sheela added, "Tell him I really appreciate it."

"Oh I will, Mum - but aren't you excited? We're already like making plans - crazy, I know, so many years in advance, but what the heck -"

"I think it's very wise to plan things in advance, and of course, my darling, I'll be with you all the way."

"Oh thank you so much, Mum - so we do have your blessing, don't we?"

"Yes, of course, you have my blessing. You will always have my blessing."

"And Daddy, he would have given his blessing, wouldn't he?"

"Yes darling, you know Daddy was the kindest of men - he would surely have given his blessing."

Yes, she said to herself as she put her phone away, I do have to carry on - for Nina's sake. But the feeling of hopelessness, briefly forgotten during the phone call, returned, this time sharpened by anger. *Who am I doing all this for? For myself? Or for others? The answer is clear: always for others - Nina, my mother-in-law, Ramu, even Max*. The thought of Max brought back the same question she had asked herself before: why had she allowed herself to fail at Kate's Point?

It was only when her eyes fell upon Copper Chimney, a restaurant that Cyrus and she had frequented in the early years of their marriage, that her attention was caught by life outside the taxi. To her left was the racecourse, to her right the Arabian Sea. She would be back at Tower View in less than twenty minutes. Back to the role of dutiful daughter-in-law. There had been a brief interlude - the tantalising prospect offered by the Alexanders of a life not dominated by the loss of Cyrus.

But now she had come full circle to the dreary existence she was fated to endure through the rest of her days.

The taxi was beginning its ascent up Pedder Road when a large Audi tried to overtake it from the left. The taxi driver shouted obscenities as he braked to avoid a collision. Sheela thought she heard a ping from somewhere in the front of the car, probably from the man's phone. He had now launched into a tirade about billionaire black marketeers who bought fancy cars to launder their ill-gotten gains. As he paused for breath, the ping returned, this time clearly from within her handbag. Somebody had sent her a message. It wouldn't be her mother-in-law - she didn't know how to send texts. It must be Nina again. Wearily she opened her bag and extracted her mobile.

At the top of the list of text messages was an announcement from 3Alerts that her latest eBill was ready to view. As she returned to the full screen she noticed there was an unopened WhatsApp message. It took a few seconds for her to take in the three-letter word in bold typeface at the top of the Chats list. She tapped on it to read the message below the name:

I'm at Bombay airport, ready to board my flight to London. Now that I don't have my Indian mobile, I decided five minutes ago to check my UK mobile and saw a missed call from you earlier this evening. Max

The taxi driver was still fulminating about the Audi motorist but all she could think of was the message staring at her: so cold and stark she wondered why he had bothered to send it. No doubt with his middle-class English upbringing he had felt that courtesy demanded a response. That was all there was to it. A reply was clearly not welcome. He had meant what he had said when he had written that he must go away. She wanted to be angry, to be the wounded party, but instead she felt herself sinking into an inescapable pit.

She put the phone back into her handbag and stared blankly at the buildings lit by the street lamps lining Hughes Road. Then she heard another ping. She wasn't going to answer it. She wasn't going to be at the beck and call of her daughter or anybody else for that matter. But she couldn't fight off the old Sheela: suppose Nina needed to speak to her urgently? suppose it was Gopal saying something serious had happened to Khorshed? or to Ramu? And what if it was something to do with Max? With that last thought she extracted the mobile from her handbag.

PS, the latest message read, *in my hurry to get to the departure gate, I forgot to mention I had tried to call you before I sent you my last message, but the phone was engaged. Boarding is anytime now, so I don't know if you'll receive this message before we take off.*

I don't know if you'll receive this message ... The plea she hoped lay behind those words conjured up an image almost forgotten since her return from Mahabaleshwar: Clarissa on her death bed, unmindful of her own condition, appealing to her to "keep an eye on Max". She slid to the right to make sure she was hidden from the driver's view: she might not be able to control the swelling in her throat.

Dear Max, she proceeded to reply, *Thank you for your message.* What was she to say next? Whatever came to mind sounded sterile, arid, like the sample emails she had prepared for her English language students. He had tried to call her, hadn't he - and the chat message was sent only because she had been on the phone speaking to Nina. But writing was so much safer - the sentences could be carefully crafted, the text properly checked, before the 'send' arrow was pressed.

He would be on the point of boarding, if he hadn't already boarded.

Keep an eye on Max. The taxi was now approaching Chowpatty Beach – the end point of the evening walks she used to take with Cyrus along Marine Drive; and as if Cyrus had just returned to her side, she heard his voice again, gently encouraging: "Sheela my darling, we need to give people the benefit of the doubt - even if that means taking emotional risks..." Cyrus, Clarissa - both spurring her on...

No more time to lose. Without letting herself think further, she deleted the message she had started writing and pressed the 'Calls' tab on WhatsApp.

With her arms tucked against her sides to steady the trembling in her hands, she tapped on 'Max', then placed the phone against her ear and waited. Nothing. He must have switched his phone off. He must have concluded that once again she had signalled her desire not to have anything to do with him.

She moved the phone away, ready to end the call.

She was about to touch the red button when she heard a faint sound. She pressed the mobile to her ear. The phone had started ringing.

She winced as the concertina lift door slammed shut. Turning the front door key of the flat as quietly as possible, she found the light in the hallway hadn't been switched off. To her surprise the lights in the dining room were also on. So typically thoughtful of

Khorshed. She tiptoed to her bedroom and switched the bedside lamp on.

Something was amiss: the chair, the dressing table, even the portable phone – they no longer belonged where she had moved them over a year ago. Tomorrow morning she would return them to their rightful place, nearer to Cyrus's side of the bed. She opened the bottom drawer of the dressing table and reached out into the furthest corner to retrieve a framed photograph that she had placed there, face down. She turned over the frame to see the portrait of her husband smiling directly at her. She smiled back but had to bite her lips to stop the tears. "My beloved Cyrus, my husband in a million, I hope you will forgive me." Through the blur in her eyes, the picture seemed to come to life, and she heard once more the chuckle in his voice as he urged her not to be perpetually distrustful – as if he were telling her this time that she should trust *him*, that he would be the first person to support whatever she chose to do. She placed the photograph on the dressing table, where it had always belonged.

"Darling?"

"Oh Mummy, you gave me such a start! Why are you up so late?"

Khorshed was in her nightdress, but looked wide awake.

"Oh, I don't know - I couldn't sleep, so I thought I'd wait until you returned, just to check that everything was OK."

"Oh everything is super-OK, Mummy - but you shouldn't have waited for me."

"I'm so glad. Look, in case you wanted a nightcap on your return I got Philomena to make some Horlicks - it's in the thermos, so it's nice and hot."

"Oh Mummy, that's lovely - you'll have some with me, won't you?"

"Yes of course, darling, I'd love to sit down with you."

The dining table had a thermos and two mugs placed on mats. Sheela's eyes fell upon the Nandi. No longer dolorous, its oversized eyes and wide mouth gave, if anything, the impression that it was about to break into a mischievous smile.

With shaky hands, Khorshed unscrewed the thermos lid and poured the Horlicks into the mugs.

"As usual, Mummy, you think of everything." Sheela turned and wrapped her arms round her mother-in-law's waist. "You are the best mother on earth."

"And *you*," said Khorshed, cupping Sheela's face with both hands, "are the best daughter in the world. Now settle yourself down and have your Horlicks."

Once Sheela was seated, Khorshed continued, "I don't wish to intrude, but am I right in feeling you might want to tell me something? I haven't seen you look so - so happy since - for a long time." Her eyes had a sparkle that belied her age.

So uncharacteristic of her mother-in-law to probe like this. Yet so characteristic of her to know when to probe, to sense that, despite the lateness of the hour, Sheela was keen to talk to her.

After a few sips of the steaming Horlicks, Khorshed looked up at Sheela with an expectant smile - the same smile Cyrus used to give whenever she needed encouragement.

"Come, now tell me all about it."

Acknowledgements

For the practical help they offered in their different ways, I would like to thank Jackie Bhabha, Farzan Bilimoria, Azmy Birdi, Mita Kapur, Alan Maher, Shireen Mistry, Aban Mukherji, Jean Nayar, Anand Pandya, Eva Rea and Anna South – but many thanks also for all the moral support and encouragement I received from family members and friends I haven't specifically mentioned here.

A big thankyou to Julian Costley and Paul Davies of Bite-Sized Books for their faith in the novel and for being such a pleasure to work with.

Very special thanks to three individuals whose investment in the success of this book led to so many improvements in the quality of the final product: Caroline Dalal, for her whole-hearted enthusiasm and unstinting support from the moment she read the manuscript, and more specifically for the professional insights that lent credibility to the psychology behind the actions of some of the protagonists; Suzie Dalal, for her suggestions on plot development - always so generous, thoughtful and wise - and for her gentle, witty and constructive critique when the prose was threatening to turn dangerously purple; and Firdaus Gandavia, for always being there, and in particular for his sensitive counsel against redundant and overwritten passages, which helped so much to tighten the structure and increase the impact of the novel.

For their efforts to help bring the book to publication I would like to thank three people in particular: Niloufer Bilimoria, whose enormous kindness and unflagging championship were pivotal in bringing my novel to the attention of people in the literary world; Farrukh Dhondy, whose encouragement and huge generosity in opening doors ensured that the book crossed the finishing line; and Zareer Masani, for his backing on the publishing front and his valuable observations on the writing in the early sections of the manuscript.

Finally, I wish to thank two family members without whose loving support this novel would never have seen the light of day: my daughter Dinu, the first person to give me the encouragement I needed, the first to read and offer thoughts - always perceptive and constructive - on the original and subsequent versions of the manuscript, and the first to moot the idea of publication; and, last but by no means least, my wife Maneck, without whose practical and emotional investment - her sharp observations on turns of phrase in the final editing of the manuscript, her care, her endless patience (and cups of tea!) - completion of the book would have remained a distant vision.

A postscript about my mother and father, Hilla and Rusi Suntook: if there is a leitmotif running through the narrative of this book it is the need for understanding and compassion, and I would like to think that the spirit of my parents, who embodied these qualities in abundance, has had a bearing on the way this novel has turned out.

Why not sign up to our mailing list here:

Find out more about Farrokh Suntook:

Why not browse our BOOKSHOP?

Find out more about Bite-Sized Books here:

Printed in Great Britain
by Amazon